THE SCARLET BLADE: THE RAKEHELLY
ADVENTURES OF CLEVE AND
D'ENTREVILLE, VOLUME 1

Blood Ritual:
The Adventures of Scarlet and Bradshaw, Volume 1
BY THEODORE ROSCOE

Champion of Lost Causes
BY MAX BRAND

The City of Stolen Lives: The Adventures
of Peter the Brazen, Volume 1
BY LORING BRENT

The Complete Cabalistic Cases of Semi Dual,
the Occult Detector, Volume 2: 1912–13
BY J.U. GIESY AND JUNIUS B. SMITH

Doan and Carstairs: Their Complete Cases
BY NORBERT DAVIS

The King Who Came Back
BY FRED MacISAAC

The Radio Gun-Runners
BY RALPH MILNE FARLEY

Sabotage
BY CLEVE F. ADAMS

South of Fifty-Three
BY JACK BECHDOLT

THE SCARLET BLADE

THE RAKEHELLY ADVENTURES OF CLEVE AND D'ENTREVILLE, VOLUME 1

MURRAY R. MONTGOMERY

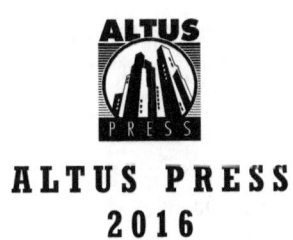

ALTUS PRESS
2016

EDITED AND DESIGNED BY
Matthew Moring

PUBLISHING HISTORY
"A Sword for the Cardinal" originally appeared in the March 26, 1938 issue of
    Argosy magazine (Vol. 280, No. 4). Copyright © 1938 by The Frank A. Munsey
    Company. Copyright renewed © 1965 and assigned to Steeger Properties, LLC.
    All rights reserved.
"Rakehelly Ride" originally appeared in the October 21, 1939 issue of *Argosy*
    magazine (Vol. 294, No. 2). Copyright © 1939 by The Frank A. Munsey
    Company. Copyright renewed © 1966 and assigned to Steeger Properties, LLC.
    All rights reserved.
"Seal of Treason" originally appeared in the January 27, 1940 issue of *Argosy*
    magazine (Vol. 296, No. 4). Copyright © 1940 by The Frank A. Munsey
    Company. Copyright renewed © 1967 and assigned to Steeger Properties, LLC.
    All rights reserved.
"The Scarlet Blade" originally appeared in the October 26 and November 2 & 9,
    1940 issues of *Argosy* magazine (Vol. 303, Nos. 1–3). Copyright © 1940 by The
    Frank A. Munsey Company. Copyright renewed © 1967 and assigned to
    Steeger Properties, LLC. All rights reserved.
"About the Author" originally appeared in the August 2, 1941 issue of *Argosy*
    magazine (Vol. 309, No. 5). Copyright © 1941 by The Frank A. Munsey
    Company. Copyright renewed © 1968 and assigned to Steeger Properties, LLC.
    All rights reserved.

THANKS TO
Everard P. Digges LaTouche and Gerd Pircher

ISBN
978-1-61827-229-4

Visit *altuspress.com* for more books like this.
Printed in the United States of America.

TABLE OF CONTENTS

I

A SWORD FOR THE CARDINAL

For the King or for Richelieu?—that question had to be answered at one time or another by every young Seventeenth Century Frenchman.

CHAPTER I

THE LARGE VENETIAN clock in the palace library was chiming seven as the Cardinal pushed aside the litter of correspondence before him and fell wearily back against the plush of his chair. There were times when this business of wresting France from the avarice of her feudal nobles tired him to a point near exhaustion.

He bit gently on his lower lip and frowned across the table to Père Joseph. There was silence. In the soft, flickering light of the candles the Cardinal's fine pallor was delicately tinted with shadow, giving his sharply chiseled features a thoughtful, profound, almost ethereal, appearance. Finally, under the steady compulsion of his gaze, Father Joseph looked up. There was an unspoken query in his glance.

"Monseigneur?"

Richelieu did not answer immediately. Outside, in the spacious corridor, a squad of guards swung by, and the rhythm of their tread sounded in muffled cadence through the library door. The velvety stillness of the high-ceilinged room was broken.

"The young Comte d'Entreville," the Cardinal said when the tramp of feet had faded into the distance, "has been writing poetry again."

Père Joseph shrugged. "Le Comte d'Entreville is a very foolish man, *Monseigneur.*"

"He is, Joseph," agreed the Cardinal flatly, reaching forward to pick a document from the table. "Either that, or very ignorant." He sighed and ran his eyes quickly over the paper. "This is a facsimile which my agents have sent me. It makes the tenth of its kind. Listen." He bent nearer the candles to better see the script and began to read:

> *When I have slain a dozen men,*
> *And robbed the treas'ry bare;*
> *When conscience, I have none to rue,*
> *In grasping thrice my share,*
> *'Tis then I'll name me Richelieu,*
> *'Tis lean I'll be—not fat.*
> *'Tis then I'll name me Richelieu,*
> *And wear a Cardinal's hat.*

He paused thoughtfully, tossed the paper atop the litter, and then offered his aide a faint, grim, smile. "Monsieur d'Entreville has been clever enough not to sign it."

"It is libel, *Monseigneur,*" said Père Joseph, his Socratic features fixed with indignation.

The Cardinal shrugged and rose. He made a graceful figure in his trailing red robe and tasseled sash, seeming taller than he was, by virtue of his lithe slenderness. With fingers interlaced, he paced silently to the end of the room and then faced about.

"Whether it be libel, or not," he replied, "makes no difference. In its effect we find the true reason for condemnation. It has discredited me before Louis—and made the Court laugh." His dark eyes hardened. "I must *not* be laughed at, Joseph!"

THERE was no vain or shallow logic behind these words; but one deeper, more impersonal and fundamental. For years France had been weakened by a feudalism which gave her noble houses the privileges of raising personal armies, levying their own taxes, and subsidizing the Throne for their own ends. Richelieu was seeking now to crush this system and the men behind it, in order to grant the nation the power of a united country under

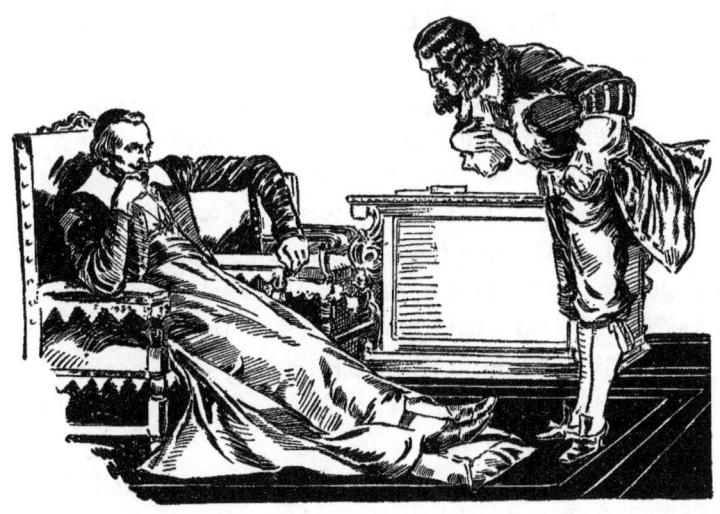

but one recognized government, namely, the King's. Bitterness, hatred—almost civil war—had been the result.

"Ridicule can be as deadly as, though more insidious than, an assassin's knife," asserted Père Joseph mildly. "I have learned that, *Monseigneur*. But if you arrest M. d'Entreville without reason, except for his verse—and he'll deny authorship of that, mind you—then you have made him a martyr and given your enemies opportunity to call you assassin. As I see it, *Monseigneur*, you can do nothing."

The Cardinal spread his fine, tapering fingers in a careless motion of resignation, and nodded.

"I will do nothing," he agreed and frowned. "But I am not thinking of d'Entreville's present impudence. I am considering his future. There will come a time, Joseph, when he will have grown bolder with his frivolous wit and sharp pen. One day, he will go too far for me to ignore—perhaps forsake his verse for an actual intrigue against me." At this juncture the Cardinal shrugged. "Chalais once started in much the same manner. He grew popular in the company of the same treacherous group: Nevers, Condé, le Duc d'Orleans, Soissons, Vendôme and the

Duchess de Chevreuse." He snapped his fingers. "Last week he met the headsman."

A soft, hesitant knock on the door; a pause, and then, a louder knock as if its author had gained sudden courage for his action, interrupted further conversation. Richelieu returned to his chair beside the table and sat down. He asked the caller to enter.

The tall, resplendent, figure of Birotteau, captain of the guard, stepped quickly into the room. His sword held stiffly to prevent its swaying, he marched formally across to the table and bowed.

"Monsieur le Comte Guy d'Entreville, requests an audience with you, *Monseigneur*," he reported. "I have told him you were not free, but he insists."

The Cardinal steepled his fingers thoughtfully and glanced over at Père Joseph. "Speak of the devil, eh, Joseph?"

He smiled dryly before returning to the captain. "Has M. d'Entreville explained why he so pressingly wishes an interview, Birotteau?"

"No, *Monseigneur.*"

"Hmmm. Well, I'm curious. Show him in."

"Oui, Monseigneur."

After the captain had left, Père Joseph snapped shut the volume from which he had been reading, and stood up. There was a frown on his forehead as he went over and took a place beside his master.

"Timeo Danaos et dona ferentes," he said.

The Cardinal heard him and smiled. "I doubt if M. d'Entreville bears gifts for *me*, Joseph. From a careful study of his poetry— I fear he is not so charitably inclined."

CAPTAIN BIROTTEAU returned to the library. He led in an elegant young man wearing high boots, and a swirling military cape. An unusually long rapier hung from his belt. He was frowning slightly and he stood before Richelieu with the silence of pride as the officer tactfully withdrew. The Cardinal regarded him without expression. His fingers toyed absently with the priceless medallion strung by a silken cord from his neck. A minute crawled into the stillness.

"You are Guy, le Comte d'Entreville, *monsieur?*"

The visitor nodded stiffly. He did not bow. Cardinal Richelieu accepted the discourtesy with an enigmatic smile. His dark eyes took a quick, accurate, accounting of the man before him. The bearing was soldiery, the cheekbones high, the nose aristocratic, and the mouth even. There was a certain young recklessness in the eyes which led the Cardinal to surmise that M. d'Entreville had escaped violent death enough times to cease fearing it.

"Well, *monsieur,*" he said after a pause. "I am waiting."

Guy d'Entreville took a deep breath. "I have come here, *Monseigneur,*" he said, "to plead for the release of Mademoiselle du Murier whom you have seen fit to have placed in the Convent of Carmelites."

Richelieu could have laughed, but he did not. Instead he frowned slightly. "Why?" he asked bluntly and dropped his hand to the arm of the chair. "For what reason?"

A flood of resentment flushed Guy d'Entreville's face. He bit angrily at his lower lip and then looked at his enemy defiantly. "Because, I love her, *Monseigneur—if you* can understand what love means," he blurted hotly. "I am her betrothed."

The expression on the Cardinal's face did not change. "Mademoiselle du Murier, recently lady-in-waiting to the Queen," he said as though reading from an unseen list of charges, "was proved to be implicated in a plot against me. She was found guilty of bearing messages from the Duchess de Chevreuse to the Queen... by her judges."

"*Your* judges, *Monseigneur.*"

Cardinal Richelieu folded his hands in his lap. "Monsieur d'Entreville," he said quietly, "you shall accomplish very little by using that tone to me."

A choked silence followed. How long Guy stood there, hot and flushed, gripped by the wild rush of two counter emotions, he did not know. He did know, however, that when he once more raised his eyes to those of the Cardinal, love for Catherine du Murier had been stronger than his hatred of Richelieu.

"I know it, *Monseigneur,*" he said simply. "But with the faith of a fool, I had hope in your compassion. I will do anything, *Monseigneur*.... Anything, if you will only give her back to me!"

The Cardinal arched his eyebrow quizzically. "I wonder?"

He leaned forward across the table and plucked a quill from the inkstand. He wrote rapidly across a sheet of paper and signed it with his seal. When he had finished, he looked up.

"The fact that you had the courage to come here, *Monsieur le Comte,* has aroused my admiration of your frankness. I shall make a bargain with you, *monsieur.*"

"*Monseigneur!*"

A FAINT, amused, smile appeared in the corners of the Cardinal's mouth. This young hothead before him had emotions which could bound from resentment to anger, to defiance, to pleading, to hope, with the facility of a mountain goat.

"*Ma foi,* d'Entreville," he said, "don't permit your spirits to rise too high. I am not one to make bargains unless I secure the larger profits." He waved the paper indicatingly. "This," he continued, "is an order for the release of your Mademoiselle du Murier whom has been so foolish as to—er, play Mercury to the wrong persons. I shall be delighted to turn it over to you provided—" He allowed the sentence to trail off and regarded the eager chevalier questioningly.

"Anything, *Monseigneur.* Anything!"

"Provided, that you renounce your treasonable friends, and accept a lieutenancy in my Guards!"

A thunderclap couldn't have hit Guy any harder. For a moment he stood there with his hands clenched while he fought to control the gusts of indignation that stormed within him.

"*Sangodemi!*" he burst out. "I offer you my soul, *Monseigneur*—and you demand my honor!"

Richelieu spread his fingers with a gesture of finality and dropped the paper back upon the table.

"*Mon dieu, Monsieur le Comte,*" he grunted, "You are a man of contradictions. And—" he smiled enigmatically—"bad verse. Very bad verse."

Guy d'Entreville glowered and sought to check the mad fury which pranced over his heart. He loathed this pale, chilly Cardinal with all the acid hatred of his class—the explosive bitterness of his youth. But, he must be humble, must forget his hatred if Catherine was to be free.

"I—I," he stammered haltingly, "I must consider, *Monseigneur*. To take your service will be to give the lie to my convictions. It is something one does not decide upon in a moment. Perhaps, by tomorrow I shall be less—confused."

The Cardinal's lips formed the words dubiously. "Perhaps," he agreed. "But it will have to be early because I leave at nine for the King's Court in Brittany."

Guy bowed. "Tomorrow at eight, then, *Monseigneur*."

"Remember, *Monsieur le Comte*," Richelieu told him as he turned to leave. "Remember, that I am the only person who can give you back your betrothed."

Guy d'Entreville stood, pale-faced, in the door frame. The knuckles on the hand which held his plumed hat were white with the strain of self-control. He managed a curt bow.

"It is a factor which I shall remember in weighing my decision, *Monseigneur*," he replied. "Good evening!"

When he had gone, Richelieu looked up at Père Joseph with a thin, bitter, little smile. "One would believe, Joseph," he shrugged, "that I serve the Devil instead of France."

CHAPTER II

THE MISERY OF indecision was never more painful than in the case of Guy d'Entreville. Four hours had passed and still no definite course of action had been decided upon. He paced the polished floor of his comfortable apartment near *le Quai de l'Ecole* frowning, and kicking at furniture with savage abandon.

Somewhere in the darkened city a clock tower tolled eleven. A mongrel barked nervously. Guy's nerves grew tighter, tighter, and a great restlessness bore down on him. Finally, he could bear it no longer. With a curse he buckled on his sword and left the place.

On previous evenings the glittering gaiety of the Hotel de Rohan had helped brighten his discontent. But tonight, it seemed only to press them lower. He wandered about the grand foyer, listlessly. He chatted disinterestedly with several acquaintances, drank a bottle of wine and finally, was in the act of leaving when a small person with a hooked nose, a jet black mustache, tapped him lightly on the shoulder.

"Monsieur d'Entreville?"

Guy turned. He did not smile when he recognised the man. The Duc de Valvasson was not the type of man one wanted to smile at.

"Good evening to you, *Monsieur le Duc,*" he said indifferently. "Your health, *monsieur.*"

De Valvasson shrugged. His eyes winked into Guy's face for a moment, and then darted nervously, almost furtively, about the room. Apparently satisfied, he pulled Guy into a corner before speaking again.

"It is most fortunate that I should find our poet," he said. "Do you ride well, *monsieur?*"

Guy was puzzled but interested. He frowned slightly and nodded. "Since childhood," he assented.

"Excellent." The speaker's voice dropped almost to a whisper. "You were a friend to Chalais, of course?"

"Naturally."

"Then, you would be willing to ride for his memory, would you not?"

"Why, er—yes, of course. But—"

De Valvasson held up a cautioning finger. "The walls have

ears, *monsieur*," he said significantly. "But, if you have the heart
for a little danger, you will follow me. Agreed?"

Guy nodded. He did know precisely what de Valvasson was
about, but the little man's furtiveness and whispered words were
baited with the tempting possibility of action and adventure.
Excitement, Guy suddenly felt, was exactly what he needed.

"Agreed, *Monsieur le Duc.*"

De Valvasson smiled. He said nothing more, but linked Guy's
arm in his and together they sought the black streets....

THE TAVERN, known as Les Trois Chiens, was admirably
situated for a conspiracy. It was a ramshackle edifice which
traced its beginnings to the days of the eighth Charles. Backed
into an obscure alley near the foot of the Pont Neuf it combined
the fine assets of being both unknown and unnoticeable. A
wretched, weed-grown inner court guarded its front entrance,
and the yellow waters of the Seine protected its rear. As de
Valvasson led the way to one of the side doors, Guy noticed
that the building was boarded up, and to all intents and purposes deserted.

"*Corbac*," he muttered. "What a miserable place."

The first two floors were deserted, but in a huge garret atop
the whole structure, twelve men were gathered. Guy knew most
of them. Richard Bovarde, Chalais' closest friend, the Marquis
de la Marnette, Marrilac, and several others, all with definite
anti-Cardinalist sympathies. They talked in soft, grim voices,
and the light from the fireplace danced crisply on their fine
swords and brocade. Conversation stopped the moment de
Valvasson and Guy entered. Dark, expectant, eyes were turned.

"I have brought another," announced de Valvasson. "I have
brought Monsieur le Comte d'Entreville."

Guy was greeted in varying degrees of cordiality. Then everyone gathered about a great table in the center of the room
while de Valvasson produced a rolled map and spread it quickly
over the surface.

"With a miserable escort of four, he leaves Paris tomorrow

at nine o'clock, *messieurs*," he told them and placed a bony finger on the parchment. "By coach he travels down this road—" The finger traced the road slowly. "Past Versailles, Lunours—ah, and here.... Here, just outside of Chartres he has planned a short rest at the Inn du Lac d'Or." The Duke glanced quickly at the ring of faces surrounding him and tapped the map lightly. "It is here that we shall meet him. The Inn of the Golden Lake!"

"To assure that his rest be permanent," said a voice.

Guy frowned. There was something to this business which did not suit his taste. He had expected some wild escapade, a furious cross-country ride, perhaps, with just a *soupçon* of lawlessness about it, sufficient to make it exciting—such as the time, he and several others had stolen the Cardinal's coach and painted it blue and green with yellow spots. This present meeting was too grim, too cold-blooded, for any merely mischievous prank. He was beginning to regret de Valvasson's cryptic invitation. He stepped up closer to the table.

"You will pardon my ignorance, *messieurs*," he said. "But, what is this that you have planned?"

Eyebrows were raised and a buzz of questions mounted. De Valvasson held up his hand. "I had no opportunity to explain, d'Entreville," he apologized. "There might have been ears listening."

Guy nodded. "What have you planned?" he reiterated.

"To kill the Cardinal, *Monsieur le Comte*."

GUY'S mouth suddenly went dry; his stomach felt icy cold. Unconsciously his hand dropped to the hilt of his rapier. "Er—all of you?" he asked foolishly.

"No," corrected de Valvasson, "only six. We will draw lots. The others will remain here and await the news."

The easy confidence with which le Duc de Valvasson stressed his words raised a sudden alarm in Guy. Quite suddenly he knew that he did not want Cardinal Richelieu to die. It was very simple. Richelieu was the only man who could release Catherine from her confinement. Guy discovered once again that his love for her was greater than his hatred of the prelate. The fingers on his hilt tightened imperceptibly.

"In either case, *Monsieur le Duc,*" he said calmly, "it is a business which will endure for many hours. Am I correct?"

"Quite correct, Monsieur d'Entreville. According to our calculations it will take our horsemen fully eight hours to ride to Chartres, accomplish their purpose, and return here to the inn."

Guy nodded. He had no illusions about his situation and he eased his legs into a position which gave him greater stability.

"*Ma foi,*" he said lightly. "I would that you had mentioned the extreme time which this shall take, when you first accosted me. It would have saved both of us our trouble. I am afraid, *messieurs*"—he turned to the assemblage "—that I must plead to be excused. I have made an important appointment for the morning."

If Guy thought that they would allow him to leave on such a flimsy pretext, he was mistaken. As he clapped on his wide-brimmed hat and started for the door the alarming bulk of Bovarde posted itself in front of him. Guy stepped back a pace and cocked his head thoughtfully. The others in the room seemed to be holding their breaths.

Finally Guy spoke. "Your pardon, *monsieur,* but you are barring my path. Step aside, please."

Bovarde grinned wolfishly. His thumbs were in his sash, close to his sword.

"Must you leave so quickly, *Monsieur le Comte?*" he asked evenly.

"Sad, Monsieur Bovarde, but I must."

"Sadder, d'Entreville," said somebody in the group, "but you mustn't."

Guy faced the gathering and spread his arms in a gesture of abjuration. "Must I believe that you do not trust me?"

De Valvasson, standing with his arms akimbo, near the fire-place, chuckled. It was not a nice chuckle. "In such a business as this," he said, "no one is trusted. I fear that you will miss your appointment, *Monsieur le Comte.*"

Guy sighed. He eyed the door thoughtfully. It was but three jumps away with no one but Bovarde in a position to interfere. He eyed the massive gentleman and scowled.

"Step aside, Bovarde. I have decided not to miss my appointment."

Bovarde shook his head. Guy took a deep breath. Suddenly, he galvanized into action. His sword jumped out of its sheath and touched lightly on Bovarde's chest. The big man retreated with an oath. *"Sacré nom de cochon!"* he exclaimed. "I do believe this fool is a Cardinlist."

Guy gripped his rapier tightly and smiled a thin, cheerless, smile. The others in the room surged forward, and then stopped, frozen.

Guy addressed them crisply. "Make a move, *messieurs,* and my friend here is a dead man. I have no quarrel to pick, but if I must fight my way out of here, I will."

Bovarde's lower lip trembled with apprehension as Guy's sword point lifted from his chest to his throat. A dead, yet terribly tense stillness had fallen into the room. Only the crackling of the fire could be heard. Guy lifted his feet cautiously and edged toward the door. He did not see de Valvasson in the background slyly grasp a wine bottle and aim it carefully.

Suddenly, the room swayed and seemed to be full of orange, green and yellow lights. Guy pitched sideward to the floor. His sword slipped from nerveless fingers and then—blackness engulfed him....

CHAPTER III

GUY COULD VAGUELY hear the soft, emotionless, voice of Richelieu saying over and over: *"Remember, monsieur, I am the only man who can give you back your bethrothed."* He groaned. They were going to kill Richelieu—murder the Cardinal at the

Inn du Lac d'Or! Catherine would grow old in the Carmelites. His heart shuddered at the thought. Slowly he opened his eyes. His head ached terrifically.

"…senseless six hours," he heard someone say. "Are you sure, *Monsieur le Duc,* that you have not killed him?"

Guy looked up. He was still in the garret of Les Trois Chiens. The fire on the hearth had simmered down to a heap of tenacious coals which glowed redly in the darkness. With a mild start he discovered that he was bound to a chair. He looked quickly in the direction of the voices. Two men were seated at the table eating little white cakes and drinking wine. Guy recognized de Valvasson and Bovarde. He closed his eyes and tried to reassemble his thoughts.

"On the contrary," he heard de Valvasson say, "he still breathes therefore he lives. *Corbac!* Who would have suspected d'Entreville of loving the Cardinal?"

A short silence fell. Dumbly, Guy wondered how he had been struck down. Apparently by a bottle, he concluded. Somewhere, the faint tones of a bell sounded. Guy counted the strokes: One, two, three, four, five, six. Six o'clock! *Sacré nom,* this would never do. He must warn the Cardinal!

It proved easier to say than to do. Whoever had bound him had done an excellent job. The thick hemp strands held his body flat against the chair. A strand was passed thrice about his chest; his feet were lashed securely to the rungs; his hands, tied and held to the chair-back, seemed to be covered by a veritable mesh of rope. Guy struggled, perspired mightily, and got nowhere. The noise he made attracted the two men at the table. Bovarde got up and walked over to him. Guy noticed that the man swayed slightly in his stride.

"Awake, eh?" he scowled.

Guy did not answer. Bovarde fingered the wine cup which he held in his hand and laughed. "Traitor!" he said and dashed the contents into Guy's face. "Cardinalist!"

"You lie, swine," said Guy and shook the wine out of his eyes. Some of it lingered there and smarted painfully.

Bovarde snarled a curse and lifted his arm to throw the cup. De Valvasson knocked it out of his hand and it shattered on the floor.

"None of that, please," said the Duke firmly. He placed a hand under Bovarde's elbow and led him to the door. "You had better go down and sleep with the others, *monsieur*. I fear that you have had too much wine."

Bovarde nodded docilely. He paused in the doorway to give Guy a parting scowl. "*Sangodemi!* How I hate traitors," he said and disappeared.

De Valvasson smiled bleakly and returned to the prisoner. "Bovarde wants your death, *Monsieur le Comte*," he told Guy pleasantly and shrugged. "So do I."

Guy bit his lower lip and stared moodily at the embers. After a long pause, he said: "Why haven't you finished the business?"

The duke shrugged again. He walked slowly to the table and poured himself a goblet of wine. Guy watched him narrowly. It occurred to him for the first time that de Valvasson looked remarkably like a big, black spider.

"Some of the men who have left for the inn still have doubts about your sympathies," the duke said. "They feel that your poetry indicates your true beliefs." He took a sip of the wine. "I don't. To me, you showed your true colors when you drew your sword last night in a desperate effort to quit this place. Only a man who had a definite place to go, would have done that. Well." De Valvasson drained the last of the wine. He picked up a cake and nibbled on it delicately. "I have agreed to wait until they return before killing you. They want to put a few questions to you, understand?" He smiled amiably. "I do believe I shall go downstairs with the others and take myself a nap."

"Six have already left for Chartres, of course?"

DE VALVASSON flicked the remainder of his cake carelessly upon the floor and brushed his hands together. He was standing by the large window at the end of the room, and for the first time since his recovery, Guy noted that the cold, leaden light of dawn was shafted through it.

De Valvasson hooked his thumbs into his doublet and nodded. "Of course," he said and walked over to Guy's chair. "They'll hold," he continued, regarding the ropes. "The man who tied them used to be a sailor."

He went to the door and upon reaching it, turned and gave the prisoner a cold smirk. "You will undoubtedly try to loose them whilst I am gone." He kicked open the door. *"Ma foi,* such foolishness!"

"A man who can kill without the heat of hatred," Guy said slowly, "isn't human."

"A thought worth considering, *monsieur,*" nodded de Valvasson. "For I am going to kill you, and I do not hate you—particularly." He frowned reflectively. "Inhuman," he muttered and disappeared. The door slammed shut after him, and Guy could hear the sound of his footsteps as they descended the stairs....

An hour of straining, jerking at the ropes which bound him filled Guy with despair and his body with agony. The ropes were cruelly tight. His struggles only made them bite deep into the flesh of his wrists and ankles. He paused and cursed sobbingly.

Outside the tolling of a distant bell told him that it was seven o'clock. *Dieu,* how time flew! He gritted his teeth and renewed the attack. Blood began to well from his wrists and its warm dampness made the rope slimy.

A half an hour passed in pain and he slumped forward, exhausted. It was hopeless. In a few hours some one would come into the room and kill him as he sat there bound hand and foot.

"What a miserable finish," he muttered and stared listlessly at the floor. Slowly the things which his eyes saw kindled new hope, new vitality. *"Mon dieu,"* he cried excitedly, "why haven't I thought of it before!"

He jerked sideward against the ropes. The chair teetered, hesitated, and then crashed him to the floor.

GASPARD VORENS, *le duc de Valvasson,* was not a cruel man—that is to say, he took no pleasure in the unnecessary sufferings of others, either mentally or physically. When he decided that a man should die, he believed in committing his decision immediately and with neatness and dispatch. A quick blow. No pain. No mental agony, which was as bad as, if not worse than torture. No unnecessary blood letting. It was typical of his cold-blooded philosophy. Consequently, he could see no need for Guy d'Entreville's natural apprehensions of a fate which he, de Valvasson, had definitely preconceived. Guy must die, so why procrastinate? With this thought in mind, the duke rose from his couch, loosened his rapier, and set out for the prisoner's room.

It was just striking eight when he thrust open the door and stepped briskly into Guy's improvised cell. The captive was still sitting on the chair, head bowed, apparently resigned to his fate. De Valvasson drew his blade and coughed politely. D'Entreville looked up.

"Monsieur," said the duke, "I regret very much what I am about to do, but it is necessary."

Guy smiled grimly and eyed the other's weapon. "You've come to kill me," he said without emotion. "What will the other gentlemen say?"

De Valvasson gripped his sword a trifle more tightly. He felt relieved that Guy was not going to embarrass him by pleading, blubbering, for his life. The duke shrugged slightly and raised the shining steel.

"I'll tell them," he said deprecatingly, "that you have confessed." He took a step toward Guy, totally unprepared for the astonishing thing which happened.

Guy suddenly seemed to leap out of his bonds. De Valvasson fell back with a curse. He saw the chair come hurtling through the air at him and tried to duck.

It struck him a stunning blow on the forehead. He heard Guy's laughter but faintly before black fog rolled over him.

The barbaric desire to mutilate, to blot out the life of an enemy by mauling it to death, shook Guy as he stood thoughtfully over de Valvasson's senseless form. It took several seconds to overcome. Guy hated the duke, but not with the passion of understanding. De Valvasson was not human enough to be hated in that manner. Guy loathed the man with a repugnance which heretofore he had always reserved for snakes and spiders and other cold, crawly things. He paused now, with a curse, and then, bent forward and picked up de Valvasson's sword. The duke moaned and slowly opened his eyes. Guy rested the blade on the man's throat.

"One mistake, *Monsieur le Duc*," he said, "and you choke on your own blood."

De Valvasson frowned, nodded, and lay still. "How did you lose the bonds?" he asked.

Guy laughed softly. "Bovarde's broken wine-glass was very sharp," he replied and took the sword point away from the other's throat. "I cut the ropes with the pieces. Arise, *monsieur*, and do it gently with no sudden movement."

DE VALVASSON sat up slowly and shook his head. "I should have killed you last night," he said with mild regret. "This is my own cursed fault."

Guy waved his rapier commandingly. "Up, *monsieur*. Where are your friends?"

"Downstairs. Some sleeping; some eating," said the duke and pulled his knees up. He rubbed a palsied hand across his eyes. "*Sacré nom,* but how dizzy I am. I'm afraid your chair has cracked my skull, *monsieur.*"

Guy shrugged indifferently. Somewhere in the hall there was a faint noise. He inclined his head slightly to listen, and thereby committed an error. For a man apparently so groggy, de Valvasson enjoyed a remarkable recovery. With a shrill yell, he leaped and wrapped his small wiry body about Guy's startled frame.

"André! Phillip! Bovarde! A moi! Help! He escapes! Help!"

Guy struggled, frenziedly, desperately. The duke clung to his chest and arms with the horrid tenacity of an octopus. Suddenly, Guy managed to rip his sword arm free. De Valvasson was too close for the use of the blade, so Guy did the next best thing. He lifted the weapon high and brought its heavy guard smashing down atop the duke's head. De Valvasson grunted and slumped to the floor.

As he stood panting over the other's prostrate form, Guy pondered what to do next. He had originally hoped that he would be able to escape by stealth. Such a move was out of the question, now. De Valvasson's shrieks had aroused the others. He could hear them calling out from below.

Finally, with an oath to the senseless figure at his feet, he bounded to the door. Perhaps there was still enough time to make a run for it. Besides, he had a weapon now. The long steel sliver gave him confidence.

He burst into the small hallway which led to the stairs. It was deserted but even as he started to congratulate himself the heads of Bovarde and de la Marnette raised themselves at its end. Both men had naked blades grasped in their hands. They saw Guy at the same time he saw them.

"Here he is! Hurry! Kill him!"

Guy met the first rush with a shower of lightning-like ripostes. Bovarde and de la Marnette fell back timidly. More men surged up the staircase behind them and they charged forward again. Guy danced backward from the flicker of their blades. The hallway was narrow and it gave him an advantage.

At the door one of the blades which had been licking hungrily for his body, bit a brief gash in the side of his head. The blood made the wound look more serious than it really was. Bovarde's blade had accomplished it, and the big man laughed in triumph.

"Look, *mes amis*. He bleeds. I have nipped him!"

Fury of the pain made Guy lash forward. His blade whipped aside other steel and buried itself in the base of Bovarde's throat. The move was entirely unexpected. With a bubbly scream the dying man slumped wearily into the arms of the men behind him.

Before anyone had time to collect his wits, Guy leaped back through the door and slammed it shut. "And I have nipped you, *monsieur,*" he panted grimly and fell to piling furniture in front of the closed door. It was shivering under the poundings of boots, shoulders, and sword hilts, before he had finished.

The assault ceased after a few moments and there was silence. Guy went over and pressed an ear to the paneling. The men outside were having a hurried but orderly discussion.

"... need a battering ram," someone said.

"Yes. The door is a sturdy one," agreed someone else. "You, *Monsieur le Marquis,* and you André, go downstairs and fetch up a long bench. Be certain it is a heavy one."

CHAPTER IV

GUY STEPPED BACK and frowned. It was apparent that his present refuge was to remain inviolable for only a very short period. The door was strong, but not strong enough to withstand forever the shattering impacts of a heavy wooden bench. His eyes whipped inquiringly around the room. To his right, the Duke de Valvasson lay sprawled loosely with a cruel gash in his head.

He was so still that Guy wondered whether he had killed him. "*Corbac!* I hope so," he muttered and walked over to the window.

The miserable court seemed to lie very far below him. If a man had a long rope, however, he might—Guy snapped his fingers. That was it!

Lacking a sheath, he placed the sword on the table and began collecting pieces of the rope which had bound him. There was a goodly amount of it, but it took time to tie the lengths together. While he was so engaged, the men on the other side of the door brought up their impromptu battering-ram and began shivering the door with it.

He eyed the tortured paneling nervously. As yet, it showed no indication of giving, but even as he watched, a small, significant crack began to appear. He picked up the rope, coiled it loosely, and went to the window.

"*Pécaire*, but I hope it holds," he said, inspecting the number of lumpy knots in its length. "If it doesn't—" He shrugged and bent down to tie the end of it to one of the table's heavy legs.

As he straightened, facing the window, something whizzed by his ear and the glass in front of him shattered into a million splinters. With a cry, he whirled about.

The Duke de Valvasson was standing in the center of the room with a snarl of disappointment creasing his blood-streaked features. For a moment, stark terror shot through Guy. What sort of a snake was de Valvasson? Would he never stay down, or would black life remain in his body until sunset? An almost hysterical laugh broke from Guy's throat.

"You'll run out of bottles, scum," he cried. "Your aim is poorer than last night!"

The duke did not answer. The two of them just stood there, frozen. Behind them the sturdy door began to splinter. Finally, de Valvasson's eyes darted to the table and saw the gleaming sword lying there. With a cry he sprang for it, but Guy's lean body arched through the space separating them and crashed numbingly into the duke. They rolled madly across the floor like a pair of spitting cats, scratching, gouging.

A bruising kick threw Guy over on his back. De Valvasson started to crawl toward the table. He reached it, picked up the sword; but Guy's arms crushed him before he could turn about. They fought madly. Suddenly, they were in front of the window. Without thinking Guy let go of the duke, placed his hands on the man's shoulders, and pushed. The sword in de Valvasson's arms flailed about wildly. Horror smeared his features for but a moment, and then he was gone. His body struck the hard cobbles of court three flights below. It shivered slightly and then lay lifeless, like a stringless puppet.

FROM the garret window Guy stared down through a haze of exhaustion. *Dieu,* how he wanted to sit down somewhere, relax over a bumper of cool refreshing wine. He pressed a hand to his forehead and it came away streaked with red. For a moment he stared at it stupidly, and then he remembered the swordcut. It had happened so long ago that he had almost forgotten.

A noise, something like that of a breaking drumhead, made him look over his shoulder in time to see the door crack open. The sight shook the weariness from his shoulders and he bent down, picked up the rope, and tossed it through the window. He was disappearing over the ledge as the first of the conspirators wiggled into the room.

Guy remembered only flashes of that wild slide to the ground. He remembered the gnawing pain in his hands as the rope burned through them; remembered seeing de la Marnette's narrow fox-like features staring down at him from the window. Suddenly, the restraint of the rope ceased and it snaked down atop him as he hit the courtyard. It hadn't broken; de la Marnette had slashed through it with his sword.

Guy's fall had been a short one, fortunately, and he picked himself up without pain. Above, de la Marnette had disappeared, but inside the building the sounds of yells and pounding feet told him that his enemies were bounding down the stairs. He hadn't a minute to waste.

He found horses at the rear of the building and mounted one quickly. The men in the courtyard shouted wildly as he galloped through their midst. Swords licked out at him. Missed. Almost sobbing his joy, Guy bent close to the horse's neck and thundered over the Pont Neuf. He was free! And the sounds of pursuit faded in the distance. It was a quarter after eight.

... Richelieu said: "Monsieur d'Entreville, your condition is deplorable. You look as though you had been brawling all night."

Guy leaned heavily on the table behind which the Cardinal was sitting. He was a ghastly sight with his blood-smeared features, his torn and dirty clothing; but his eyes were clear and determined.

"At the Inn du Lac d'Or," he said hoarsely, "a party of six men is waiting to kill you."

"Go on, *monsieur.*"

"They have found out that you shall have only an escort of four, and that you have planned to rest there." The speaker straightened with a touch of his former disdain. "There," he said, "I have warned you. I have struggled through a century of horror to do it. But, do not feel complimented, *Monseigneur.* I have done this only because of my Catherine. If her freedom had not been at stake, I would have allowed your enemies to—"

Richelieu held up his hand. "I am most grateful to Mademoiselle du Murier," he said with a smile.

Guy brushed the words aside. "About our bargain, *Monseigneur!* I accept it. You may expect courtesy, obedience and loyalty from me, but—" The man's eyes grew cold. "Never respect, or friendship."

Richelieu nodded. He picked a sheet of paper from the table and handed it to Guy.

"Our bargain is already completed, *Monsieur le Comte,*" he said quietly. "That paper which you hold is Mademoiselle du Murier's release. I have no use for you in my guard."

Guy stared at the paper in his hand and then at the Cardinal. His mouth gaped. "Oh, so I am not good enough for your guard, now, eh? You are in character, *Monseigneur.* First, you allow me to make enemies of my friends so that I shall never be again trusted by them; then, you let me risk my very life for your safety; and now, you refuse me entrance to your guard. *Corbac!* What am I to do?"

The Cardinal shrugged. "Perhaps, you had better leave France, *monsieur!*"

Guy leaned forward and pounded the table with his fist. The injustice of the whole business infuriated him.

"No!" he exclaimed. "No! You have made a bargain with me, and I'll accept no withdrawal." He straightened up angrily and shoved Catherine's release into his belt. "First," said he more quietly, "I shall go to the Convent of Carmelites. Then, I shall be married. And then, *Monseigneur,* I shall take up my duties as lieutenant of your guards!" With a brisk nod, he turned on his heel and strode out of the room.

Richelieu looked slyly up at Père Joseph who stood beside him. For the first time in many years he actually laughed.

"Joseph," he said between bursts, "someday our erstwhile poet is going to make a fine officer."

Père Joseph smiled wryly. *"Oui, Monseigneur,"* he agreed. "If we can ever keep pace with his change of mind."

II

RAKEHELLY RIDE

Ride and sing, Cavaliers! Does any man scorn your poetry? Will there be fighting? You have fists, and good blades; cannon, muskets, broken bottles, or anything. And is France to be saved? Well, then, there's more sport for two resourceful rogues.

CHAPTER I

CAVALIER'S DOWNFALL

THE MAN WAS rash. Entirely too rash for duty at the Louvre. He refused to recognize the diplomacy demanded of an officer in the Queen's Guard despite de Guitaut's repeated lectures about it.

De Guitaut eyed him now, in the precise confines of his quarters, and shook his head. This slim malefactor of the court's etiquette; this exiled Englishman who bore the title of Lord Richard Cleve with such amiability, had to be reprimanded.

He had to be chastised in a manner which would show him the error of taking a young peer of France by the ear, and leading him from a Paris pot-house while onlookers howled in merriment.

The *capitaine* shrugged. To make a reprimand stick to this smiling iconoclast was a poser. Richard Cleve seemed born for trouble and verbal punishment had lost potency through overuse. De Guitaut tugged his spade-beard, scowled.

"Of course you realize, Lieutenant," he said, "last night's affair will cause me embarrassment. I am responsible for the conduct of my officers. La Duchesse d'Argonne does not take kindly to being made a laughing-stock. Her son's prestige is important, and she is very close to Her Majesty's ear!"

Cleve shrugged. There was grace in the way his broad shoulders moved. He rested a lean hand on his sword-hilt and used the other to brush back a strand of unruly chestnut hair.

"The Duchess asked me to save her wandering son from the evils of Paris," he said smilingly. "And I did."

De Guitaut snorted. "You made a fool of him!"

"That's impossible."

The *capitaine* choked. He glared at his junior officer. Richard Cleve reminded him of his younger days. The Englishman had the same gay restlessness in his eye; the same devil-may-care manner of dressing.

The black doublet he wore was slashed with silver. His short maroon military cape was faced with *fleur de lis*, and his thigh-high cordovan boots encased his legs without a crease.

Gallant! Rakish! But a devil for trouble, nevertheless. The *capitaine* threw up his hands.

"*Sangodemi!*" he exploded. "I despair of you! But for that cursed wild streak, you'd be perfect. Mark your past actions, *monsieur:* Last week, three duels. Yesterday, two Cardinal's guards thrown into a fountain. Last night, a fool made of a nobleman!"

Cleve looked uncomfortable. Until now those adventures

The Englishman fought alone—until D'Entreville arrived.

had seemed fun. He picked up his hat with its scarlet plume and inspected it intently.

"Sorry," he said looking up. "I joined the Guard for action, *Capitaine*. I'm not made for court life. Social hypocrisy stifles me. There is something in my nature that prevents me fawning for favors from fops and courtiers."

He eyed his *commandante* obliquely. "Perchance," he continued hopefully, "another regiment such as the...."

But de Guitaut was already shaking his grizzled head. The court was rife with rumors of war and civil war. Cardinal Richelieu's latest coup d'état had sparked new jealousy amongst the nobility. Richard Cleve might be an irrepressible madcap, but he was also a fine soldier. A leader. And the *capitaine* wanted to keep him in the troop.

"No!" he said flatly. "If this is another request for a transfer to the King's Horse, I refuse in advance."

"Oh." The young officer hesitated. "I was afraid of that." Then the slow smile, typical of him, crept across his lean bronzed features. "But what of the Duchess, *monsieur?*"

De Guitaut scratched his chin and paced the length of the room. "A month's suspension without pay should placate her," he decided. "Yes. A month without pay."

Cleve nodded. He had seen little of France since his arrival from England. Here was an opportunity. "Why, that is excellent, *mon Capitaine,*" he agreed. "I really need a vacation, you know. Been getting stuffy, here at the palace."

De Guitaut collapsed into a chair. He made a hopeless gesture. "There it is," he muttered to himself. "I punish him, and he turns it into a holiday!" Suddenly he got to his feet. "*Corbac,*" he roared. "Get out! Get out of here before I lose my patience!"

OUTSIDE the *capitaine's* room Cleve paused, adjusted his hat, and blew out his cheeks. "Hmmmm. The old boy is getting touchy!" he muttered, and strode off down the long hallway.

The remark was typical. Cleve had never learned the penalty of an irresponsible tongue or an impulsive act. The trouble he found himself constantly embroiled in came for the most part as a complete surprise. His intentions were honest, but opinionated. They were the reason for his present exile.

Two months ago he had been home, secure in the luxury of the English peerage. And then he had said the wrong things about Buckingham, the King's favorite. And Buckingham had seen to it that he left England before he had had a chance to prove them. Personally, Cleve considered the whole affair unwarranted.

Outside the Louvre it was a beautiful morning. Blue and gold, with sunshine sweeping the Capitainerie and glinting on the green-yellow waters of the Seine. Stepping into the warmth of it, Cleve decided to walk. The sun was too pleasant to waste.

There was a tavern, L'Oiseau Bleu on the other side of town, so he bent his course in that direction.

The Quai de l'École was quiet as he passed, somnolent in the spring warmth. He loitered through the market at the foot of the Pont Neuf because the booths, with their variety of merchandise—great slabs of gory meat to the finest examples of metal work—fascinated him.

He paused to watch a group of tumblers do their act; threw them a coin and continued his way.

Rounding the corner which led to the tavern, he was greeted by the sight of a small crowd. A heaving, yelling, cursing crowd, gripped in the spirit of combat. The nucleus of the fray was clotted around the tavern's door. Cleve approached slowly, his fingers caressing the steel of his rapier.

He stood at the fringe and glanced curiously in the direction of the entrance. He weighed his chances of reaching it, and decided that the passage would be too rough. Not worth a bottle of *sacque.*

"Well, there are other inns." He shrugged, and started to leave. Splattering out of the fracas came a large gob of mud. It struck his shoulder and streaked upward, dirtying his cheek.

He removed the grime and turned slowly. Ten feet away was a little man standing in the attitude of a discus-thrower after the throw. The man stared uncertainly, and Cleve wagged a reprimanding finger.

"Ah, you want to play, eh?" he asked advancing.

The little man seemed hypnotized at first by what he'd done; then he let out a howl and scuttled into the mob. The cavalier hitched up his rapier and plunged after him. Somebody stuck out a foot and he found himself sprawled on the ground.

"By Gad, that settles it," he muttered, getting to his feet. With the righteous indignation of an aroused neutral, he drew his blade and slapped the flat of it across an exposed rear. "Disperse you brawlers! Disperse!"

He waded in, his blade whistling as he spanked right and left. "Come gentlemen," he laughed. "Let's have order. Disperse and go home! Disperse!"

The mob was quick to understand. It felt the cavalier's smarting blade; heard his yelled command. Same spotted the *fleur de lis* on his cape, and sent up the cry: "Run! The Guard has come! Run! Run!"

THE CROWD scattered like marbles. There was still a knot of four struggling inside the tavern. Cleve sheathed his blade and stepped through the door.

He took the first by the scruff of the neck, and sent him bowling into the street. A second followed. The third left quickly of his own accord; but as the Englishman seized the fourth, the fellow objected.

"Mais non, m'sieu. I am the proprietor!"

Cleve noted the rolled-up sleeves; the apron. He released the man with a laugh. *"Pecaire, m'sieu le maitre,* you have remarkable entertainment at your tavern. I enjoyed it, but it has given me a thirst. Fetch me a bottle of wine, eh?"

"Mais oui, m'sieu le grand," said the inn-keeper, hastening to obey. "For you I fetch the very best in my cellar. One moment, *m'sieu."*

Cleve found an overturned table and righted it. He discovered a chair and was about to sit down when his eye caught a portion of the floor near the entrance. There was a long shadow stretched across it. He looked up.

In the door-frame, with a bared sword slanted across his boots, stood the resplendent figure of a Cardinal Guards officer. Behind him were his men. A squad of eight, standing at ease in the bright sunshine of the street.

Cleve's hand which had instinctively dropped to his hilt fell away, and he laughed. "Egad! To the rescue come the Cardinal's brave men. But, late as usual." He bowed mockingly. "Pray enter, *monsieur.* It is quite safe—now."

The newcomer frowned, sheathed his sword, and stepped into the taproom. His flashing dark eyes swept the wreckage. He didn't speak for a moment, but stood arms akimbo as if undecided.

"A small war, no doubt," he finally muttered to himself, and turned to the Englishman. "All right, *monsieur*. What was the cause of this?"

Cleve's jaw tightened. There was a stiff authority in the other's voice which didn't quite suit his taste. He sat down leisurely. "A high wind, *monsieur*," he said pleasantly. "A tornado."

The Cardinalist didn't consider it funny. "Who are you?"

"Richard Cleve, of Her Majesty's Guards. I have the situation well in control. You may run on back to your master and tell him that."

The officer pierced the speaker with a glance. "Ah," he grated, "a clown, from a regiment of clowns." He stared at Cleve with sudden decision in his eyes. "A man with your sense of comedy would naturally start something like this. Where is the proprietor?"

"Below. In the cellar. Shall I fetch him?"

"And escape? Oh no! You're under arrest, *monsieur*."

Cleve stood up. He kicked the chair aside so that he could have room. "What?"

The Cardinalist beckoned and the squad poured into the inn. "I said," he repeated. "You are under arrest."

Cleve eyed the guards. His sword seemed to leap from its sheath. "Well"—he laughed—"the odds are about even. Come and take me!"

The Cardinalist shrugged. He turned to his men. "My pleasure," he warned. "Don't interfere." With great calmness he drew his blade. His even lips beneath the clipped mustache verged on a smile. "I'm coming for you, clown. *En garde!*"

Cleve laughed. He crouched; dropped a foot back for balance. The heel came down heavily on the neck of a bottle; and then things began to happen. His feet shot up; his sword flew one way and his hat another. He landed with a soul-jarring crash.

"*Ooff!*"

The Cardinalist howled. He sheathed his blade and assisted the Englishman to his feet. "My quickest capture, *monsieur*," he chuckled. "Consider yourself arrested!"

Cleve glared, then hobbled two steps forward. The floor hadn't been soft. " 'Tis considered," he accorded wryly. "A downfall both figurative and literal."

"Shall I have the men carry you?"

"I'll walk," Cleve said. "Lead on."

CHAPTER II

OUT CLAWS, KITTEN!

DURING THE MARCH to the Palais de Richelieu, Cleve studied his captor. The man's bearing was soldierly, the cheekbones high, the nose aristocratic, the mouth personable.

He was taller than Cleve by two inches, and if he hadn't such an air of self-sufficiency the Englishman felt that he would be likeable.

This trait annoyed Cleve. Then he smiled considering how this smug martinet would look when he discovered that he had arrested the wrong man. Cleve was counting on the keeper of L'Oiseau Bleu to aid him.

His thoughts were interrupted as the squad tramped through the main gate of the Cardinal's palace. The building was magnificent, a true proclamation of Richelieu's power: for it far exceeded the Louvre in beauty and size.

The captive stared; then nodded agreeably. The Cardinal was very wise. Having incurred Louis XIII's jealousy by building this edifice, he had soothed the pangs by giving it to the Crown—after his death, of course.

Cleve smiled. "Very pretty quarters," he said to the Cardinalist.

The other nodded pleasantly. "Glad you like them, *monsieur,*" he said. "I trust the dungeon will meet with your approval, also."

They went deep into the bowels of the palace where the light was grey and the air damp. The smell of mould was heavy.

Walking through the grim atmosphere Cleve wondered whether he hadn't bit off more than he could chew. The Cardinalist ushered him into a dismal little room and smiled charmingly.

"Fine view," he said, indicating the blank wall. "Well heated and cosy. Of course, I must apologize for the slight leak in the roof. But we can't have everything, can we?"

Cleve looked at his uncomfortable surroundings. The grin on his captor's face suddenly irked him, and he lost his sense of humor. "No," he said in a strangled voice. "*We* can't."

The Cardinalist pursed his lips. He stepped out of the cell and locked the door. *"Au revoir, mon ami.* I trust that your sense of comedy will make you comfortable."

The Englishman stood spread-legged in the center of the cell, now thoroughly aroused. "I trust yours will, when I get out of here!" he roared. "You'll need it."

AN HOUR crawled into the gloom. Cleve paced and cursed and thought up tortures. Finally a bearded guardsman came and opened the cell.

He led Cleve silently up the grimy stone steps into a reception hall, then down a corridor to a gilded anteroom carpeted in red. There was a set of high-paneled doors at one side.

"Monseigneur le Cardinal will see you presently, m'lord," the guard said, and withdrew.

Alone in the large room Cleve grew thoughtful. He had a distinct sense of impending adventure. He was not being treated as a prisoner but rather as a guest. And then too, the guard had used his English title. With a frown, the Englishman shrugged and waited.

Shortly, there was the firm tread of footsteps approaching the other side of the paneled doors. He straightened as they swung back to reveal a bearded figure on the threshold.

The newcomer was garbed in a monk's habit which somehow added to his height and lent dignity to his years. Cleve recognised the man immediately. This was Père Joseph, Richelieu's only true friend, his only confidant.

The monk nodded. His voice had a soft timbre which fell pleasantly.

"Monseigneur will see you now, m'lord."

He ushered Cleve into a vast library heavy with furnishings and an atmosphere of thought. Except for the two patterned shafts of sunlight cast through the latticed windows, it was almost dark. At the end, behind a heavy Venetian desk, sat Richelieu.

The Cardinal's fine pallor was delicately tinted with shadow, giving his sharply chiseled features a thoughtful, profound, nearly ethereal appearance. He was leaning forward over the desk and speaking in sharp tones to a young man standing before him.

Cleve recognized the officer who had arrested him, and he grinned with impish glee.

"…and from the testimony of the proprietor," Richelieu was saying, "your patrol was fifteen minutes late in answering his call for aid. Furthermore, Capitaine Cordeau assures me that you were spending that time finishing one of your silly poems. Monsieur d'Entreville, I'll not tolerate such inefficiency!"

The stern reprimand ended as Cleve and Père Joseph came up. The Cardinalist officer, d'Entreville, glanced out of the corner of his eye, saw the Englishman and flushed.

"Rather warm isn't it, *mon ami?*" Cleve greeted him out of the corner of his mouth.

D'Entreville didn't say anything but there was murder in his dark eyes. Cleve chuckled happily. And then Richelieu looked up and pinned him with cold black eyes. The happy chuckle died away.

"And here we have the man who did d'Entreville's work for him," said Richelieu. "I have long desired to meet you, my lord Cleve. *Mais oui.* Your *commandante* tells such interesting things of you."

The speaker rose. He made a graceful figure in his trailing red robe, seeming taller than he was by virtue of his slenderness.

There was an authoritative crack to his words which revealed the man's dynamic personality.

Here was a ruler. A molder of destiny. He paced to the side of the room now, turned with a lithe panther-like movement, and fixed Cleve again with his eyes.

"There is a little matter of two Cardinal's guards and a fountain that needs explaining, Monsieur Cleve," he said, and returned to the desk. "Also a few illegal duels."

The Englishman looked for his glib tongue and couldn't find it. "Oh I—I—that is, *Monseigneur....*"

The Cardinal made a peremptory gesture. "Don't waste my time in inventing excuses. You're a rascal, and you know it!" He looked up and caught d'Entreville wearing a crooked smile. "Ah. It amuses you, *monsieur le comte?*"

The Frenchman shifted uneasily. "Eh—no, *Monseigneur,*" he replied.

A SILENCE fell. Finally Richelieu sat down. He shrugged and interlaced his long tapering fingers. "Two of the wildest young rogues in Paris," he said ruefully to Père Joseph.

Then he directed a thoughtful glance in Cleve's direction. "Your arrest was a fortunate error, *monsieur.* It saves me the trouble of sending for you."

"Sending for me, *Monseigneur?*"

"Yes. One of the guards whom you pitched into the fountain has developed a cold. Poetic justice, *monsieur,* for you shall take his place. You are transferred to my guards, m'lord. Not only that—you are about to be sent on your first mission. I have notified your *commandante.*"

Cleve saw his month of freedom flying out of the window. He'd wanted that month. Besides, he had small heart for running any of the Cardinal's errands.

"But—but *Monseigneur,*" he protested. "You said yourself that I was a rascal. Surely, so fine a regiment as the Cardinal's Guards doesn't deserve a rascal such as I."

The Cardinal's lips quivered into a near smile. "The guard has one rascal in it already, *monsieur*," he said with a nod toward d'Entreville. "Another should make little difference. Besides, I have checked your record thoroughly.

"I need swordsmen now, and you are one of the best. Except for rashness, you are the soul of honor. You are loyal also, and that is all that I demand of a man."

Cleve decided that he was a gone goose. He attempted to put a good face on it by saying, "Thank you, *Monseigneur.*" But the words fell unheeded. Richelieu had dropped him and was speaking to d'Entreville.

"As for you, *monsieur le comte,*" he said, "I tremble at the responsibility I am forced to put in your hands. If I were not starved for resourceful rogues, I'd have you in la Bastille. Your foolhardiness is well proven. Yesterday, you saw fit to duck two musketeers in a fountain for laughing at your poetry...."

Cleve choked at this, and Richelieu eyed him coldly.

"Yes," he snapped. "It was the same fountain. One would believe it was a public bath." He shrugged and fell back in his chair. "Bah! I do Paris a favor by sending you two out of it. You're both madcaps, *messieurs.* Impudent fools!"

Guy d'Entreville shifted expectantly. Beside him, Cleve scowled. "I wish the old rake would get to the point," he thought.

The Cardinal did. Having established his acid censure of their respective misdeeds, he dropped the stern tone. He beckoned Père Joseph to him. "Have Beaucaire come in."

"Oui, Monseigneur."

As Père Joseph departed, the Cardinal searched among a litter of papers and finally drew for a parchment map of Royal France. He regarded it thoughtfully; and when he looked up, his face was grave.

He said: *"Messieurs,* your mission is vital. You may not know it, but France is on the brink of civil war. I have just had word that le Duc d'Orleans has crossed the border with a rebel army of 6,000 men."

GUY D'ENTREVILLE frowned. Being French he knew the political situation of his country, and the news did not come too much as a surprise. D'Orleans had sworn to ruin Richelieu.

But Cleve didn't know this. He only considered that the Duke of Orleans was the King's brother and heir to the throne; and knowing that, was definitely startled.

"Gad's teeth!" he exploded. "Against the Crown?"

Richelieu's dark eyes hardened. He shook his head. "No," he said quietly. "Against me!"

And then Cleve understood. He had been in France long enough to hear the political gossip about Richelieu's aims. The nation had been weakened for years by a feudalism which gave the nobility right to raise private armies, to levy personal taxes, and to subsidize the throne.

The Cardinal was trying to crush this system. He wanted a united France powerful under but one recognized and centralized government—the kings! Bitterness, hatred, constant intrigue had been the result.

Richelieu picked a quill from the inkstand and tapped its tip lightly on the map. "D'Orleans is not strong enough to try storming Paris," he said softly. "He is passing down the west side of the Rhone River toward Nîmes. There he hopes to enlist more hot-heads and also to effect junction with certain disloyal noblemen in southern France."

He paused, and then, raised the tip of the quill and placed it at Bordeaux on the western edge of the map.

"And here," he continued, "we have the royal army under Marshal Schomberg, It is moving east now, at right angles, to intercept d'Orleans. If my calculations are correct it should meet the rebels near Privas."

The speaker looked up. Père Joseph had returned and with him was a swarthy man of medium height, resplendent in red and black. Père Joseph said, "Le Marquis de Beaucaire, *Monseigneur.*"

The Cardinal nodded. Cleve bent close to d'Entreville. "Important?" he asked.

Guy nodded. "Cardinal's agent."

"These are the two who shall officer your escort south, *monsieur le marquis*," said Richelieu. "May I present le Comte d'Entreville and m'Lord Cleve. They are rogues, but the resourcefulness of their roguery is suited for my purpose."

Beaucaire smiled. It was a nice smile, flashing in white contrast to his skin. He nodded to Cleve but his hawkish features were curious when he regarded d'Entreville.

He said: "*Ma foi!* Aren't you that acid-versed poet with such sharp claws that you are known as the Kitten? The Cardinal's Kitten?"

Cleve felt d'Entreville go rigid. The Frenchman nodded stiffly. "I am," he admitted. His face was red.

Beaucaire smiled politely.

THEN Richelieu stood up. He spoke crisply to Cleve and Guy. "I have selected you, *messieurs*, to escort a shipment of gold south. Understand, it is not a routine detail. Marshal Schomberg's troops have not been paid for two months. The last convoys sent him have been robbed and the men are growing restless. They threaten to desert.

"As the situation stands now, they are either paid or d'Orleans will not be stopped."

D'Entreville nodded understandingly. During the early seventeenth century armies were mercenary; rapidly levied, disbanded again, haphazard.

"I have arranged," Richelieu continued, "for the royal army to pass Beaucaire's Castle on their way to meet the rebels. They must be paid there, or they will mutiny! We have five days to prevent that, *messieurs*."

The speaker frowned. "Now, concerning your mode of transportation. The other convoys have been waylaid, so this time I will change my tactics."

D'Entreville chewed his lip. He lacked the subtlety of his red-robed superior. To him the way to prevent further robberies would be to increase the escort—a regiment if need be. Richelieu could spare no regiments. With Austria threatening on one side and Spain on another, he needed them at home.

"*Le marquis* is returning to his castle at Beaucaire," he said slowly, "as an innocent traveler. He shall have a traveler's escort. Six men. However, within his coach will be a secret compartment. The gold will be hidden there."

Richard Cleve understood. "*Oui, Monseigneur,*" he said.

"Good." The steel in Richelieu's voice denied failure. "Now leave me and return prepared to quit Paris within the hour. Cordeau is waiting in the guardroom with Beaucaire's personal liveries. Select four men. See that they are dressed in them."

Outside the library, Cleve stared at his new companion reproachfully. "Had you let me alone at the tavern—" he began to say; then changed his mind and smiled. "Hmph! The old man works quickly, eh? Two hours ago I was in the Queen's Guard, suspended and anticipating a holiday."

D'Entreville regarded him thoughtfully, and the faint frown left his forehead. "I wouldn't," he cautioned, "let anyone hear you refer to the Cardinal as 'the old man'. It isn't healthy."

The good intention was lost. Cleve bowed and said mockingly: "Words of wisdom, Kitten, fall upon my poor ears as dew upon parched grass."

Guy d'Entreville's breath caught up short. "Very funny," he snapped. "Mark you, Cleve. Fate insists that we become companions. But if you desire harmony, don't use that title!"

The Englishman inclined his head. " 'Tis remembered, old comrade," he promised.

They swung down the corridor side by side. Cleve eyed his lean companion obliquely, and the devil in him started dancing. He stared ahead.

"Here Kitty, Kitty, Kitty!"

D'Entreville's lips became a tight line. His hand on the hilt of his sword balled into a lump. Without breaking stride, he jerked it to his stomach. The sword-length swung out; slipped between Cleve's scissoring legs.

A yell—a crash, and Guy d'Entreville continued his way—alone. Smiling.

CHAPTER III

SWORD-SPORT FOR TWO

TWO DAYS LATER, the treasure-train reached the halfway mark. Sitting his horse in the orange wash of the setting sun, Cleve scowled and reviewed them remorsefully.

Everything had been quiet. The days—monotonous. In a way he felt cheated. When one humbles himself by masquerading as a part of a petty noble's retinue, there should be compensation. But, so far, Richelieu's subterfuge had been so perfect as to make him nearly pray for action.

He cursed silently between his teeth as his eyes swept the surrounding hills lying pale green in the sun. The convoy was threading through lower Bourbonnais, and tonight the stop would be at the village of Lamont.

"Peaceful," he growled, eyeing the landscape. "It makes me itchy."

Behind him, Beaucaire's gaudy blue-and-gold coach rumbled along with the pompousness of a dowager. It was flanked by two riders with another pair trailing and trotting carefully outside the rolling dust of the coach-wheels.

Back there someone was singing. Cleve knew that fine tenor voice. It was d'Entreville's. The song blended pleasantly with the cadence of horse's hoofs.

> *So I ride, ride, ride.*
> *With a good blade at my side,*

And a horse without an equal in the land.
'Tis the gayest life I know....

The Englishman twisted in the saddle. His association with Guy had, for the past forty-eight hours, been painful. Despite their mutual animosity, however, he secretly liked the Frenchman. D'Entreville had the nerve and courage which he admired in a man.

Nevertheless, the two of them argued like fish-wives, and only their subconscious congeniality prevented physical violence. Now, as Cleve heard Guy's self-made song, he raised his own baritone in an ill-intentioned parody.

So I ride, ride, ride.
With the Kitten at my side.
He's a Kitten without equal in the land!
Though he dabbles hard with verse,
I can think of nothing worse,
Than an ode which he has written with his—

Whap!

The song ended as a round hard apple, snatched from a low-hanging limb, caromed off the back of the singer's neck. Cleve grinned and spurred his horse to a trot.

The two managed to complete the journey that day without further song or comedy—or hostilities.

Lamont was small. It was a village barely out of swaddling clothes. But it was a favorite coach-stop and boasted of two large hostelries—one at either end of its central thoroughfare. The treasure-train clattered into the courtyard of the first inn, as the last glow in the west faded into purple-pink.

The footman leaped nimbly from the coach, placed a step-stool on the ground and opened the door. But Beaucaire did not step out. He hesitated, scrutinized the inn; then smiled ruefully.

"We shall stay at the other hostelry," he decided, and waved at Cleve and d'Entreville. "Drive on!"

The cavaliers exchanged glances. They didn't speak until they were again on the move. This was the fourth time Beaucaire had taken advantage of the masquerade to make the decisions for the party and they didn't like the idea.

"You know," Cleve said softly, "I am beginning to wonder if Beaucaire has forgotten that we are in charge. The manner in which he acts makes me actually feel like a lackey!"

He paused, scowled, and batted road-dust from his gauntlets. "My first impression of *le marquis* has changed. He smiles too much for my fancy."

D'ENTREVILLE nodded. Those were his sentiments exactly. Beaucaire had not turned out to be the charming companion that they had first believed. His amiable smile and pleasant manners only cloaked a stubborn officiousness.

As Guy became aware of the man's ruthlessness, his ironic humor and his arrogant vanity, he often thought of himself as guardian to a mysterious powder-keg which might erupt at any moment.

He mentioned this feeling now: "Beaucaire seems waiting for something to happen."

Cleve laughed. "Aren't we all? We carry enough gold to tempt a saint."

But that wasn't what d'Entreville had meant. Last evening an Nevers, where the coach had put up for the night, he had caught the marquis in earnest conversation with a strange horseman. Possibly there was nothing to the incident; but the stranger had spurred quickly away at his approach.

Guy hadn't liked that. There had been something furtive about it. Considered now, however, the affair seemed trifling.

He shrugged. He said, "Perhaps," and spurred his horse into he courtyard of the second tavern.

As was customary, the marquis was given the best suite in the tavern while the rest of the party wrapped themselves in cloaks and slept near the coach in the yard behind. The vehicle itself was shared by Cleve and d'Entreville.

Tonight however, as the Frenchman groped his way into the dark tonneau, Cleve was missing. D'Entreville cursed. He had stayed late in the tavern, talking over tomorrow's itinerary with Beaucaire under the impression that the Englishman was on duty.

He turned and called: "Étienne. Sergeant Étienne!"

A lumpish figure on the ground stirred. "*Oui, m'sieu.*"

"Where is Cleve?"

Sergeant Étienne scratched his head. Mental agility was not one of his virtues. He waited a long time and then he said, "Oh, Cleve? Hmmmm. He went for a holiday."

D'Entreville stiffened. His jaw grew tight. The fate of a nation was in Beaucaire's coach. Guy felt its responsibility keenly. But Cleve! *Sangodemi!* It was so like that irresponsible fool to walk away and forget it. The Englishman had irked him many times; but now d'Entreville was thoroughly angered.

He snapped, "Where did he go?"

"The tavern at the other end of town, *monsieur.*"

D'Entreville hitched up his rapier. There was going to be a showdown between him and this English rakehelly.

"You're in charge," he told Étienne briefly. "Cut down all prowlers first. Challenge later."

He went past the strong smell of the stable; through the torch-lit courtyard, and into the dark of Lamont's streets. Somewhere off to the right a bell tolled the hour. It was nearly midnight.

A small troop of horsemen thundered by. He stared curiously. They were Montmorency's men. He could tell by the embroidered cross-blades that they carried on their green surcoats. He wondered what the Duke of Montmorency could be doing so far from court, and shrugged.

The matter of Richard Cleve seemed more important. He strode on through the night toward the other tavern without answering the self-posed question.

THE FIRST inn was called Le Gant Blanc. It was trim, well lighted, peaceful-looking from a distance. But as he came up to it the clash and cry of battle greeted him.

Inside, tables were being overturned; glass was being smashed with abandon. He reached the polished door. It burst open and a man stumbled out, hands clutching a blood-soaked side. Guy shook his head. He had found Cleve.

He stepped over the wounded man and drew his basket-hilt rapier. Inside was shambles. The wreckage indicated a battle far above the average tavern brawl. He eyed it appreciatively.

In the corner was a knot of struggling figures. Five in all. They had Cleve backed to the wall and were straining to pin him there. D'Entreville flexed his sword and walked leisurely toward them. In the center of the room he stopped and shook his head.

"Cleve, if it wasn't that I'd miss a good fight, I'd let them split your worthless hide."

The Englishman had a smile on his lips. It was tired, strained. Someone had ripped a crimson gash over his left eye and blood trickled into it. He kept wiping the flow back with his free hand as he danced in and out of lancing steel. He was like a wraith. His blade seemed five places at once.

Now he looked up; saw d'Entreville. A steel tip arrowed for his throat. He darted under it and pricked the owner's arm and laughed.

"Hello, Kitten. Join the fun?"

His laugh was forced, thrown recklessly into the teeth of five thirsting blades. A fool's gesture when every breath counted. D'Entreville shook his head. His indignation at Cleve for leaving the coach was washed away in a flood of admiration, although he'd never have admitted it.

"Why not?" he cried. "Do you want all of it?"

A man appeared on the stair-landing directly above the Englishman. A knife glittered in his hand. Guy scooped up a full wine bottle and hurled it. The man caught it full in the face. He wilted over the bannister and crashed to the floor.

"War's declared," the Frenchman grunted.

He hurdled a wrecked bench. Two of Cleve's opponents whirled. He put his steel through one and turned for the other.

But the fight was over. Having lost half their original number, the remaining four dropped their swords and rushed for the door. They'd had enough.

Richard Cleve watched them go, a vacant grin fixed to his lips. He said: "And thus endeth another lesson," and sagged suddenly around the knees. He'd have fallen if Guy hadn't caught him.

"Cleve! Did they pin steel into you?"

The Englishman straightened. He chuckled. "Ridiculous!" Then he slogged across the room, collapsed on a bench and grinned at Guy crookedly. "Among the bottles on the floor," he croaked. "Find a good one. I need a drink, Kitten. I'm cursed near the exhaustion point."

D'Entreville found an unbroken bottle of brandy, and they both drank deep from it before speaking again. The liquor's potent sting did things to Cleve. The mist of fatigue slipped from his eyes.

"Thanks, Guy," he said awkwardly. "I—I'm glad you dropped by. I was but two minutes removed from being made a pincushion."

It was the first time he had used d'Entreville's first name, and the Frenchman caught the significance. There was a pause. Then, he shrugged. "Bah! I did nothing." He stared at Cleve sincerely. "You're a real man, Rick."

FOR TWO who had always concealed their sentiments beneath a barrage of banter and criticism the conversation was naturally stilted, almost shy. They both felt it, and it made them more uncomfortable. A pledge had been given. A pledge of friendship welded in the fires of danger.

Cleve laughed. "Egad! Had I known that we were going to carry on this way, I'd have written a sonnet or something."

Guy felt relieved. The words put them back on the old familiar footing. He stood up and glowered. "*Corbac!* And what are you doing here, anyway? Ours is not a pleasure jaunt, *monsieur!* We are entrusted with a vital mission. You have a duty!"

"A curiosity," grinned Cleve. He sampled the brandy some more. "I came to discover Beaucaire's aversion to this particular tavern." He gestured to include the whole room. " 'Tis a pleasant place. As neat as the other. Well, perhaps not at present. But, before the argument…."

Guy snorted. "Brawling!" he said. "You are always brawling. Why can't you behave? Must you continually provoke battles?"

Cleve looked offended. "Me?" he asked in an injured voice. "Me? Why I was minding my own business. And then, two popinjays…." He pointed to a corpse on the floor. "That fellow in particular began to insult me. The next thing I knew, I was fighting half the tavern. Am I to blame for that?"

Guy didn't say anything. Instead he walked over and looked at the body. His eyes narrowed. The insignia on the dead man's green surcoat was crossed blades. Montmorency's man.

Suddenly he realized that they had all been Montmorency's men. He thought of the hard-riding cavalcade which had passed him on the way to the tavern. A frown cut vertical lines in his forehead. Montmorency had once been a constant companion of le Duc d'Orleans! He remembered that now, with a start.

Cleve was saying: "One thing I know; my late friend there and his comrades didn't want me to leave alive. In fact, the whole battle was planned. But why?" He stood up. "Something's rotten, Kitten."

D'Entreville stared at him and nodded. He had been piecing suspicions together himself and he didn't like the pattern they were making. "Let's get out of here," he said.

They returned to the second tavern with unease tugging at their hearts. It was quiet as they marched up to it. Cleve didn't like that quiet. It was death-like, brooding. Two of the torches had gone out and now only one remained to illuminate the courtyard.

Menace hung in the deep shadows. The heavy stillness shrieked with it. The door ajar; the windows dark and staring. The tavern was gutted of life. Disaster had struck—they knew it instinctively.

Huddled against the dark archway with its sword half unsheathed, a bullet in its head, was a corpse. D'Entreville found it. He recognized Pierre, one of the guardsmen he had selected for the journey.

The cavalier took a swift breath and started to run toward the stables. He felt sick inside. Intuitively, he knew that the coach was gone. Cleve grabbed his shoulder. "Hold on! There may be someone waiting—in the shadows."

Guy relaxed. Cleve was using his head. He steadied himself and let his blade whisper from its sheath. They advanced then. Shoulders touching; eyes probing.

CHAPTER IV

POWDER PUFF IN GREEN

THEY FOUND THE others in the rear. They were all dead. Cleve bent beside one and turned him over. It was a stranger. He wore a green surcoat with crossed blades embroidered on it. D'Entreville's lips formed the word hollowly: "Montmorency!"

Cleve nodded and stood up, "They hit the place like a plague. Wiped everything out." He walked over to a pair of parallel ruts. "And they took what they had come for!"

Guy stood with his sword slanted across his boots. Now the realization of the calamity struck like a cudgel.

Sickly he thought, "Schomberg's troops won't be paid. There won't be a royal army. D'Orleans will have time to gather strength now for a war which will wrack France with the horror of internal strife. And, it's my fault! Mine!"

From somewhere in the shadows a faint moan sounded. He glanced in its direction, and then walked over to a clump of bushes. Cleve followed. There was a man lumped under the briar. They picked him up and carried him nearer the light.

It was Sergeant Étienne. Cleve noted the dark stain on the sergeant's chest and shook his head.

"Bad," he said. "Not much hope."

Étienne opened his eyes as they lowered him to the ground. Guy bent close.

"Étienne. Do you hear me?"

"*Oui.*" The voice was faint, pitifully weak. "*Oui, mon lieutenant.*" The speaker looked into Cleve's lean face and chuckled feebly. "Enjoy your holiday, *m'sieu?*"

Cleve had brought the brandy from the first tavern. He gave some of it to the sergeant, and it helped a little.

"What happened, Sergeant?"

Étienne shrugged. "Twelve of them," he croaked. "They swooped into the yard. Killed all before we had chance. I got one, though. Gave an account of myself before—before—" His voice dribbled off.

D'Entreville shook him slightly. "Where's Beaucaire?"

Étienne opened his eyes. They were becoming glazed; he was going fast. "Beaucaire," he muttered. "Hmmm. Beaucaire. He came with them, out of the inn. They got him first. Put him in coach. Kidnaped Beaucaire. Going to make him tell—"

The voice faded into a rattle; and Étienne was staring at them blankly. D'Entreville lowered the head to the ground and stood up.

His voice had ice in it when he said, "And *that* leaves our work cut out for us."

The Englishman nodded absently. His eyes were bleak question marks. Where d'Entreville had been thinking of the consequence, he had been pondering the cause. Now he sent his long sword riding back into its sheath and stared at his tall companion.

HE KNEW that twelve blades against two were long odds. But when he thought of Étienne and the others, the ease with which one could trace a blue-and-gold coach; the stake, and his own cold anger, the odds shrank. He tilted his hat cockily.

"Damme, Guy. We have of a certainty!"

They found the inn-keeper, his family and lackies, hiding in the horse-stalls. D'Entreville routed them out. He showered them with questions, but they were all too terrified to answer sensibly.

"Well!" He finally shrugged. "Which way did they go—or don't you know that, either?"

The lanky inn-keeper washed his hands nervously. The events of the night would be graven in his mind for the rest of his life. He made a sweeping gesture. "To—to the south, *monsieur.*"

D'Entreville's eyes sought Cleve's over the man's shoulder, and the slim Englishman shrugged. "Naturally, Kitten. What did you expect?"

The French cavalier frowned. Things had been happening rapidly. He hadn't had time to consider them closely. But the fact which had lurked at the borderline of his mind since the discovery of the missing coach suddenly loomed into expression.

He shoved the inn-keeper aside, told him to saddle two fresh horses, and walked up to Cleve.

"*Sacré nom!*" he burst out. "There's been a leak! How did Montmorency know that our coach was...."

Richard Cleve looked amused. He shook his head and patted the Frenchman's shoulder. "Very clever, Kitten," he commented soothingly. "Relax. Of course, there's been a leak. As a matter of fact, there's been more than a leak. There's been a whole cursed fountain of treachery."

The jibe in Cleve's tone made Guy angry. "Now mark me,

Richard Cleve—" he started. But the laughter in the English-man's eyes stopped him. He shook his head hopelessly. "All right, wise man. Perhaps you can tell me who the traitor is."

Cleve cocked an eyebrow. "It couldn't be you?" he said.

D'Entreville grew purple. "No!"

"Temper, Kitten," the other continued smoothly. "And, it wasn't I." His face grew serious. "So that leaves but one!"

D'Entreville looked startled. "Beaucaire!"

Cleve nodded.

"But that is impossible!"

"Is it?" asked the Englishman softly.

"Yes."

Cleve plucked a wisp of straw from a nearby bale, and eyed it thoughtfully.

"For a poet, Kitten," he said at length, "you have a singular lack of imagination, Mark this."

He put the straw in his mouth and stared at the Frenchman. "Tonight I visit the first tavern and stumble into a nest of green-coats. They attempt to kill me. Why?" He shrugged. "Because they are waiting to butcher the coach's escort. I know that now."

"But that has nothing to do with Beaucaire," Guy said.

"Hasn't it? Very well, I shall go further. This evening when le Marquis de Beaucaire arrived at the first inn, he did not care to stay there. Damme! He didn't care to stay, because he knew that the place was stuffed with traitors. It's all quite simple, you see."

D'Entreville was thoughtful. Cleve made sense. But the Frenchman found it hard to believe. Whatever his faults Beau-caire was one of Richelieu's trusted agents. The wily Cardinal was not one to select faulty material for his secret police. This knowledge kept nagging at Guy.

"*Mordi!* Your logic is sound, Cleve; but Étienne told us that

Beaucaire was a prisoner, a captive, when last seen. Does that sound like treachery?"

Cleve shrugged. "No. But Étienne was dying. Death blurs the vision."

"Possibly."

"Possibly indeed! I tell you, the marquis is hand in glove with Montmorency!"

D'ENTREVILLE shrugged. He was almost convinced, but he wouldn't give Cleve the satisfaction of knowing it. As he considered Beaucaire's treason that episode back at Nevers suddenly became clear. The marquis had sent that rider on ahead to prepare Montmorency's men.

"I think you're babbling nonsense," he told the Englishman.

The inn-keeper led the horses to them personally. He was anxious to see them go. As they swung to the saddle Guy tossed him a small pouch of gold.

"See that a padre attends the men in the rear," he commanded.

"Mais oui, m'sieu. Even now I shall go to the parish. Your brave comrades shall be buried decently."

Cleve started forward. "No tricks," he said. "We'll pass this way again." He waited until Guy had drawn abreast him in the dark of the street. "We hope," he finished softly.

D'Entreville nodded. The thing that they were about to attempt wasn't wise. Only a caprice of fate had saved them from the massacre. Next time fortune might not smile. Guy frowned, shrugged indifferently. "Who knows?"

The slim Briton put spurs to his horse. "At best it's a game of chance," he said lightly. "Two against twelve and devil take the odds."

But as they thundered into the night, Cleve couldn't help remembering that had he used his wits to catch the reason for the fight at the tavern, the game would never have had to be played. An ounce of prevention would have saved all.

Dawn found them on the grey ribbon of road leading to Clermont. They were saddle-stained and weary; a trifle worried. They had come many miles. So far, no sign of the coach.

Their horses were beginning to labor beneath the crazy pace. They whipped them on with the cruelty of desperation. A coach can not outrun riders. Although the Marquis had had two hours start, they knew he couldn't be far ahead.

"Fresh mounts!" D'Entreville yelled above the pounding hoofs. "*Corbac!* And soon!"

Cleve nodded. His horse stumbled a trifle and he reached forward and patted its straining neck. "Steady. One more league, boy! Keep heart!"

They careened around the bend and almost overlooked the small tavern hidden there. It was a ramshackle affair, seamed with cracks and vari-colored in greys and browns. Cleve drew up and slipped lightly from the saddle. He eyed the staggered chimney wisping smoke on the gold light of the rising day and grinned.

"Some one is astir. Take the horses to the stable and see about fresh ones. I'll order a breakfast."

Guy clutched the reins of the Englishman's horse and held up two fingers. "Two breakfasts," he said. "Big ones. And pump the landlord dry about the coach. *Parbleu!* I hope we're on the right trail." He shrugged and set his horse to a shambling walk.

IN THE rear, the tavern's stables matched the main building in decay—exceeded it in solitude. Guy found them deserted. He stamped about the stalls calling loudly. Finally, he shrugged, led the horses to the trough, watered them and installed them in separate booths.

He started out; then, paused. The animals regarded him pleadingly.

"*Sangodemi!*" he muttered. "I have other things to do. Be patient. Some one will bring you fodder." One of the horses whinnied softly and he laughed. "Oh, very well. I'll find something."

He discovered a pile of hay near the entrance to the stable. There was a pitchfork against the jamb. He picked it up and thrust the prongs deep into the pile. A startled yelp greeted the effort and a green-clad figure, trailing hay, shot out of the pile. D'Entreville dropped the pitchfork and dove. That green surcoat meant only one thing. Montmorency!

He caught the fugitive cleanly with his shoulder and marveled at the fellow's light softness. The Montmorency guard slammed hard to the floor. A hollow *"Ooof!"* whooshed out—and the figure went limp.

With a scowl d'Entreville arose from the body. *"Pecaire!"* he shrugged. "Snuffed like a candle. Montmorency must be hiring powder puffs for guards." He bent down and rolled the unconscious figure over on its back. "Powder puffs," he chuckled, "Or women...."

He gagged. It *was* a woman! A dark, red-lipped girl of twenty with delicate features made more beautiful by the luster of perfect skin.

She was dressed in man's clothes. Pleasingly, too, but Guy was too flabbergasted to notice. The surcoat of green with its crossed-blades insignia was the only thing that registered. He gulped. *"Sacré nom d'un cochon!* What is a gentleman supposed to do now?"

He attempted patting the face, then the wrists. He rested the head on one knee and fanned it with his big hat. Still the dark lashes did not quiver. The girl was out, definitely!

"Well, my lady," he decided at last, "perhaps cognac will do."

He lifted her. The lightness made him feel sheepish. "Guy d'Entreville—brute," he muttered wryly. But his eyes were narrowed, asking questions. Who was she? Why was she hidden in that hay-pile? And what connection did she have with Montmorency and Beaucaire?

That there was a connection, he was positive. The green surcoat spoke volumes.

CHAPTER V

SING FOR YOUR BREAKFAST

RICHARD CLEVE FOUND the Tavern hushed when he entered. There was a brisk fire in the hearth over which a pot of porridge bubbled sloppily. He grinned. "Faith! There must be a strain of Scot in my host."

There were two guests asleep and snoring softly in the window-seats near the front of the taproom. Cleve hadn't noticed them at first, and he regarded them thoughtfully, wondering faintly how men could sleep in such uncomfortable-looking positions.

He considered waking them; but at that moment the side door burst open and a paunchy little man entered. The Englishman smiled.

"Well, landlord! Do you practice leaving your new-come guests alone? My friend and I have traveled hard through the night. We expect service."

The inn-keeper had been napping in the kitchen. He was fresh awake and peevish. His eyes, sunk deep in fatty sockets, blinked meanly. "This inn serves no breakfasts, *m'sieu!*"

Cleve looked at the porridge cooking in the hearth and his arm flickered out like a snake. His fingers curled about the dirty collar and he yanked he inn-keeper up short.

"Really now!" he laughed. "No breakfasts, eh?"

His prisoner wiggled vainly. Then he saw the cold devilment in the Englishman's eyes and he stopped.

"But there are exceptions, *monsieur.* There are—*ouch*—exceptions."

Cleve didn't release him yet. "Naturally," he said. "My friend and I are exceptional persons. We enjoy the best of food, and we like information with it."

"*Oui, m'sieu.* I am your servant."

"At what time did a blue-and-gold coach pass here this morning?"

The fat landlord hesitated. His little eyes swept craftily over Cleve's shoulder. Then widened. The Englishman caught the expression. He heard a slight movement behind.

Without warning he ducked and hurled the screaming inn-keeper over his shoulder. There was a grunt followed by the thud of two bodies hitting the floor.

A knife clattered in spinning circles to his feet.

Cleve whirled. The other guest was plunging toward him a stiletto poised high. Cleve grabbed the striking arm with his left hand. He let fly a savage right and the man's head snapped back.

Cleve blew on his knuckles. He kicked the groaning landlord aside, and pulled the first assailant to his knees by the hair. The man was barely conscious. The impact of the inn-keeper's body had knocked most of the wind out of him. Cleve shook the fellow.

"Nice people," he said. "I should have suspected you two, when I first entered. You looked too uncomfortable to be actually slumbering. Egad! I'm growing careless."

The prisoner cringed. "Mercy," he pleaded groggily. "Mercy, in the name of God."

Cleve reached back for a bottle on the mantel over the hearth. He cracked it shatteringly against the stone and held the remaining half in front of his prisoner's horrified eyes. The glass was jagged, vicious-looking.

"All right," said the Englishman. "Sing out, my pretty bird."

In the background the landlord groaned. "Not in my inn, *m'sieu*, please. Not his eyes!" he implored.

Cleve's voice was cold, "Silence, dolt!" He yanked the prisoner's face closer to the broken bottle. "Do you tell your tale, or have I to twist this into your ugly face?"

The prisoner collapsed. "I'll talk, you devil," he blubbered. "I'll talk."

Cleve nodded. "Good." He smiled grimly. "And never mind your opinions of me. When did Beaucaire pass through here?"

"Three hours past, *monsieur.*"

"He expected us?"

"Yes. When he learned that you and d'Entreville hadn't been killed last night, he left René and me behind to take care of you."

Cleve shrugged. The man's words cleared all doubts about Beaucaire. The marquis was in the plot, up to his neck.

"Where is Beaucaire going?"

A slight stubbornness edged into the prisoner's eyes. He closed his lips. With a curse Cleve gave him a small taste of the glass. Just a scratch. But it was enough. The man wilted.

"To his castle, at Beaucaire."

Cleve lifted the bottle. "You lie! Schomberg will be at Beaucaire within a week. The marquis will want none of him."

"The marquis will have a thousand men by then."

CLEVE'S eyes widened. So that was it! Beaucaire was going to use the gold to raise his own troops. The Englishman bit his lip thoughtfully. It followed that Montmorency had done the same with the other robbed shipments.

Then there would be two well-equipped forces to act in accord with d'Orleans!

"A war," Cleve muttered, "of no mean size." He smiled grimly. The whole plot had an ironic jest to it. The conspirators were using Richelieu's gold to defeat Richelieu. He stared down at his captive. "Montmorency's army. Where is—"

But, the question was interrupted. Cleve released the prisoner, flashed out with his blade, then relaxed. It was d'Entreville, standing in the doorway with a limp figure in his arms.

"You'll fetch trouble, sneaking up on people that way, Kitten," Cleve said. "You should sing, or something."

D'Entreville strode into the room. He frowned at the prisoner and at the unconscious form on the floor. "Brawling again, eh? What happened?"

Cleve told him. When he had finished the Frenchman had a tight expression around his lips. "You realize what it means, of course," he said.

"Certainly. Unless something is done quickly, France will not be independent much longer. The moment civil war weakens her enough, Spain and Austria will step in to establish order."

"I hadn't thought of it that way," d'Entreville admitted gravely. "But you're right." He shrugged and stared down at the girl in his arms. He didn't like to think about it.

"Look what I found," he said.

Cleve stared. "Why damme!" he exclaimed. "It's a girl. A beautiful girl!"

At his feet the prisoner gasped. The Englishman tapped him with the rapier. "No tricks. Understand?" He returned to Guy. "Faith, Kitten, from now on, *I'll* take care of the horses." Then, he frowned. "Hmm. Green surcoat?"

D'Entreville nodded. His voice was loaded with significance. "Precisely. A green surcoat!"

In his arms the girl moaned softly, stirred. He carried her to a bench and sat her down on it. "Inn-keeper," he yelled. "Fetch some brandy."

Cleve's other prisoner grunted and sat up groggily. "Wha-what happened?" he wanted to know.

"You forgot to duck," Cleve told him. He snagged the inn-keeper's arm as that worthy appeared from the kitchen carrying a bottle. "Give me your keys, landlord."

The inn-keeper had seen enough and heard enough to make him respect this Englishman. He surrendered the keys without question and scuttled over to Guy with the brandy.

Cleve forced his grumbling captives upstairs. He locked them in a small closet, pocketed the key and returned to the taproom. He found d'Entreville pouring brandy down the girl's throat, the inn-keeper watching fascinatedly.

"Breakfast, you lout!" Cleve bellowed, bringing the flat of his blade across the fat man's breeches. "And be quick about it!"

The landlord bounded into the kitchen yelping "*Oui's.*" The girl opened her eyes. They were beautiful eyes, soft brown and at the moment confused. Cleve sat down opposite her so that he could see them better.

"Good morning, m'dear," he said pleasantly and frowned at d'Entreville. "I'll take care of her now."

Guy's arms held firmly to the girl's shoulders. "You are too cursed kind for your own good," he said.

Cleve shrugged. The girl said, "Good morning." Her voice was soft, rather faint. Cleve liked it. He began to tell d'Entreville that if he was a true gentleman—but the French cavalier wasn't heeding him.

"You feel better, *mademoiselle?*" he asked.

"Yes. What—what happened?"

Cleve looked at the Frenchman bitterly. "This lout would know," he told her.

Guy flashed. "Wait till I get you alone."

THEN the girl gasped. "Now I remember. I was in the barn. *Oui!* I was hiding." At this point her eyes blazed. "And you,"—she turned on Guy—"tried to stab me; you hurled me to the floor!"

Cleve made sympathetic sounds and glared at d'Entreville. The crimson Frenchman attempted a weak defense.

"But, *mademoiselle*—"

The girl's hand flashed up and slapped across the startled Frenchman's lips.

"*Cochon!*"

Guy caught her hands in self-defense. Cleve started to laugh, but the girl's hot gaze swept him and he frowned and shook his finger at d'Entreville.

"Shame on you, Kitten!" he said.

"Never mind being gallant," Guy snapped. "We have a lot

of questions to ask this young lady. In the first place, I want to know why she was hiding, and in the second place why she is garbed in Montmorency's uniform."

Cleve stood up and shook his head. "I merely want to know her name," he admitted.

The girl said, "I'll answer nothing! Nothing! Do you understand?"

D'Entreville got to his feet. He was still holding her hands in a strong grip and his eyes were determined.

"Mademoiselle," he said patiently, "boorishness is not my habit to one so beautiful as you. But—" His voice became flint-like. "I have a duty to France. You'll answer my questions."

Cleve said: "Egad! You'd be a good poet, if you hadn't such a strong love of duty, Kitten." He looked at the girl. "But, he's right, m'dear. Duty knows no courtesy. We're on the King's business."

She laughed. "Liar!" she cried. "Do you not think that I know the uniform you wear? The King's business indeed! Those sky-blue surcoats with their gold trim are the very liveries of my own brother!"

CHAPTER VI

RIDE A SLOW HORSE

THE STATEMENT FELL like a blow on their credulity. D'Entreville recovered first. *"Corbac!* It's true! Her face has been teasing my memory and now I see it. Two years past—presented at court." He stared. "Am I correct, *mademoiselle?"*

She nodded.

Cleve pursed his lips. He wanted to know why le Marquis de Beaucaire's sister was dressed like a man. Why she had hidden in the stable of a decrepit little hostelry half a league from Clermont.

"I shall tell you nothing," the girl snapped.

The Englishman bowed and said, "Your beauty is exceeded only by your stubbornness."

The girl regarded him defiantly. "Precisely, *monsieur!*"

Cleve shrugged. He was tempted to shake her, but his better instincts prevailed. He had been brought up to be a gentleman; and although he had often doubted the wisdom of it, the fact remained that he couldn't lay violent hands on a woman.

Just then, the pudgy inn-keeper appeared staggering beneath a full tray. The sight of food made up the Englishman's mind and he took the girl firmly by the arm.

"Very well, m'lady. For the present, you win."

She wrenched free of him. "What are you going to do?"

Cleve smiled faintly. "First I'm going to lock you in a room; and then I intend to enjoy the first meal I've had in twelve long hours." He bowed graciously. "After you, *mademoiselle.*"

The girl hesitated, contemplating rebellion, but the dancing light in the Englishman's eyes dissuaded her. She shrugged and preceded him up the creaking stairs at the end of the room.

… Breakfast was good. Stewed fruit, porridge, bacon, and frothy chocolate. When they had finished Cleve pushed aside the naked plates and regarded d'Entreville. He saw that the Frenchman was thinking the same thoughts as he, and chuckled.

" 'Tis a simple kettle of trouble, Kitten," he said. "And it has but four ingredients.

"First, there is the Duke of Orleans marching his army down the west side of the Rhone. Second, there is Schomberg's royal army marching from the west to intercept him. Third, there is a traitor who had made off with the gold for his own ends."

Cleve sighed. "And fourth, there are two foolish cavaliers—ourselves. Add these ingredients one by one. Season with a mysterious lady who is the traitor's sister and two futile assassins, and you have a devil's brew."

D'ENTREVILLE didn't appreciate the whimsy. He was thinking about Schomberg's army marching toward Beaucaire Castle in hope of being paid. The French cavalier could visualize the scene. The royal army would be paid. Paid in bullets! Beaucaire Castle was strong and with a small force Beaucaire could hold it for months. The royal army would disband.

"*Corbac!*" he exclaimed. "We should warn Marshal Schomberg."

"Why?" The Englishman's tone was amused. "Do you wish to disband his army sooner than expected?"

"*Sacré nom!* That is right, too. Hmmph! We are in a *cul de sac*, eh?"

Cleve picked up a crust of bread, tore off a piece and popped it into his mouth. "It appears that way. I fear that there is small hope of catching Beaucaire now. Of course we could try."

D'Entreville leaned forward. "That is precisely what I am going to do, Cleve." His dark eyes held a challenge; a question in them. "I'll follow that swine into his castle."

Cleve knew that he was being sounded. The mere fact that D'Entreville thought it necessary made him grin wryly.

"Really?" he said. "You realize of course, that when Beaucaire does not hear from his hirelings, he'll be on guard. He knows us for fools. He'll be expecting us."

"*Sangodemi!* What of it?"

Cleve nodded and stood up. He gave Guy's head a push and laughed. "Come on, fool. We'll see about fresh horses."

They found the landlord and went out to the stables. Beaucaire had taken all the fresh horses for his coach and the only mounts remaining were at pasture. They went to the field behind the barn and inspected the beasts.

"*Mordi!* Do you call those things horses?" D'Entreville cried. "They're insults to their breed."

The inn-keeper looked apologetic. He observed that the horses were rather jaded, but Beaucaire had given them a hard ride. He was very sorry. In fact, he verged into tears when Guy scowled at him.

"Well," the Frenchman decided, "there is not much we can do. Saddle the two best, and we'll pray that they carry us as far as Clermont without collapsing."

DURING this exchange Cleve leaned against the fence and said nothing. Now he turned. "Never mind the best. Saddle the oldest horse, the most disreputable of the lot. The dappled-grey mare over there in the corner will do."

The pudgy proprietor's mouth gaped, but Cleve eyed him sternly. *"Oui, monsieur.* Immediately. *Oui!"*

He waddled off like a frightened penguin. D'Entreville tapped Cleve's shoulder gently.

"More comedy, *mon ami?"*

"On the contrary. I'm becoming clever."

"Or a trifle addled."

"Why, Kitten!"

"Sangodemi! Don't call me Kitten!"

"All right."

"Hmmph! You're a liar. Now perhaps you'll tell me what you've dug up with your presumed mind."

Cleve relaxed against the fence, crossed one booted leg over the other. He grinned. "Beaucaire is a very clever fellow!"

D'Entreville's foot shot out, caught under Cleve's supporting leg and yanked. The Englishman crashed to the ground.

"Pecaire! Cleve, some day you shall learn to answer simple questions—simply!"

From his sitting position Cleve shook his head, plucked a blade of grass and inserted it between his teeth. The rough handling did not affect him in the least. "Temper, Kitten," he said. "You did not give me opportunity to finish."

"Well, finish then. Here, give me your hand."

The Englishman shook his head wisely. "Ah no. I feel safer on the ground, thank you." He inspected the blade of grass thoughtfully before looking up again. "As I was saying, Beaucaire is clever and if we are to beat him we must—"

Suddenly his voice trailed. He had shifted his gaze indifferently toward the rear of the tavern, but now his eyes blinked wide and he vaulted to his feet.

"The prisoners," he cried. "They're escaping."

D'Entreville whirled. He saw the girl and the two men climbing into the saddles of the horses he had put into the stables earlier. The girl seemed to be objecting about something. Suddenly one of the men reached down and swept her to the pommel. Then they were galloping away before Cleve had taken three steps.

"Ah well," the Englishman sighed. "They made it. But they shan't get far. Those mounts are about done in." He turned to Guy. "Come on, Kitten. Let's retire to our host's kitchen and see how many pots and pans he has."

D'Entreville's eyes widened. Then narrowed. Cleve had something on his mind but he didn't trust him. "If this is some more of your putrid comedy—" he threatened.

But the Englishman was already striding toward the tavern.

CHAPTER VII

COME INTO MY DUNGEON

BEAUCAIRE WAS A small town of a few thousand, standing opposite Avignon and dominated by a huge feudal castle which had been renovated during the reign of Francis I.

It was a town not easily startled by the bizarre appearance of its many transients because it was on one of the major arteries which connected Paris with southern France.

The advent of a wandering tinker, seated upon a sway-backed mare, led by a dirty-faced apprentice, caused no more than an incurious stare from a few idle citizens.

The tinker had come from the north. For lack of a more convenient place, he carried the implements of his trade—an unholy conglomeration of pots and pans—upon the swaying rump of his horse. His hat was grey, smudgy and brimless; the hair beneath matted, unkempt.

He rolled in his saddle, arms dangling, and left no doubt in the minds of many as to the utterly shiftless mode of his living.

The apprentice was cut from the same cloth. He trudged along at a listless pace, hand on the bridle more as in need of support than to lead, with a blank grin on his unshaven face and a low tune in his throat.

Had any of the hurrying burghers bothered to listen they would have heard,

> *So I walk, walk, walk,*
> *With the Kitten at my hock,*
> *He's a Kitten without equal in the land*

But, even had the burghers listened and understood the droned words, they could not have understood the tinker's crazy reaction.

He reached back deliberately, gripped a pot, and banged it smartly atop the coned hat of his musical assistant.

"*Sangodemi!* Quiet, Cleve, or by—"

The Englishman grinned through the grime. "*Ssh!*" he cautioned. "Remember, my name is Jacques."

"Very well, Jacques. If you value your life don't—"

Cleve pulled the mare to a stop. They were in the middle of the marketplace near the foot of the castle. Busy crowds surged about them and the shadow of the castle's great bastion lent solidness to the movement.

It was late in the afternoon. The townsfolk clustered about the food vendors intent upon buying the evening meal. The babble of voices unending.

"Well, Kitten. Here we are."

D'Entreville slid from the saddle with an experienced grace

entirely out of keeping with a tinker's manner. He sent a thoughtful glance toward the portcullis of the castle and noted the guards in green surcoats standing there.

"*Corbac,*" he muttered. "To get past them will be a problem." He looked at Cleve. "I presume the next move for us is to rent a stall, set up a business, and trust that trade is bad. If someone asks me to mend a kettle I'll be in a pretty fix."

Cleve grinned. "You could develop a sore hand or something," he suggested, and pointed toward a stall twenty yards to the right whose occupant seemed engaged in moving. "There is our place."

They approached the owner of the booth. He was a leather worker of long proportions both of body and face. He was piling his merchandise angrily into a two-wheeled cart, muttering as he did so.

D'Entreville said, "Hola, *mon ami*. You are moving out, eh?"

The lanky leather worker paused, put his hands on his hips and spat forcefully. "Yes! And if you are wise you'll do the same. Hell will break in Beaucaire shortly. I'm leaving while the leaving is good!"

"Really? And, what will cause this Hell?"

THE MAN cast a black look at the castle. "Rebellion," he said frankly. "Le Marquis de Beaucaire and le Duc de Montmorency are recruiting. Every day for the past week unemployed soldiers have been drifting into town. I know the signs. The war-drums are getting ready to roll, and when they do, it is no place for an honest worker."

"But the other booths are full," Guy observed.

"They'll be gone tomorrow. Word has just come that Schomberg's army is on the march here. Note the crowds around you, *m'sieu*. The townsfolk are smart. They are buying provisions from a long siege."

D'Entreville shook his head. "I don't believe you," he said bluntly. "I have been told that Beaucaire is a good place to trade.

I have traveled far, and here I stay! How much for your stall, *monsieur?*"

The leather worker laughed bleakly. He threw the last of his goods into the cart and climbed aboard. "Nothing," he said. "To take money from a fool is bad luck."

Then he slapped leather on the rump of his horse and went away, bumping awkwardly across the square, and leaving d'Entreville red-laced and speechless with anger. Cleve rubbed a thoughtful finger along the stubble on his chin. Suddenly he laughed and clapped Guy upon the back.

"Well, come on, fool," he said heartily, "let's get unpacked!"

D'Entreville's foot shot out. But Cleve evaded it merrily, spinning lightly on his heels. The maneuver carried him swiftly over the cobbles.

He didn't see the two guards, resplendent in their plumed hats and green surcoats, and they didn't see him. Mutual ignorance resulted in a heavy impact. Cleve struck them like a bowling ball.

"*Corbac et Sacré nom d'un cochon!*" One of the guards roared struggling to a sitting position. His comrade was not as verbal. He lay face down in the mud with Cleve sprawled atop him. "What is this?"

"A mistake," Cleve assured him and bounded to his feet. "A thousand pardons, *monsieur.*" He looked closely at the mud-packed face of the other who was now rising, and added hastily, "A million pardons to you."

"*Sangodemi!* I'll murder him! I'll cut his heart out!" howled he of the mud-filled face.

D'Entreville stepped up. In his hand he held a heavy soldering iron. He glared at Cleve. "Brawling again, eh?" he said. "*Mordi!* Can't you keep out of trouble!"

"But, it wasn't my—" Cleve began to protest.

AT THAT moment, the guards decided to avenge the indignity done them. Muddy-face whirled Cleve around with the intention of cuffing him soundly, only d'Entreville interrupted. He rapped Muddy-face across the knuckles and Muddy-face danced away howling.

And then the other guard started to go for his sword, but Cleve drove his fist into the fellow's belly.

From up the square, six more guards witnessed the outrages being committed on their comrades and charged to the rescue. D'Entreville bent his soldering iron over the head of the first one and Cleve lashed out with his fist and sent another back on his heels. Guy regarded the Englishman in amazement.

"*Parbleu!* With your fists? Where did you learn to fight that way?"

"England," puffed Cleve. "The common people on my father's estate call it boxing."

The battle was short, after that. Bare fists and a soldering iron are no match for a quartet of rapiers. Cleve and d'Entreville took one look at the steel, shrugged, and surrendered.

"Take them to the dungeon," bawled one of the guards, a sergeant. "They have attacked the soldiers of the duke. *Le marquis* will judge them."

"Fine mess," d'Entreville growled to Cleve, as they were marched away.

"Hush, Kitten." The Englishman grinned. "We are getting into the castle."

Montmorency's guards marched them through the gate, across the outer bailey, and into the armory building which adjoined the north wall and surmounted the dungeon. With each step d'Entreville's hopes diminished.

As itinerant tinkers he and Cleve had plotted to enter the walls under guise of being commissioned to repair the pots and pans of the kitchen. Then they would have had opportunity to reconnoiter without suspicion. But now—they were trapped. And destined to languish in a stinking cell until their fate was decided.

They were pitched roughly into a large room. It was dirty,

deserted. It wasn't a regular cell but seemed to be a sort of forgotten guardroom unused for decades. Cleve inspected it thoughtfully and wondered why they had been put here instead of in the main dungeon. He asked the jailer. The man shrugged.

"The dungeon's being used to store arms. Ball and powder," he said.

Cleve nodded. Recruits had been drilling in the bailey when he and Guy had come through it. This sight and now the knowledge of the vast amounts of munitions being stored away, converged into one fact. Beaucaire Castle was to be used as a seat of war.

He turned to mention it to his companion. Guy was over in a corner, bending beneath a worm-eaten table, the cell's lone piece of furniture.

"Faith. What the devil are you up to?"

The French cavalier threw a furtive glance over his shoulder. Then he settled on his haunches and displayed that which he had in his hands. It gleamed dully in the half-light.

"I found it behind this table," he said softly.

Cleve looked closer. It was the latter part of a broken broadsword. Its hilt was green with corrosion and extended for exactly half of the whole piece. "Damme! That's an old thing. Been here for a hundred years, no doubt. They can't have cleaned this room very thoroughly before pitching us into it. Perchance there is more to be found."

Without another word they bent down and combed the cell for further weapons. It was futile, but they continued with the stubbornness of hope. So engrossed were they in the task that they didn't notice the door swing open to admit an officer of the guards and his squad of eight.

CLEVE made the discovery. On hands and knees he had worked himself nearer the door. His hands sifted through the dust on the floor, fluttered across the toe of a jack-boot.

His eyes followed the toe to the heel; from the heel to the

calf; to the thigh, to the red velvet sash, and then into the officer's frowning face.

The Englishman grinned weakly.

"Hello," he said.

The officer snorted. *"Nom du Diable!* What is this?"

Guy d'Entreville, engaged in a corner, whirled at the voice and leaped to his feet. The sword-hilt tinkled to the floor and an alert guardsman scooped it up.

"A broken sword?" the officer asked, staring at it. He shoved it into his sash and laughed. "Tricky varlets, aren't you? Well, it will do you no good. Fall in. I'm taking you up to the main hall for your judgment. It won't go any easier with you when I tell *monsieur le marquis* of this attempt to escape."

Le Marquis de Beaucaire sat behind the elevated table in the main hall and stared indifferently at the two ragamuffins who had been led before him.

As a rule he liked the prerogative which, as a noble of a semi-feudal domain, gave him the right to sit in judgment over his fellow men. But tonight he was tired, listless. Beside him, le Duc de Montmorency crossed his legs and sighed.

Montmorency was a handsome man still under forty, and looked younger than his years. He was a dashing sort of person, adored by women, hot-blooded, impulsive. The present scene bored him.

"Sandieu!" he muttered to Beaucaire, "this sort of thing went out with plate armor. Why don't you turn it over to the civil courts in the town? We're living in the Seventeenth Century, Mazo! Not in 1266."

Beaucaire shrugged, rested his hawkish face on the palm of his hand and stared at the prisoners. "It amuses me," he said. "Life can be boring at times, and the tales that some of these wretches tell me are laughable." He eyed the officer who had brought in the culprits. "Very well, *capitaine.* The charges?"

"Assaulting eight guardsmen, interfering with a patrol, attempting murder with a broken sword, conspiring to escape their just punishment, disturbing the peace—"

One of the prisoners, the slighter of the two, turned.

"Damme!" he erupted, "either you are a proficient liar, or you've mistaken us for two other prisoners!"

The *capitaine* raised his hand to smash the face of his accuser. Beaucaire's crisp command stopped him. The marquis was straight in his chair now. No longer indifferent, bored. He sank his dark eyes into the men before him; stripped aside the rags, the grime; and smiled.

"Ma foi!" he said. "Le Comte d'Entreville and m'Lord Cleve."

CHAPTER VIII

TURN OF THE DICE

SILENCE FELL LIKE a mantle over the great hall. Time seemed frozen. Beaucaire remained sitting with that triumphant smile smearing his face. Montmorency was astounded, the *capitaine* and guards confused. And Guy d'Entreville's heart filled with despair.

It was Cleve who broke the quiet. He cursed the English accent which had given them away, but it was typical of him to smile.

"Hmmm," he said and shrugged. "Well, the jig's up." He thrust hands into his pockets and looked impudently at the marquis. "Greetings—swine!"

Beaucaire started as if slapped. The smile left his lips. His eyes glittered with a cruel coldness. "You are most welcome, *messieurs*," he said with great control. "We've been expecting you."

Cleve nodded. "I thought as much. The two that you left to murder us are better messengers than assassins."

Beaucaire stood up. The Englishman's manner infuriated

him. "You're a clever one, aren't you. What did you intend to do in those disguises?"

Cleve folded his arms. "Guess," he said pleasantly.

Beaucaire shook his head. "I don't need to. The fact that you are here is all that I need to know." He turned to Montmorency who was leaning back in his chair regarding Cleve and d'Entreville narrowly. "These are the two, *monsieur le duc.*"

"I've gathered that," Montmorency nodded. "They've caused a deal of mischief, haven't they?"

"Enough," Beaucaire replied. He smiled. "In war time, Henri, when an enemy is caught wearing a disguise, what is the penalty?"

"Death. Naturally."

Beaucaire folded his hands and nodded. "Naturally," he said.

D'Entreville surged forward. Two guards grabbed his arms and jerked him back. "You filthy dog! You wouldn't dare!"

Beaucaire raised his eyebrows and shrugged. "Wouldn't I?" he asked. Suddenly, his fist hit the table.

"You'll hang! I'll string you from the wall for Schomberg to admire. Yes, and in your vile rags! 'Twill be a fine sight to see two gentlemen, a French *comte* and an English lord, dangling in rags like common felons. A fine sight!"

Cleve, still with his hands in his pockets, rolled easily on his heels. He had been whistling softly through his teeth during Beaucaire's vituperation. Now he stopped and eyed the marquis calmly.

"Faith! You lose composure quickly. Aren't you a little mad, *monsieur!* A trifle drunk with petty power?"

Beaucaire was livid. His hand trembled. "Take them away," he shouted. "Take them out of my sight, until morning!"

"Your wish," smiled Cleve, "is their command. Good evening gentlemen. And if you sleep—pleasant dreams!"

THEIR cell was clean when they returned to it. The fat jailer, having witnessed the episode with the broken sword, had

guarded against possible recurrence. The floor had been swept
of its ancient dust; even the lone piece of furniture had been
removed.

In the corner were two mattresses of straw, a pitcher of water.
Nothing more. Cleve flopped down, cradled his head and regarded d'Entreville.

The Frenchman was pacing the room like a caged tiger. His
fate wasn't what bothered him. He wasn't afraid. He was angry
clear through.

"The filthy swine! The scabby traitor! Oh, had I but one
minute alone with him…."

"Half a minute," Cleve said and chuckled. "Ah relax, Kitten.
That is your trouble. You anger too easily."

Guy came over and sat down. He didn't speak. His eyes swept
the cell. It was long, low-ceilinged, with solid stone walls on
four sides unpierced by windows.

The only egress, the lone means of ventilation, was the iron
door at the further end. He stared at this carefully. The lower
half was solid metal; the upper portion, striped with iron bars.
It was escape-proof.

"*Corbac!* This is a tight little nest. It leaves nothing to the
imagination."

"True," Cleve nodded, "Too true." He raised his head and
squinted at the door. Fortunately there was a torch-pot opposite it in the corridor. He watched the file of men passing by
and said, "I wonder why our friends out there are so busy?
They've been carrying powder-kegs and ball from below ever
since we've arrived."

Guy shrugged. "Our cell is adjacent to the castle's main
bastion. That corridor connects the armory with the tower room.
There is a forty-pound Carthoun cannon mounted atop it. I
overheard one of the guards talking while we were being led
back. They expect to do great things when Schomberg arrives
tomorrow. Height will double the Carthoun's ordinary range."

"Faith! A pretty idea! A cannon in the tower-top and a whole army marching up to it unsuspecting. That's about all Schomberg's troops need. No pay for months and a gun hurling death down on them after a long trek."

The Englishman sat up and smiled wryly. "Our friend the marquis has plotted well. After the first two charges, Schomberg will have trouble in keeping his men from desertion, much less having them storm the castle."

"Mordi! Had we but a way to warn them!"

"False hope, Kitten. We'll be too cursed busy kicking our lives out on the wall to care much about the royal army."

Four hours crawled into the gloom. At midnight the castle settled down. From the wall-walks sleepy sentinels called their post tunelessly. Cleve and Guy had borrowed a set of dice from the jailer. Now, as the muffled "All's well" cries seeped down to them, they paused in the play.

Twelve o'clock! They had six possibly seven hours left of life. Finally the Englishman laughed.

"Ten thousand you owe me," he said. "Your luck has run out, Guy."

D'Entreville stared through the dimness. The torch in the corridor was guttering. Its light coated the side of his face in wavery orange. His lips were drawn, his eyes helpless. He had made the mistake of allowing his imagination to work. Cleve's chiding words cracked it. *"Corbac!* And that is true!"

He raised his hand to hurl the senseless dice away, but Cleve's voice came solidly through the half murk. "Play them, Kitten!"

Guy relaxed. He rattled the cubes, half ashamed. "Of course, clown. My luck will turn. Wager a thousand."

Suddenly his hand stopped in mid-air. His eyes were fixed on the door. *"Parbleu,* Cleve. We have a visitor."

CLEVE didn't turn. His voice came soft: "Better to go down fighting than to hang. I'll knock his legs from under him. Grab his sword."

"But it isn't a he!"

"Eh?" The Englishman stood up and turned. Coming toward them, outlined sharply, was the figure of a woman. A young woman, lithe and graceful in her step. She held her finger to her lips.

D'Entreville gasped. "You!"

"Yes, it is I," she said softly.

It was the girl of the tavern, Beaucaire's sister. Cleve said, "Thoughtful of you to come to gloat."

"You are cruel, *monsieur*. I have come to help you."

"A likely tale."

" 'Tis the truth. Had I believed you two days ago at the tavern, this might not have happened."

Cleve glanced at d'Entreville. The Frenchman was serious, intent. The Briton shrugged. "Pray continue, *mademoiselle*. We have little else to do, and no appointments until tomorrow morning."

The girl bit her lip at his casual reference to the execution. She looked over her shoulder at the jailer who was standing indifferently in the doorway with a torch in his fist.

"Please believe me, *monsieur*," she said. "I am a loyal subject. I want no part in the treason that my mad brother has started. For two months he has kept me a virtual prisoner in the castle; then three nights ago I escaped dressed in a guard's uniform. I tried to reach Paris to warn the King of this plot and plead clemency for my brother."

"He'll need more than clemency now," d'Entreville said.

The girl cast him a despairing look. "It's not Mazo's fault," she replied. "He has fallen under the influence of that devil Montmorency. The promise of great glories has made him mad. He's like a child. Blind to the wrong he's doing. Surely, you can understand that?"

"We can try," Cleve compromised. He eyed her closely. "You were trying to reach Paris…."

"Yes. I stopped at that little inn where you found me, to change horses. While I was there my brother's coach drew into the courtyard. I was frantic. Should he see me he would know my business and take me back."

"So you hid in the stable."

"Yes. I covered myself with hay. It was soft and I was tired. I was asleep—" Here she paused, smiled ruefully at Guy "—when you awakened me, *monsieur*."

"Er—Yes."

"Afterward in the tavern, when I saw both of you in my brother's livery, I refused to believe your loyalty to the Crown. It wasn't until Pierre and René broke into my room that I realized my error."

Guy asked: "Pierre and René?"

"The lads who tried to knife me," Cleve said. "Continue, *mademoiselle*."

"René had recognized me in the taproom. He and Pierre forced me to return with them to Beaucaire." She looked earnestly into the faces of the two cavaliers.

"AND THAT is all. I have heard the sentence which my poor mad brother has passed on you. I have come to aid. I ask only that you speak a kind word in his behalf after this rebellion collapses. For your Richelieu will pardon him."

She fumbled in her handbag and furtively withdrew a large key. "Take this. It is the duplicate of the one which opens he door to this room."

Cleve felt the cool thrill of the metal in his palm. He inclined his head. "You are a brave woman, *mademoiselle*."

Her earnestness disregarded the words. "Tonight the gate will be opened to allow Montmorency's coach to leave."

D'Entreville frowned. "The duke is not staying?"

"No. He is on his way to inform le Duc d'Orleans of Schomberg's collapse."

"Confident fellow," Cleve said.

"That is all I can do for you, *messieurs*," he girl shrugged. "Go to Schomberg and warn him of the ambuscade that the rebels have awaiting him."

D'Entreville bowed over her hand. "My gratitude shall be eternally yours, *mademoiselle.*"

Cleve sniffed. "We're not out of here yet, Kitten." Then he softened. He stared at her and finished simply. "Thanks."

She smiled, laughed softly. "You English are so clipped, yet so sincere," she laid. "I trust you will be equally sincere in practicing your gratitude. When this is over, pay it by saving my brother's life."

"Richelieu is a hard man, *mademoiselle,*" Guy pointed out. "He is ruthless to his enemies, implacable."

"Promise that you will intercede for my brother," she insisted.

D'Entreville shrugged. "I promise," he said.

And then she was gone. Gone in a swirl of satin through the iron door at the end of the room. The jailer followed heavily and Cleve stared at d'Entreville.

"The dead live again," he said and flipped the key in his hand. "How do you feel, Kitten?"

"Like singing. Come. Let's get out of here!"

"Not so fast, my friend. What plan have we?"

"To leave, of course; and then, to warn Schomberg."

Cleve shook his head. "And what good would it do? Beaucaire still has the gold. He has a dungeon crammed with munitions. Warning Schomberg will not save France from a civil war. We must find the treasure, Kitten. And, if we can't steal it—destroy it."

Guy stared. "*Parbleu!* You speak of miracles!"

The Briton looked at the key in his hand and then at the door through which the girl had gone. "After this," he said, "I believe in miracles! Come on."

THEY found the jailer. He was seated on a stool in the tower room which prefixed the short stair-flight leading down to their cell. At the right, stone steps spiraled upward into the bastion. The jailer sat facing them, intent upon his midnight snack. He didn't suspect the figures creeping up behind him.

They pounced.

"One outcry, *mon ami*," d'Entreville murmured, his lean fingers taloned about the jailer's fat neck. "One peep, and I squeeze. Get his keys. We'll lock him below."

The prisoner remained passive. The Englishman fumbled, removed a large keyring and a knife. For a moment d'Entreville's fingers relaxed. Like a greased fish the chubby jailer slipped away.

"Ho the watch!" he howled. *"A moi!* There's villainy afoot! They escape!"

Cleve made a despairing dive. The man scuttled through the door as the Englishman fell heavily across the table. Guy charging forward tripped over him. Then the jailer was in the bailey dancing excitedly and shouting.

Lights appeared. Yelled questions rang through the night. From around a corner in the court the officer of the Guard trotted, closely followed by a squad. Cleve and Guy saw him. They struggled to their feet, grabbed the door, swung it shut and dropped its bar into place.

"Thank God it's made of iron," d'Entreville gasped. "They'll not batter it down quickly."

Cleve didn't answer. He left the door in a bound and mounted the spiral stairs two at a time. On the first landing a confused guardsman was coming in off the wall-walk.

"What's the clamor for?" he asked. Cleve's fist slammed up sharply and he grunted.

The Englishman kicked the body out of the way, banged the door closed and leaned against it relievedly. That had been close!

But, now the door was shut. It was made of iron, small and compact. It would take a long time to batter down. He caught his breath and moved across to the one opposite. He barred this too.

Then, to be on the safe side, he trotted half-way up the stairs and called, "Ho, up there! Come down at once. You're needed!" When there was no reply he nodded, satisfied. He and Guy had the tower to themselves.

CHAPTER IX

BLASTING PARTY

WHEN HE RETURNED to the ground floor the main door was ringing beneath blows. Guy was nowhere in sight. Cleve darted to the doorway leading toward the dungeon and the armory and met the Frenchman carrying an armload of muskets, ball and powder.

"Remember the door to the armory," Guy explained. "It's six-inch oak and studded with steel. It'll take them two hours or more to smash through it."

He carried the muskets to the center of the tower room. "In the meantime, let's see if we cannot discourage the din our friends are making at the main door."

He went to a cruciformed loop-hole and thrust the muzzle of a musket through it. By craning the gun against the stone he could command part of the tower door. He aimed low and pulled the trigger. A howl of pain rewarded the effort. The pounding ceased.

"Well. It's quieter now."

"Yes. But they'll be at the other entrances in a moment," Cleve said. He picked up a musket with a pouch of powder and ball, and walked to the stairs.

D'Entreville smiled. Reckless confidence was pounding through his veins. *"Pecaire!* We've a fighting chance, now."

Suddenly the tower vibrated to the thud of something heavy being smashed against one of the iron doors leading to the wall. Outside, the whole castle blazed with light. The babble of countless voices.

Yelling, angry voices tinged with surprise and confusion seeped through the thick stone walls. Cleve listened and laughed. He said: "I fear we have interrupted our host's slumber."

Guy sent a warning shot through the loop-hole. "Too bad," he said wryly. Then, frowning, "I wonder how long we can keep this up?"

The Englishman's eyes were reckless. "I'm pondering the same thing, Kitten!"

He shrugged and mounted the stairs.

At the top of the bastion he found the castle crouched at his feet like a sullen dog. It was crawling with lights, and in the darkness they reminded him of scattered pearls on sable. He frowned away this fancy and bent over the parapet.

Below he could make out the dim lane of the wall-walk. There was a dark cluster on it, near the foot of the tower. The cluster moved in rhythmic surges. It battered a log against the iron side door.

"We'll have none of that, boys!" Cleve muttered.

He sent a musket ball whistling earthward. The cluster burst apart, retreated down the walk. Startled cries and loud commands lifted on the night air. The Englishman nodded, satisfied.

He left the parapet and started to cross the platform. At his right a huge metal object, glinting dull in the moonlight, attracted him. It was the Carthoun cannon. He stared thoughtfully. Grouped about its base, neatly stacked, were pyramids of forty-pound iron ball. He counted twenty. Powder kegs lined the left side of the tower rampart.

Suddenly he laughed and bent over and lifted a ball. He held it poised on the parapet a moment. The battering crew assigned to the main entrance had started again. He could see them outlined sharply against torch-light. They were far to one side, well out of d'Entreville's musket range.

Cleve shrugged. With an almost indifferent motion he brushed the cannon ball off the stone.

IT MISSED. But its purpose was obtained. The battering crew withdrew to a safe distance. The ball had plunged half its weight into the ground. The sight unnerved onlookers. For the first time in fifteen minutes, silence fell. A tense, confused silence.

Cleve picked up another cannon ball and waited.

A tiny figure burst the ring of men surrounding the base of the tower, and stepped into the clear. It was Beaucaire, half-dressed, still wearing a nightcap, and very angry.

"Ho! You in the bastion!"

D'Entreville's voice cane back, easy, unruffled. "Good evening, *monsieur*. Have we disturbed you?"

"Disturb—*Sacré nom!* Come out and surrender! You cannot hope to fight off a whole garrison."

"But we can, *monsieur*."

In the tower, Cleve rested his chin on his fist and sighed. "We can try, my friend," he corrected.

Beaucaire shouted, "*Sangodemi!* You fools! You mad fools! It's a matter of minutes before my men break into the tower. Surrender now! Things will go easier with you!"

"You don't lie convincingly, *monsieur*. I think we shall stay here. Thanks all the same."

"This is your last chance to surrender!"

"*Pecaire!* If there is any surrendering to be done, *monsieur*— you had better do it to the Crown. And quickly!"

"Very well, then! Remember your words when I have you both on the rack!"

Beaucaire stepped back into the shadows. Cleve could hear him giving orders. A squad of men rushed toward the door. D'Entreville's musket cracked sharply. One of the men collapsed like a stringless puppet. The others came on.

Cleve arranged two more cannon balls beside the one he had already had posed. He waited until the battering crew was directly below; then pushed them off one by one. He didn't have to watch the result. The ugly thuds told everything.

A musket ball whined off the lip of the parapet. Two more followed it. Cleve ducked. He broke open a powder keg and reloaded his musket. He had expected this. The enemy would keep him blanketed with musketry while their comrades once more tried to crash the door.

He crawled to the trap door and slid down the stairs. There was a slitted loophole at his right. He inserted the musket and waited. Two hundred feet away rose the dim column of another bastion. A flame winked in it. Cleve smiled. He located the place and sent a shot tearing into it.

Somebody screamed. Below he heard the crash of a musket shattering on the ground.

He went back to the tower top and dropped three more balls on ambitious assault parties. Further attacks ceased, and a period of watchful waiting set in. It continued for more than an hour.

CLEVE frowned and went down to the tower room in the base. D'Entreville greeted him cheerfully. He had brought up more arms from the dungeon and they were scattered all over.

"I feel like a one-man army," said he, indicating them.

Cleve nodded. "You're going to have to act like one. The lads outside aren't sleeping, you know. They're up to something."

"I feel that, too. But, what? The game seems a stalemate at present."

"Yes. It can't last. Have you checked the door leading to the dungeon from the armory?"

"Half an hour ago."

"Anything stirring?"

"No."

Cleve shifted uneasily. "I'll have a look," he said. "Keep your eyes open."

Guy rested three muskets across his knees. "They won't try anything. They still think you are up there in the tower."

Cleve laughed. He went below, down the shadowy corridor and past the cell which they had recently occupied. At the end of this passageway, a series of stone steps ran up to a large studded door.

Cleve inspected it thoughtfully. It led to the armory and was the only entrance which could not be defended externally. The fact that it was not being shivered by blows puzzled him.

He placed his ear to the wood. From the other side came vague murmurings and the sound of things being dragged. He sat down on a step and scratched his chin.

To his right was a dingy little cell, stacked high with powder-kegs. At his left was another. A series of stone steps, flanking those upon which he sat, staggered down to the depths. The dungeon was down there and crammed, he knew, with muni-tions.

"Faith!" he breathed. "We could blow the north wall—"

Suddenly he snapped his fingers. Now he knew what they were doing on the other side. They were clearing the armory of explosives. Then they would plant a charge—a small one, just enough to blast aside the six-inch door without endangering anything else.

With a curse he stood up, kicked heavily against the lower panel. "Ho! You on the other side!"

Sounds of labor ceased, and Beaucaire's voice rasped harsh and triumphant through the door. "Ah! Cleve. You desire sur-render, eh? Well, it's too late! We'll blow down this partition and take you. Your death will not be quick, *monsieur*. Not after this! Cease begging!"

"I'm not begging, Beaucaire. I'm warning! Blow down his door and you'll be splattered from here to Paris."

The marquis laughed. "I have foreseen that, *mon ami*. For the past two hours my men have been removing the powder from this room."

"Very wise," Cleve snapped. "Only while you've been taking powder from your side, I've been piling it high on mine!" He paused, waited to catch the effect of the lie. When there was no reply, he decided to improve on it.

"Furthermore, m'lad, I have placed a lighted candle atop the whole conglomeration. The moment you jar this door in any way, the candle will fall into the powder. It will end our dispute, old boy—definitely. Frankly, you had better forget this entrance and try the others. It's safer!"

He heard Beaucaire choking blasphemies from the other side. There was quite an argument as to whether to believe the Englishman, or not. After a while, Cleve left the door. He'd heard enough.

"That'll hold them," he muttered.

He broke into a whistle and swaggered back to the tower room.

CHAPTER X

RAKEHELLY RESCUE

MORNING FOUND HIM atop the tower. The past hours had been crammed. He was sodden with fatigue. Having abandoned the door to the armory as too risky, Beaucaire had resorted to other methods.

First, he'd sent a stream of men to scale the tower; another to assault the main door. Cleve had rimmed the parapet with cannon balls. The accuracy with which they dropped discouraged the enemy. The scaling party hadn't succeeded. Neither had the battering crew.

Then Beaucaire had tried to blow down the door. He sent men to plant powder in front of it. D'Entreville dropped the first four. And when a fifth succeeded, Cleve leaned over the parapet and doused the explosives with water. This had happened three times.

Sitting beside the Carthoun in the rays of the newborn sun, the Englishman considered their position. They had battled the marquis to a standstill, but it couldn't last.

If Beaucaire succeeded in putting one more powder keg in

front of the door, the game would be over. The defenders of the tower were out of water. Perhaps two cupfuls remained in the tank on the ground floor. Cleve shrugged.

"But, fortunately our friend doesn't know that."

In the base of the tower he could hear d'Entreville moving about. During the siege the Frenchman had composed a verse, and he was now trying to fit a tune to it. The results were not very satisfactory. And every now and then, he would stop in the middle of a note and curse.

Cleve smiled. Guy d'Entreville was a man of extremes. His emotions leaped from despair to hope, to indifference, to recklessness, and back to despair with the agility of a mountain goat.

Suddenly Cleve frowned. Above Guy's muffled tenor he had caught another sound. A sound from a distance. A rhythmic throbbing which pulsed faintly through the warm morning air. Martial. Stirring. He cursed. Drums! Military drums!

"Schomberg!" he cried. He had almost forgotten. He scrambled to his feet and a bullet whined off the rim of the parapet. The musketeers Beaucaire had placed in the neighboring bastion were alert.

He paid them no heed. Excitedly his eyes swept the western horizon. He saw it: a glint of steel in the sun; a thin plume of dust rising on the rim to his right. He turned and charged down the steps.

"They're coming!" he yelled, hurdling the last of the steps. "Egad! They're coming."

D'Entreville stood up. "Schomberg?"

"Yes!" Suddenly Cleve laughed. "I have an idea. Come upstairs."

He was gasping when they reached the tower-top again. He pointed in wordless emphasis at the thread-like columns marching out of the northwest.

The sound of drums was much louder now. The lookouts in other towers had caught it. Below the castle churned into feverish activity. The two defenders of the bastion were momentarily forgotten.

D'Entreville watched the old fashioned drawbridge being pulled up and turned to his companion.

"You said something of an idea?"

"Yes." The Englishman grinned and pointed to the Carthoun. "It will take two men to handle it."

Guy caught on and laughed. He made no comment. They swung into action. The cannon was heavy, unwieldy, and it took them ten minutes to roll it into position so that its muzzle pointed over the top of the portcullis.

At intervals Guy darted to the edge for a quick glance at the scene below. The base of the tower was deserted. For the time being, Beaucaire had forgotten them.

"I'll need deep deflection," Cleve decided, throwing aside a rammer and setting the first fuse. He reached down and picked up an armful of wooden jacks and hammered them clumsily between the breech and the carriage with a musket butt. "This brings me back to the year I served on a king's ship."

HE SIGHTED along the barrel. It ran in steep decline toward the center of the gate. The shot would be made at a thirty-degree angle. With Guy's aid he moved the Carthoun a trifle to the right.

He wanted ample opportunity to carom the ball off the gate and into the exposed hand-winch which had raised it.

"Keep your eye on the doors below, Kitten!"

He lit a match from one of the muskets. Guy nodded. He had been doing just that when he wasn't needed.

Cleve stepped aside. He touched the match to the fuse. Flame-pierced smoke enveloped the top of the bastion. The Carthoun strained back with a belching roar.

Dextrously Guy leaped forward, plunged a damp sponge into the muzzle. Cleve seconded with the rammer and a fresh charge. They were working swiftly, flawlessly. The wadding followed. Then the ball. Another wad.

"Ready!"

"Fire!"

From below astounded, dismayed yells soared into the air. A squad dashed for the bastion door. Guy was waiting for them. The Carthoun crashed for the second time. He dropped three balls and smashed two of the assault sortie and the rest withdrew.

Four shots were sent plunging into the gate. And then a new noise punctuated the yells of the garrison below. It was a sharper roar, not so deep as the Carthoun's rumble. The enemy had mounted an eighteen-pound culverin on the neighboring bastion. Its first ball struck the lip of the parapet. Guy brushed stone chips out of his hair and reached for a musket.

"*Corbac!* This is becoming too warm for comfort."

Cleve nodded. His fire had wrecked the winch. One of the gate-chains hung despairingly and the gate itself was leaning at a crazy angle. Another shot would bring it down.

He loaded the Carthoun by himself. Guy was busy dropping death notices on another assault party. Two more balls from the culverin jarred the tower. They were getting closer.

Finally Cleve stepped back and touched the match to the fuse. Through heaving billows of smoke he saw the gate reel. It started to fall. He gripped d'Entreville's arm.

"Come on, Kitten. Let's get out of here!"

At the bottom of the bastion they paused.

D'Entreville went to a loop-hole and glanced out. A squad was inching cautiously toward the door and he raised a musket, dropped a man and the rest retreated. He looked at Cleve.

"What now? *Mordi!* We've stirred up a hornet's nest."

The Englishman was triumphant. "But we've opened the door for Schomberg." He stepped up and peered through the loop-hole. "Yes. They're trying to build breastworks across the gate now, and—" He choked. "Damme! We must get out of here!"

The tower shuddered as another ball from the culverin hit it low. D'Entreville said, "Why?"

Cleve laughed. "Beaucaire has become smart. A squad has just dragged a Carthoun opposite this door. Two shots will blow it to splinters."

Guy stared through the loop-hole. He saw the gun being drawn; a hasty breastwork of earth being thrown up. For luck he sent a ball rapping toward it. Then he turned.

"Where to?"

"The armory. I have an idea that the door is not well guarded in all this excitement."

THEY trotted swiftly down the corridor between the tower room and the armory. At the great studded door they paused, lifted the iron bar and opened it softly. There were two guards on its other side and both were looking toward the noise in the bailey. They struck them simultaneously—d'Entreville with a clubbed musket; Cleve with the knife he had taken from the jailer. The guards hadn't a chance.

"Neatly and with dispatch," d'Entreville breathed.

Cleve nodded. On a shelf beside him was a box of candles. He dipped into it and withdrew one. Carefully he stripped tallow from it until there was only an inch left with the long naked wick dangling limply. Guy frowned. The Englishman held up the stub.

"This will burn for perhaps three or four minutes," he said. "Wait here. I'm going down into the dungeon, knock in the top of a powder keg and put this little invention atop it."

Then he was gone. D'Entreville heard him clatter down the steps. He bit his lip nervously. He bent down and took the rapiers from the belts of the two dead guards.

He stared at the layers of arms and ammunition piled at the far end of the armory. Soon someone would come to fetch it.

"Sacré nom," he groaned, "why doesn't he return?"

Then Cleve was back. He wore a devilish grin. He gripped d'Entreville's arm, grabbed one of the swords, and said, "We have approximately three minutes to go somewhere else. The candle is burning in the center of several tons of explosives and when it burns low enough—" He laughed. "Come on!"

They darted furtively out of the door, along the wall and into a small garden which flanked the keep. Nobody stopped them. There was too much confusion. All eyes were concentrated on the tower.

In the garden Cleve and Guy paused to catch their breath. The past half-hour had been exhausting. They crouched beneath a heavy bush panting softly and smiling.

"Damme," Cleve said at length, "we have reached this far safely. Why not go the full way? Where do you suppose Beaucaire has stored the gold?"

A soft voice behind him said, "In the strong-room, Monsieur Cleve."

As one man the two cavaliers wheeled. Their swords gleamed. Ready. It was Beaucaire's sister, standing on the other side of the bush, unsmiling, serious.

"I watched you enter the garden from there," she said indicating a window. "I felt that you might need my aid."

Gallantly d'Entreville started to get up and bow. Cleve yanked him earthward. "Sit down, fool! Someone might see you." He looked up at the girl. "I am sorry that we bungled our escape, *mademoiselle.*"

"It was a brave bungle." She smiled. "Come. I will lead you to the strong-room. I have the keys here at my waist."

"The King shall hear of your loyalty, *mademoiselle,*" said Guy.

"I desire my brother's pardon. Nothing more."

SHE LED them into the keep. The residence of the lord of the castle was quiet. The customary guards were gone, leaving the carpeted halls deserted.

Cleve paused at a window. He had been counting the time. It was nearing the point where the north wall would erupt if his invention worked. The girl and d'Entreville crowded behind him.

They were looking out into the main bailey directly across from the tower which he and Guy had defended. Even as he watched, the Carthoun which Beaucaire had been setting up roared. The heavy door to the bastion sagged. The girl murmured, "They still think you are in the tower, *messieurs.*"

Guy d'Entreville nodded. He too was waiting. Waiting to see the bastion, the wall, the armory, go up in thunder. Nothing happened. He looked at Cleve uneasily. Had the candle gone out?

Cleve shrugged. He stared bleakly into the bailey. Down there, in all his lace and finery, stood Beaucaire gesturing and shouting orders.

He kicked a slow powder-boy, slapped a gunner and stamped his foot at the delay. Finally the Carthoun vomited again, and the door in the bastion disappeared.

With a shout of triumph, Beaucaire drew his sword. He and fifty men charged forward, rushed into the tower room—and Cleve turned to Guy. The Englishman crossed his fingers and held them up. D'Entreville did the same thing.

Between them the girl stared bewildered. She did not understand. She didn't know. Almost pityingly Cleve drew her close.

"There are times, *mademoiselle,* when Fate creates a justice which—" But, looking into the soft luster of her eyes he suddenly discovered that he couldn't tell her.

"Yes, *monsieur?* You were saying—?"

And then it came! A monstrous roar which thundered over the castle in a great cloud of dust, smoke and flame. The impact shattered the glass of the window. There was a moment stunned by sheer force; then debris began to crash earthward.

Great pieces of stone, parts of armor, earth-clods, twisted

gory things that had been men. Through the holocaust Cleve felt her eyes probing him. Wide, horrified, stricken eyes. Incredulous.

"You knew! God! You knew and you didn't warn him. You didn't—" She broke down completely. Cleve held her. She clawed away. "Mazo!" she sobbed.

She fainted.

Cleve carried her to the divan; placed her gently upon it. He unhooked the keyring she wore at her waist and stood staring. The tragic whiteness of her beauty killed all of the reckless triumph in him. The fool's luck in which he and Guy had played had had a price. The girl before him was paying it.

He felt suddenly humble.

"Damme!" he burst out savagely to Guy. "Come on! To the strong-room!"

The Frenchman nodded. He cast a glance out of the broken window. Where the bastion and armory had stood was now a great hole which gaped foolishly. Through it, breasting the slope, came the lily banners of the royal army.

"It's over," he said. "We've won! Beaucaire's men are throwing down their arms."

Cleve shrugged. "Come on," he said.

THE STAFF of Marshal Schomberg had taken over the keep of the castle when Beaucaire's sister recovered. She heard the sound of their voices, their laughing triumphant voices, coming from the strong-room at the end of the hall. Stifling the great aching void in her heart, she left the divan. From the treasure-vault, she heard Richard Cleve's voice.

"Le Duc de Montmorency left last night, *monsieur le maréchal.* Else he too would be captured."

A deep bass rumbled a hearty reply. *"Mordi!* You two must be wizards!"

"But this was not all of our doing," she heard Guy say.

"No? Then who else?"

"The Marquis de Beaucaire gave his life for his King, *monsieur*. When he, Cleve, and I arrived here with the treasure, we found that—that the castle had been betrayed. Without Beaucaire's valiant aid we would never have escaped from the cell in which Montmorency had us thrown."

"Precisely," Cleve's pleasant baritone seconded. "Le Marquis de Beaucaire was a brave, loyal subject. When all else seemed lost he seized a flaming torch, ran through a hail of bullets into the powder room, and blew himself and the north wall to bits so that you and your troops could enter safely. Such courage is rarely seen on this earth, *monsieur*. Le Marquis de Beaucaire should be honored forever."

Marshal Schomberg's bass voice replied emphatically. "And he shall, *messieurs!*"

And in the hall a slim girl turned away, her dark eyes glimmering. "Thank you, Monsieur Cleve and Monsieur d'Entreville," she whispered softly. "You have kept your word."

III

SEAL OF TREASON

They're loose again! Those two trouble-jabbing trouble shooters for Richelieu: Cleve, the Cardinal's Madman, who laughs with a hot steel-point at his eyeball; D'Entreville, the Cardinal's Kitten, who scratches deepest when men laugh at his purr. Where they ride, Hell whips loose from its moorings.

CHAPTER I

DOUBLE MURDER

THE LARGE VENETIAN clock in the palace library was chiming seven as portly Capitaine Cordeau entered the high-ceilinged room, paced smartly over the thick rug and came to a halt in front of the Cardinal's desk.

He essayed a jerky bow which made the full white plume on his hat ripple gracefully, and smiled, the quick false smile of a politician.

"You sent for me, *Monseigneur?*"

Cardinal Richelieu thrust aside the litter of correspondence before him and fell wearily against the plush of his chair. It had been a busy day. An important day. But not without headaches—two headaches in particular.

"*Oui, Capitaine,*" he answered dryly, "I sent for you. It is my wish that you take a squad and search Paris for a pair of lawless scoundrels bearing the names Cleve and d'Entreville."

The smile on Cordeau's lips wavered. "Again, *Monseigneur?*"

The Cardinal inclined his head. "Again, *monsieur.*" He steepled his thin tapering fingers and stared at the tips absently, "And when you have found them, place them under arrest and throw them into the deepest dungeon. Understand?"

"Er—*oui, Monseigneur.*"

"*Bien.* That will be all."

Cordeau's muddy eyes had a glint of sarcasm in them. The Cardinal spoke as if the command were nothing. Belittled it with the careless expression: "That will be all!" *Corbac!* Richard

Cleve and Guy d'Entreville were as amenable to arrest as wild-cats.

The *capitaine's* black spade-beard trembled and he no longer wore a smile, but he managed to keep his mouth shut. It wasn't prudent to say foolish things before Richelieu. With curses kicking rebelliously behind his lips, Cordeau bowed. He left the library with the stiff dignity of a man trudging to an un-worthy fate.

Richelieu frowned across the table at Père Joseph. In the soft flickering light of the candles his fine pallor was delicately tinted with shadow, giving his sharply chiseled features a thoughtful, profound, and at the moment, stern appearance.

"Some day, Joseph," he observed, "Messieurs Cleve and d'Entreville shall learn that they cannot play their rogue-tricks in my guard!"

Father Joseph, the Cardinal's large, Socratic aide, allowed a look of resignation to flit across his unhandsome face. He sighed

and laid aside the volume he had been scanning. The incorrigibility of the two in question was an old story.

FIRST, there was Count Guy d'Entreville: satirist, poet and swordsman. Guy had been a gnat in the great Cardinal's ear until forced, by Richelieu, into shifting his alliance.

Four months ago, d'Entreville's indiscreet fiancée had been made the innocent dupe of a treasonous plot. Guy had sworn himself to the Cardinal's service to save her from going to *la Bastille.*

And then there was Lord Richard Cleve. Cleve was an Englishman who had been exiled from his native land because of his fondness for speaking the truth at the wrong times. A matter of ten thousand pounds which was going into the Duke of Buckingham's pockets instead of into the Royal Treasury.

He was an enigma. A man of contradictions. The brilliance

of his mind was exceeded only by his penchant for getting into and then out of trouble. This trait, abetted by the hot-headedness of Guy d'Entreville, combined to make a devil's partnership indeed.

Père Joseph folded his large hands. "What have they done this time, Armand?" he asked.

"Ma foi! It would be easier to ask what they have left undone!" Richelieu selected a document from the pile in front of him and held it up to the light. "Their misdeeds for the day," he said ominously.

In the spacious corridor, outside, a squad of Guards swung by, the rhythm of their tread sounding in muffled cadence through the door. He waited until it had faded before reading the report aloud.

" 'At noon,'" he read, " 'on this the tenth day of October, 1630, officers Cleve and d'Entreville fell to bickering between themselves on the ramp of the Pont Neuf. Six of His Majesty's Musketeers attempted to quiet them, and were promptly hurled into the River Seine.'"

Père Joseph shrugged. The tale was typical. He had often wondered how Cleve and d'Entreville could argue so constantly and still remain fast friends. The incongruity of madmen, he decided.

Richelieu continued, and his voice shook with cold indignation. "That was the lesser of their offenses, Joseph." He bent nearer the candles. " 'In the market-place near the Capitainerie of the Louvre, le Comte d'Entreville did wilfully and with malice aforethought hurl an egg into the face of the King's brother, heir apparent to the Throne, Monsieur le Duc d'Orleans.'"

This time, Père Joseph was honestly shocked. *"Mon dieu!"* he exclaimed. "What ever possessed d'Entreville to do that?"

Richelieu crumpled the report into a hard ball and hurled it to the floor. "Cleve did," he said icily and got to his feet. "D'Entreville aimed for him and missed!"

"The King is offended?"

"Naturally. One does not splatter royalty with eggyolk. And he blames me! Cleve and d'Entreville are in my Guard and consequently, my responsibility."

Richelieu interlaced his fingers and paced angrily. He made a graceful, commanding figure in his trailing red robe, seeming taller because of his extreme slenderness. It was a source of constant wonder to his contemporaries that such a frail-looking man could control the destiny of France. Not even the King dared rule the powerful nobles as did Richelieu. And therein lay the drama of the times.

FRANCE, in the early Seventeenth Century, was still subject to the whims of her ruling princes. The nobility retained its feudal right to levy taxes, to raise personal armies, and to subsidize the Throne for its own ends.

To combat this, Richelieu was trying to evolve France into a strong nation, united under but one leader—the King. He had to strip power from the nobles to do this and they hated him for it. Their plots against him were myriad, but as yet unavailing.

"Naturally, those rakehellies *would* wait to perpetrate their impudences when I am too busy to deal with them personally," Richelieu said returning to the desk.

Père Joseph shifted uneasily. He feared an outburst of nerves. In these critical times Richelieu's temper was stretched to the snapping point and minor irritations, such as furnished by Cleve and d'Entreville, could easily serve as the necessary cutting-edge. He was relieved when a Guardsman entered the library.

"Your Eminence, le Duc de Montauban has just returned to the Palace. He wishes me to extend regret that he is indisposed and will be unable to bid you good evening personally."

The Duke of Montauban was Richelieu's house guest, representing one of the major moves in the Cardinal's plans to unite France. The Cardinal frowned.

"De Montauban is well, I trust," he said.

"*Oui, Monseigneur.* He has retired to his suite."

"Then why? It is too early to go abed as yet."

The Guardsman moistened his lips uncertainly. "Er—you'll pardon me, *Monseigneur,* but le Duc de Montauban is drunk."

Richelieu stared at the treaty he had been hoping to persuade de Montauban to sign. He sighed. "The irresponsible young fool. The progress of a nation awaits his name, but he prefers to amuse himself."

The Guardsman nodded uneasily and left. Richelieu poured himself a tumbler of water and sipped it slowly. His dark eyes were pools of thought. De Montauban had been a guest in his Palace for a week, and still the reason for his visit lay unsigned. Something always came up. Fate? The Cardinal was beginning to wonder.

Prior to a month ago de Montauban had hated him with the fire and unreason of a very young and very reactionary noble. Now he was accepting his sworn enemy's hospitality with the promise of signing a pledge that would bind him by honor to the Cardinal's theory of government. Why? Richelieu set aside the tumbler of water and stared at Joseph.

"**YOUNG** de Montauban troubles me, Joseph," he confessed. "I have never fully believed his sudden reversal of opinion. Yet my agents have learned nothing to prove otherwise. *Ma foi!* It is an uncertain business. Intuition warns me of a trap, but reason and my desire for peace urge credulity."

"I have a profound respect for your intuition, Armand," Père Joseph said. "However, I think that the young duke is too shallow to formulate a clever plot."

"My opinion also, Joseph. And still, that vague suspicion has been gnawing steadily at the back of my brain and tonight it is stronger than usual."

The speaker rose to his feet and once more started pacing. Père Joseph frowned. It wasn't like the cold-minded Cardinal to act in this manner. The monk stood up.

"If it will relieve your mind, *Monseigneur,* I shall look in on *le duc* as I go to my room."

Richelieu's fingers played absently with the heavy pendant on his chest. He nodded. "Do that, Joseph," he said.

The elaborate suite given to le Duc de Montauban was on the second story. Père Joseph strode easily along the wide corridor leading to it; and then a sudden questioning expression began to cloud his features. Usually there was a guard posted before the ducal door. Tonight the space was deserted; the guard missing.

Quickening his step, Père Joseph reached the door and knocked tentatively. There was no answer. The frown on his forehead deepened. He paused, struggling to maintain an illusion that everything was all right; then entered the room.

The body of the guard was sprawled grotesquely in the middle of the foyer. Faint light from the adjoining room washed his dead staring face in ghastly yellow. His throat had been cut.

Père Joseph stood for one frozen moment experiencing the numb nausea of a man plummeting through a scaffold-trap. He carefully closed the door and stepped across the body.

"De Montauban!"

The young duke was in bed. He lay smiling, his long hair a dark froth on the pillow, his eyes closed as if in sleep. The jeweled haft of a needle-like stiletto protruded stiffly from his chest. Père Joseph moved closer and stopped. Le Duc de Montauban was quite dead.

The monk bit his lip and retired, locking the door after him. Disaster had struck. A murder that threatened to wreck France with the revolt of her nobility. A murder that threatened Richelieu's very existence. Père Joseph broke into a horrified, anxious, dog-trot.

CHAPTER II

SCRATCHER AND CUTTER

IN THE MEANTIME, Capitaine Cordeau was rapidly losing his patience. For almost an hour he had led a stumbling squad of Guardsmen through the pitchy dark of Paris streets, without a sign of his quarry.

From tavern to tavern, house to house; scuffing his new boots on the rough cobbles; staining the fine lace of his collar with sweat, and always listening to the same story:

"No, *monsieur*, I have not seen them."… "No, *mon Capitaine*, they have not been here and they owe me ten livres."… "No, Cordeau, not tonight." And to make matters worse, the Guards were growing restive and he was running out of possibilities.

"We have visited le Coq Rouge, l'Oiseau Bleu and le Palais d'Or," Sergeant Burdet complained. "*Ventre saint gris, Capitaine,* Cleve and d'Entreville have left the city!"

"Orders to bring them in," Cordeau snapped. "So I bring them in, if we walk to Bordeaux!"

Burdet shrugged and fell silent. In the face of the *capitaine's* martinet attitude, there wasn't anything else to do. One does not argue with a duty-mad slave driver.

"Close up, men," he snarled. "*Corbac!* We are not out for an evening's stroll. Close up, curse you!"

They threaded their way past le Quai de l'Ecle, across the Pont Neuf and into the velvet dark of the market-place on the other side.

Two thick torches, carried in the van, thrust aside the night in flickering orange candescence, highlighting the stubborn flush on Cordeau's cheek. Boots cracked hard on the rough cobblestones; rapiers tinkled rhythmically against buckles; a pair of narrow-eyed footpads stared fearfully at them from a darkened alley and melted discreetly into the murk.

And then, rounding the corner which led to the Henri IV Tavern, they were greeted by the sight of a small crowd. A curious, apprehensive crowd, outlined sharply in the torch-lit courtyard, staring in fascination at the trim little inn. A battle was progressing inside.

Cordeau gripped his rapier and ordered the squad forward on the double.

The miniature war seemed to be located on the second floor; for as he approached, a window shattered open and a disheveled individual leaped from it feet first. He landed in a heap; got up and kept running. Arms akimbo, and with feet astraddle in the center of the court, the captain eyed the broken window.

"Cleve! D'Entreville!" he roared.

"Present!"

A clean-shaven face with keen brown eyes and a lean jaw line appeared through the ragged aperture. *"Hola,* Cordeau," it greeted cheerfully.

The captain raised himself to his full rotund dignity. "M'Lord," he shouted. "In the name of his Eminence the Cardinal, I command you to come down!"

Richard Cleve looked back over his shoulder. The light from inside marked the deep bronze of his skin and the slight impudent tilt of his rather small nose. It shot glints of copper through the deep chestnut of his hair.

As he turned, he ducked. A gurgling bottle somersaulted past his ear and exploded against the side of the watering-trough below. He raked a few strands of hair from his eyes and shook his head.

"Can't make it, *Capitaine.* We're entertaining."

He waved cheerfully and disappeared before Cordeau had time to erupt suitably.

THE ROOM was small, cramped. It had no furniture outside of a saggy cot and a large walnut table against the far wall. In the corner a tall, rangy young man, encased in maroon with a dancing red plume in his broad-brimmed hat, was holding a doorless portal against three gentlemen.

The three were backed up by a dozen more, all shouting and brandishing swords. Cleve went over and lounged against the table and surveyed the scene with the critical eye of a connoisseur.

"All because you decided to read poetry." he snorted. "Faith, Guy, this is one brawl that I didn't commence."

Guy d'Entreville caught a vicious thrust on the length of his blade and nipped its author in the shoulder. "*Pecaire!* Fine time for recriminations! Lend your blade to this, you English lout!"

He ducked a particularly high slash at his head and needled an exposed thigh. "No man can call my verse putrid. Especially these swine." He sent his sword into a flashing series of ripostes that caused the door-jammed trio to curse and retreat.

"Temper, Kitten," Cleve observed.

D'Entreville half rose from his couch. He was a full two inches taller than his companion. There was a glint of anger in his dark eyes. His hair, like rippled pitch, clustered in dark contrast against the white lace of his collar. The nose above his clipped mustache was high-bridged and aristocratic. It lent a slight hawkishness to his features which was abetted by high cheekbones and thin though even lips.

"*Sapristi,* Cleve! Don't call me Kitten!"

Cleve grinned. The name Cardinal's Kitten had been pinned on d'Entreville several months before by Prince Conde who considered Guy extremely young for his ability to claw adversaries first with his poetry and then with his sword. Guy had never taken to the title. To him it sounded faintly derisive.

"Some day, Cleve, you'll call me Kitten once too—"

Cleve stiffened. "Watch out, you fool!" There was a bottle on the table beside him. He scooped it up; hurled it past d'Entreville's shoulder and scored. A man staggered back holding a badly mashed nose. The sword he had been about to stick in d'Entreville's back clattered to the floor.

"Pay attention to business!"

D'Entreville nodded. "But damned to you, Cleve. À moi. I'm not cut to play Horatius forever!"

Cleve put on his hat carefully, sheathed his blade, and picked up the table. In contrast to his friend he was unusually slight, but the ease with which he handled the heavy piece evidenced amazing strength.

"Step aside, Kitten. We've lingered too long. Cordeau is without and he has his army with him plus a jailer's expression in his eyes."

"*Sangodemi!* Why didn't you say so?"

THE SPEAKER knitted his adversaries into a short retreat and then did a neat pirouette. Cleve came up behind with the table held shield-like in front of him.

The besieging horde surged into the room. They clogged loosely in the doorway as the table crashed into them. It was like a huge bowling ball striking half-set pins.

D'Entreville leaped a sprawling figure and came in behind Cleve. Opposition melted before their combined weight. The two cavaliers chased the others down the hallway as far as the stairs and hurled the table after them. Three of Cordeau's squad were caught in the deluge of falling bodies.

"Now to leave this hole," d'Entreville panted, snapping his rapier into its sheath. "The front seems best in the confusion. Keep the brim of your hat well over your face."

Cleve shook his head. "The rear. Cordeau has three men at the foot of the stairs already. Damned if I'll again return to the Palace under guard like a felon. We skip through the back, *mon ami.*"

D'Entreville's jaw snapped shut at a stubborn angle. "I still say the front. Last time, Cordeau was waiting at the back."

Cleve sighed. He planted the sole of his thigh-high cordovan boot on the chest of an ambitious climber and sent him crashing back to join his milling comrades at the foot of the stairs.

He looked at d'Entreville and frowned. Argument, spirited verbal recrimination, seemed to be the tie that bound their deep friendship.

"The last time," he said patiently, "*you* suggested the back. Not I. We were caught."

D'Entreville glared at his companion with disgust, and said:

"We wouldn't have been, if you hadn't tripped over your own clumsy feet. Besides, you started the brawl in the first place."

"Me?" Cleve looked hurt. "Why, all I did was laugh a small bit when the duchess commenced to sing."

"The woman was not a duchess. She was the mistress of le Duc de Vas."

The climber had returned with a companion. Cleve kicked them both down the stairs again. Their return restarted the turmoil of arms and legs which had been slowly reorganizing. "The woman looked like a duchess," he said. "She was fat and she sang off-key."

From the door of the grog room Sergeant Burdet appeared and caught them thus arguing. He emitted a hoarse bellow: "*Messieurs.* Stand! You are under arrest."

Both men stared down at him; and d'Entreville gripped Cleve's elbow. "You're right," he said. "The rear is the best wager."

They fled back through the L-shaped hall. It was a long narrow corridor, dingy with warped doors lining either side. The very gloom of it seemed to deaden the noise from below. Behind them Burdet was yelling curses and fighting his way up the clogged staircase.

"Damme! There's no rear entrance!" Cleve exclaimed as they pounded around the corner up against a dead end. Then he snapped his fingers and smiled. "But there's a window."

The window overlooked an extremely narrow alleyway, and stared directly across into the dark square of another. D'Entreville put his boot through the pane.

"No time for niceties," he explained, kicking aside the jagged remains. "I'll repay the innkeeper tomorrow."

"If you are able to," Cleve said, and stared at the neighboring window. He shifted to the depth of the alleyway and shrugged. "About five feet across," he decided. "Come, *mon ami.*"

They vaulted over the black chasm between buildings and stood, concealed by shadow, on the sill of the window. Burdet and three Cardinalists clattered down the hall they had just quitted. Cleve held his breath. The men finally withdrew without glancing across the alley.

"All right," he muttered, releasing his grip on a weather-warped eve. "In we go, and pray that the room is unoccupied."

IT WAS. The room appeared to be a small alcove. A thick drape blocked the single egress but allowed the light from the adjacent room to seep around its edges. Voices came in muffled accents through the folds.

Cleve hitched his rapier closer to his waist and glided across the rug on the balls of his feet. D'Entreville was close behind, breathing in softly, quickly. He had his sword drawn. He touched Cleve's shoulder and pointed to the curtain.

"Pecaire. Is that the only way out?"

Cleve nodded. He realized that they couldn't stay holed in the little room too long. The moment Cordeau discovered that they had eluded his men, nothing but a complete search of the neighboring buildings would satisfy him.

"We'll have to put a bold face on it," the Englishman said with a shrug. "Damme, I hope that our friends in there are amenable."

A whining voice from the other side was saying: "But I left my dagger there... I deserve the price of it."

With a sweep, Cleve armed aside the curtain and stepped into the room. It presented a tableau.

Three men were seated at a table around a black wine bottle. One was dark, swarthy, with a black mustache and goatee, glittering grey eyes and a rich costume studded with seed pearls.

Beside him, a veritable paunch of a man sat, blubber-lips agape and eyes pooling terror.

The third of the trio was a hard-faced individual, whom Cleve and d'Entreville had never seen, although he wore the white crossed surcoat of the Cardinal's Guard.

An imposter! Cleve's fingers felt the cool hill of his blade.

"I trust you will pardon us, *messieurs*," he said smilingly. "We have lost our way, and must pass through to find it."

The swarthy fellow with the pearl-studded doublet cursed, but the man in the Cardinalist uniform acted. With a yell he drew a knife from his belt and leaped. Cleve didn't have time to draw and d'Entreville's blade was tangled with the curtain.

"Spies!" the knife-man howled.

Cleve's left hand darted out and gripped the fellow's dagger arm. His right grasped his heavy sword-hilt from behind; raised it, and bashed it cruelly into the imposter's writhing lips. The basket hilt of the rapier was heavy. The man crumpled.

"Anyone else?" d'Entreville snapped, letting the light of the candles shimmer on his bared blade.

The swarthy man and his fat companion sat still. The knife-man, blood dripping from his lacerated lips, sat in the corner and cursed monotonously. Cleve kicked his knife into a pile of debris on the opposite wall and stepped to the door.

"Good evening, *messieurs*," he said. "Come on, Guy."

The two cavaliers closed the door firmly behind them and groped hurriedly down the house's paint-blistered stairs.

"*Corbac!* It's dark. A wonder they wouldn't have a lamp."

Cleve laughed. "Apparently our friends upstairs desire privacy. Incidentally, wasn't that swarthy fellow Vendome, the King's illegitimate brother?"

D'Entreville stumbled; caught himself and cursed. "Yes," he replied after a moment. "I'm rather curious. What in the name of Heaven has he to do with Sarasanac? I wasn't even aware that they knew one another."

"Which one was he?"

"The fat sluggard. Owns le Theatre de Paris and claims to be a dramatist. *Corbac!* He doesn't know good verse from bad."

"Meaning," Cleve interposed, "that he doesn't like yours."

THEY reached the first landing and stepped stealthily into the street. Behind, the noise from L'Henri IV had quieted. Moonlight silvered the cobbles, lending a false serenity to the night. Somewhere in the distance a clock tolled.

But instead of striding boldly away, Cleve came to a dead halt.

"What's the matter?"

Cleve said: "I don't know." Then he snapped his fingers. "Faith, now I do. Observe the street, Kitten."

"What about it? 'Tis deserted. Quiet. Excellent for our purpose."

Cleve chuckled. "And that is the point, m'lad. It is too deserted and too quiet to be natural. With the battle fresh over at the tavern the crowd should be coming home now."

"*Sangodemi!* Don't be stupid. We're free and out of it."

"And about to step into it again. I think we had better retreat."

D'Entreville snorted. "I'm not doubling back into Cordeau's waiting arms and neither are you," he said.

"But it's wise. I'm warning you, Kitten...."

A thin edge came into the French cavalier's voice. "*Sapristi!* Don't call me Kitten!" He gripped Cleve's arm. "Come on!"

They marched quickly along the house-front, rounded the corner, and struck full into a large, heavy body that cursed. It was Cordeau.

He smiled triumphantly. "Good evening, gentlemen," he said. "I've been expecting you."

His voice suddenly rasped harshly. "And now, fall in. You are both under arrest, and after I report to *Monseigneur le Cardinal* about tonight's business you'll be fortunate to escape the block."

And as the prisoners marched away surrounded by their

guards, one said to the other: "So, we are free and out of it, eh? Nice work, Kitten."

And the other replied fiercely: "Quiet!"

WHO'S DEAD NOW?

RICHELIEU SPOKE IN an iced tone and the soft composure of it terrified. "*Messieurs,* you have outraged me, my regiment, and your King. There remains but one course."

Cleve eyed d'Entreville obliquely. The two were standing alone before the Cardinal's library desk where Cordeau had escorted them after a short stay in the dungeon. D'Entreville's face was tense.

Cleve sighed. D'Entreville was allowing the curse of his vivid imagination to run away with him again.

"You mean La Bastille, of course," he said easily.

Richelieu nodded. He folded his hand and eyed them enigmatically. "Have you anything to say in your defense, *messieurs?*"

Guy d'Entreville gulped audibly. He preferred death to imprisonment, and yet he could only stand there, hot and flushed, gripped in the wild rush various of mental protests, all of which contrived to choke him speechless.

The Venetian clock ticked a minute into the silence. Cleve found himself staring at the ornate candelabrum on the table. He looked past it at the white mask of Richelieu's face; into the man's dark eyes.

The Cardinal's gaze wavered for an instant, and in the wavering revealed an emotion that Cleve had never expected to see. Haunting, apprehensive with worry! Something had cracked the chill self-assurance of the great man.

The Englishman shrugged. "You did not call us here to ask us that, *Monseigneur,*" he said. "Damme, if you had decided that the Bastille should be our lot—we would now be making friends with the jailer."

It was a bold speech. The Cardinal demanded complete deference from the officers of his Guard. But Cleve was filled with the recklessness of the foredoomed plus his natural lack of tact.

Surprisingly, Richelieu did not erupt. Instead, a look of relief seemed to flicker through his eyes. He mastered it quickly.

"You are impertinent, m'Lord," he said, "But the astuteness of your remarks pleases me." He arose, paced slowly to the window and turned. "You are quite right. I have a reason. A gamble, if you care to call it that."

"Yes?"

Richelieu frowned. *"Messieurs,"* he said, "you are scoundrels. Your roistering escapades have caused many to wonder whether the firmness of my hand has slipped. Mark you, gentlemen, it hasn't.

"It is only because I realize that two resourceful rogues are sometimes worth a regiment of ordinary men, that I suffer your repeated impertinences. And you have proved the truth of my theory in two noteworthy actions that have saved my life.

"Candidly, it is your rare ability to discover trouble that has caused me to bring you here."

The two rakehellies exchanged glances. The Cardinal was building up to something, and from past experience they knew it was something dangerous. Of the two, d'Entreville was the less apprehensive. He felt that at least they were still outside of the Bastille.

Cleve waited.

THE CARDINAL seemed to be weighing his next words carefully. He returned to his desk and sat down. The waxen mask which Cleve had first noticed returned to his thin features, and the earlier tension again clogged the atmosphere.

When Richelieu finally spoke, his voice was free of its icy smoothness. It rang in harsh accents upon their startled ears.

"Upstairs, *messieurs,*" he said, "behind the locked door of his room, lies le Duc de Montauban with a knife in his heart—murdered."

"Murdered?"

The Cardinal smiled grimly. "I see you understand the disastrous implications of the affair." He fell back against his chair and fingered the pendant-ribbon at his throat. It was a habit he had acquired while in deep thought.

"A peer of the realm has been slain, *messieurs,* beneath my roof, and that is all my court enemies need to discredit my position. Naturally, they shall fail, but it may cause a civil war."

He eyed the two gravely. "With Spain and Austria land-hungry and thirsting to pounce upon France's border provinces, it will not do to have the nation weakened internally."

Cleve wasn't interested in politics. "About de Montauban, *Monseigneur,*" he said. "Who murdered him?"

The Cardinal's lips thinned harshly. "That, my dear Cleve, is the gamble I offer you. Find the duke's assassin within the week and we shall forget La Bastille.

"I shall paint the problem more graphically. Père Joseph discovered the body two hours ago. The Guardsman at de Montauban's door had been silenced, then dragged out of sight into the ducal chamber. De Montauban was slain in his sleep. No one was seen. Nothing was heard."

He paused. "Well, *messieurs?*" Then, with a chuckle:

"Oh, I had almost forgotten. If you accept this challenge and win, you have your liberty and a princely bounty. If you accept and fail, your original term of imprisonment doubles. It is a gamble, gentlemen, fit only for lawless rakehellies such as yourselves."

Cleve shook his head. If the assassin was clever enough to outwit Richelieu, then he was clever enough to escape discovery. The Cardinal was the originator of intrigue. Besides, Cleve had heard that the Bastille was not so bad. Good food, cards, pleasant companions. The odds were too high.

"Faith, if it is all the same to you, *Monseigneur*," he grinned, "I prefer to idle my days in the—"

But d'Entreville interrupted. "We accept," he said crisply. "After all, *Monseigneur*, what have we to lose?"

"Twice as much," Cleve muttered dryly.

LATER, in the corridor outside the library, he regarded his tall comrade sarcastically. "A month was the original length of our sentence," he snapped. "Damme, now it's two. Admirable, Kitten. In fact, brilliant!"

D'Entreville was defiant. "Anything is better than rotting in La Bastille. *Corbac!* Besides, we may win."

Cleve looked at the ceiling and sighed regretfully. "He believes we may win," he told no one in particular.

Then he smiled. "Faith, Kitten, your poetic fancy has led you to some wild impulses, but this beats all. Solving an escape from the Bastille will be child's play compared to His Eminence's little task."

"Mark me, Cleve, when I begin an adventure, something always happens!"

"True, m'lad. Quite true. Only it always happens to *me!*" The Englishman chuckled and set his hat aslant over one eye.

"But lackaday, fellow. Once bitten twice warned. 'Tis your show, so I'll bid you *au revoir*. Drop in now and again, and let me know how you progress. I'll be at the Blue Boar Tavern improving this last week of freedom with a keg or so of ale."

D'Entreville swore fervently. He hadn't considered the possibility of this exigency. It was against his principles to admit it, but the irrepressible Cleve was almost as necessary to him as his right arm.

"Ah, now listen, Richard...."

But Cleve was twenty feet away and whistling cheerily. D'Entreville shook his head, reached down and picked up the edge of the long roller-rug. He jerked it once—powerfully.

Cleve's feet flew one way and his hat another. He landed with a soul-jarring bump.

"Well, *Monsieur le Comte?*"

Richelieu was standing in the door of the library and his eyes were chill. D'Entreville flushed furiously and fought to bring his stomach up from his boots. He still held on to one part of the rug.

"Er—*Monseigneur,*" he stammered. "I—that is. We were on our way to—I mean, Cleve was...."

"I know precisely what you mean," interposed the Cardinal. "I suggest that you cease your playing and commence the business at hand." His dark eyes shifted suddenly to the other. "I can see nothing to grin about, m'Lord."

Cleve nodded. He felt as if a mule had sneaked up behind him. "I agree, *Monseigneur,*" he said arising and massaging the spot solicitously.

"I understand you were planning to visit de Montauban's suite, *monsieur.*"

Cleve sighed, picked up his hat and nodded. "Yes, Your Eminence," he said.

PÈRE JOSEPH was in the Duke's room when they knocked. He had been collecting the dead man's personal effects. Frowning, he left the task to unbolt the door cautiously.

"There is little to see, *messieurs,*" he said after d'Entreville had explained their mission. "I have spoken to the captain of the Watch and no person, other than members of His Eminence's household, have been in the Palace tonight. Any person walking the halls alone would have been noticed and halted."

He ushered them into a large luxuriously furnished room, ceilinged in royal gold-trimmed blue and thick with carpets. The huge canopied bed had had the drapes drawn around it, but upon d'Entreville's suggestion they were opened to reveal the dark-haired corpse.

"I must caution you," Père Joseph said, "not to breathe a word of this misfortune. To the public the Cardinal will announce the sudden illness of the duke to allay suspicion until we have discovered the murderer."

"Or a reasonable scapegoat." Cleve nodded and collapsed into a pot-bellied chair. When Père Joseph had left, he stared at the ghastly vacancy of the room and said cheerfully: "Well, Kitten. Here is your problem. Solve it."

But, the mystery, on the face of it, seemed unsolvable. A *cul de sac.* D'Entreville found himself regretting his words to the Cardinal. He nosed uncertainly around the room, each step darkening his hopes until they were completely black.

Cleve had moved his chair to a neighboring table whereon sat an interesting-looking bottle and four silver goblets. Beside the liquor tray was Père Joseph's collection of de Montauban's personal articles. The Englishman sipped his drink and eyed the assortment of rings, pendants, brooches and medallions distastefully.

"Fop's baubles," he remarked. He picked up the largest.

Beside the bed, d'Entreville was staring unseeingly at the body. He started to turn away; then halted. With a muttered imprecation he pulled the stiletto from the duke's chest. The feel of the weapon seemed to jar his memory.

"Pecaire!"

"Speak up, Kitten."

D'Entreville looked annoyed. "Don't refer to me by that name." He held up the blood-clotted stiletto. "This has made me remember."

Cleve stood up, joggling the huge pendant ring idly in his hand. "Find the other half of that blade," he observed. "The human half, I mean. And you'll win out, m'lad."

"I am remembering," d'Entreville continued evenly, "about the visit we paid Vendome and that fat slug of a Sarasanac. There was a third man, an imposter wearing the surcoat of the Cardinal's Guard. He was complaining about losing his dagger when we burst in on them. Remember?"

Suddenly his eyes widened. *"Sacré Nom!* That's it. The imposter is the murderer." Then, he stared triumphantly at the Englishman.

"Don't look at me." Cleve shrugged. "I'm merely a spectator." He crossed to the bedside. He still had the large ring in his hand, but he slipped it over his little finger as he took the stiletto from the other's grip.

"But I believe you have stumbled upon half the truth, Kitten. A man garbed in the Cardinal's uniform would not, of a certainty, excite suspicion."

D'Entreville was vibrant. "But of course! Who would suspect a Cardinal's guard? He would pass unnoticed. That is the only way it could be done."

BUT CLEVE wasn't listening. He had his eyes riveted upon the porcelain-white fingers of the corpse. They were large fingers. Blunt-ended and heavy.

And what was more—those fingers were singularly undecorated. The few times Cleve had seen de Montauban, he had noticed the near foppishness of the man.

He took the large pendant-ring from his finger and placed it on the dead man's—rather, he attempted to place it there. The ornament wouldn't fit.

"Strange," he muttered; and went back to the table for more rings. He attempted to jam them onto de Montauban's cold fingers and failed.

D'Entreville showered questions on him.

"Sacré nom du cochon, you English fool. What are you about, anyway?"

Cleve stepped back from the bed and shrugged. His eyes were thoughtful. "Something is amiss, my friend. He has not been dead long enough to bloat."

"What are you talking about?"

Cleve handed the speaker a fistful of precious rings. "Try to place them on his fingers," he challenged. "I'll wager ten livres to one that you fail."

D'Entreville snorted. "Taken," he said, and selected two diamonds. After struggling futilely he looked up, a scowl deepening his forehead. "*Sangodemi!* They are too small. I owe you a livre."

Cleve nodded. He stared at the mole marking the left cheek of the dead man. With a gesture, he reached out and dug his thumbnail beneath its edge. The mole tilted, came off, and rolled from the corpse's face onto the pillow.

"Just as I suspected." The English cavalier stared at d'Entreville's scowling face and grinned. "Sorry, Kitten. You have not solved the murder of le Duc de Montauban."

D'Entreville's chin assumed a belligerent attitude. "No?"

"No." Cleve shrugged. "That fellow abed is no more de Montauban than am I. He can't wear the duke's rings and he hasn't got the duke's mole."

AFTER some hesitation d'Entreville conceded the point. "But *sandiou,*" he exclaimed. "The resemblance is amazing." He peered thoughtfully into the impostor's dead face, and sighed.

"Amazing," he repeated and stepped away. "But I'm still positive that I am right about the way this fellow was murdered. Vendome's hired assassin undoubtedly made a mistake."

"I thought Vendome was a friend of de Montauban. They have been seen together often," Cleve observed.

D'Entreville pressed his fingers to his head. "You are right," he groaned, "Of course, Vendome hates Richelieu and perhaps that hatred exceeds his fondness for de Montauban. *Mon dieu!* The deeper we delve into this affair the more confused it becomes. Why should Vendome murder his friend? What was he doing with Sarasanac and that bogus Cardinalist? And where is le Duc de Montauban?"

"Sounds like the ingredients for a wonderful headache," Cleve chuckled. "However, it belongs to you, Kitten. Jerking the rug from beneath me does not force me into this problem. And, incidentally, that is one I owe you."

Suddenly, d'Entreville snapped his fingers. "*Corbac,* Cleve. This business passes all understanding, particularly mine; but if de Montauban is not dead, I intend to find him. And, I think I know where to start. The house beside the Henri IV Tavern. Vendome and the others may still be there."

"Possibly." Cleve nodded, starting for the door. "But while you are finding out, I believe I shall keep my appointment with a keg at the Blue Boar. *Bonne chance, mon ami.*"

D'Entreville shrugged, scowled.

CHAPTER IV

TRAP FOR A MADMAN

CLOUDS WERE BEGINNING to clog the moonlight as he rode alone up to the house beside the Henri IV. He tied his mount to a rusted hitching post and paused to inspect the place.

It stared back ominously. Silently. The tavern next door was closed, its pudgy proprietor deciding in favor of rest after a hectic evening.

With steel lending cool assurance beneath his touch, the French rakehelly tried the door. It swung back silently.

At the top of the staircase, a glimmer of light threaded along the base of the door. He paused tensely and listened. No voices rewarded the effort. Only a brooding, uncomfortable silence. It seemed to hang over his senses like a heavy cloak. Mentally, he cursed Richard Cleve for his desertion.

He put his hand on the door and kicked it open.

Charging into the room with blade aglitter, he was forced to a surprised, skidding halt. In the corner behind the table was Sarasanac. The fat dramatist was staring mildly at him, a seeming question in his eyes. He was alone. Only the black wine bottle and the flanking trio of glasses gave evidence that there had previously been guests.

"Ha! Sarasanac, you fat slug! Where is le Duc de Vendome? Where is that henchman of his? That hard-faced killer, that masquerading bravo. Answer me, you paunchy pig, before I ram this blade down your gullet. Come on, curse you. Speak!'

But the fat dramatist said nothing. He merely stared in mild amazement, A chill lumped in d'Entreville's stomach. He lowered his rapier, stepped across, and shook the man. Sarasanac, still staring, wavered hesitantly, then slid off his chair to the floor. He was quite dead.

How long d'Entreville stood there staring at the body he never knew. All at once he stiffened. The stealthy creak of a floor-board outside the door announced a visitor.

Sword held ready, he flattened against the wall. The candle guttering on the table, wavered in weird shadows and flicked out. The ensuing darkness became crammed with tensity. D'Entreville licked his lips and waited.

Suddenly a raucous sneeze rent the silence to shreds, and a baritone voice near the door said: "Damn the dust!"

All of the breath went out of the Frenchman in a gasp. His sword-point dropped and he stepped out into the room. *"Sangodemi!"* he erupted. "Cleve!"

The Englishman's voice cut through the black. "Eh? Oh, er, hello, Guy. Thought I'd drop in. Where the de'il is a light?"

D'Entreville jerked a tinder-box from his sash and lit a taper. He found a fresh candle and touched flame to it.

"Understood that you weren't interested in this affair, *mon ami,"* he said,

The candle-light made the silver-facings on Cleve's black velvet doublet gleam in white contrast. It softened the hardness of his sword-hilt and threw shadows along one side of his face beneath its broad-brimmed plumed hat. The Englishman shrugged back the folds of his cape and smiled.

"I'm not," he replied.

"Then what are you doing here?"

"Keeping you out of harm's way, Kitten—nothing more. You are such a rash fool. I feared that you might uncover some insurmountable difficulty." He stepped across and stared at Sarasanac. "And I see that you have.... Dead?"

D'Entreville nodded. He sheathed his blade and bent over the body. "No wounds," he said. "Possibly his heart gave out. He was subject to attacks."

CLEVE jerked off a gauntlet and picked up a wine goblet. He sniffed the glass and replaced it. "Poisoned, Kitten. Gad, I'd know that odor anywhere. Friend of mine had a jealous wife and she used precisely the same stuff on him. Pleasant woman."

He picked up the bottle and inspected it thoughtfully.

D'Entreville, standing with arms akimbo in the center of the room, suddenly grew angry. The frustration that dogged every one of his conclusions was beginning to stick in his throat. He cursed.

"I'm getting a belly full of this," he growled. *"Corbac!* Vendome was here. Therefore, Vendome finished him. I'm wasting no more time. Come along, Cleve; we're going to see Vendome right now."

"That will be very interesting," observed the Englishman mildly. "Vendome apparently isn't to be visited. I have made inquiries and as far as I can ascertain he's—"

"For a person who is not interested in this affair," d'Entreville interrupted crisply, "you're wasting a cursed amount of time worrying about it."

Cleve tucked the bottle beneath his cloak. He eyed his companion brightly. "That I am, Kitten," he said, chuckling. "That I am."

D'Entreville looked murderously in his direction and strode out of the room.

They returned to the Cardinal's Palace. The French rakehelly had smoldering impatience in his eyes as he threw his mount's reins to a waiting groom and stumped across the court. He knew much and could prove little and the sensation was annoying.

For example, he was pretty certain that de Montauban lived; that he was working in accord with the Duke of Vendome, and that their joint effort was to depose Richelieu.

"They'll have the Cardinal accused of de Montauban's death and force his execution," he told Cleve as they entered the grand foyer.

Cleve nodded. Basically, he believed in the theory, but there were several loose ends. He fingered the poison bottle beneath his cape and said: "A good opinion, Guy. Only what happens if it succeeds? If de Montauban is declared dead, then it will be dangerous for him to return to life. He would be prosecuted for treasonous subterfuge. He must live for the rest of his life incognito and surrender his wealthy estate to his heirs. Damme! Will he make such a sacrifice? Frankly, I doubt it."

D'Entreville pursed his lips tightly. *"Monsieur,"* he said, "if you care to lend a hand in this affair, pray say so. Otherwise—" His voice broke sharply. "Cease blasting my theories!"

And with a swirl of his cape he marched away to report to Richelieu. Cleve remained behind, chuckling. After his friend had disappeared, the English cavalier fell to inspecting the bottle he had carried from Sarasanac's room.

Cordeau came up.

"M'Lord," he snapped authoritatively, "it is against regulations for a Guardsman to drink in the corridors. And especially from the bottle."

"A good rule," Cleve conceded, and held the bottle higher in the light. "I say, *Capitaine,* you know your Paris. Where would you say I got this bottle?"

Cordeau looked flattered. Some of his stiffness departed. "Allow me, *monsieur,*" he said, taking the bottle. "I must see the seal. Of course," he cast a suspicious eye, "you took this from a reputable house?"

"Quite," Cleve nodded. He was thinking of Sarasanac's hovel.

Cordeau stared at the waxen seal on the neck. "Hotel Rambouillet," he adjudged. *"Pecaire,* I'd know that seal anywhere. An excellent vintage, too. '07."

"You are certain, *Capitaine?"*

"Positive. A moment and I shall sample it."

CLEVE struck like a snake. Fingers curling he ripped the bottle from Cordeau's startled lips. An angry flush crimsoned the captain's cheeks. He half-drew his blade.

"Put it back," Cleve snapped. "This bottle is crammed with poison!"

Cordeau's face grayed, "Poison?" he gasped.

"Exactly." Cleve thrust the bottle into his surprised hands. "Here. Take it and get rid of it. I'm off to discover whether Hotel Rambouillet makes a practice of fatal beverages."

Leaving Cordeau gaping, he went out to the stables and mounted a horse. When he rode up to the large hotel, fifteen minutes later, there was cold calculation in his eyes.

If he had guessed correctly, Vendome would be here and well protected. That meant caution. A hundred feet to one side of the main entrance he slid quietly from the saddle. Stealth would have to be the mode of his attack. In some tower a clock tolled a leisurely twelve.

Hotel Rambouillet was located on the border of a large public square, murky now in the uncertain silver of a cloud-ridden moon. At the main portal, two huge torches lighted the scene.

Keeping deep in the velvet shadows Cleve drew near. There was a huge lackey dozing beside an ornate palanquin at the foot of the stone steps. He was supposed to be guarding the vehicle. A seaman's cutlass was girded to his thick middle.

Cleve swung past the outer fringe of light and came up on the fellow from the shadows. He sent a swift challenging glance about to assure himself that no one was astir. Satisfied, he tapped the lackey on the shoulder with the point of his rapier. The man started; fumbled for his weapon.

"Forget it," Cleve warned him, and emphasized the command with a sword-prick. "I desire some information. On which floor is Vendome staying? You know, because you wear his livery."

The lackey shrugged and said nothing. He had a look of stubbornness on his lips. Cleve laid the point of his blade on the fellow's cheek just below the eye.

"A flick of my wrist and you lose half your vision, friend," he said softly. "Understand that I'm not in the mood to quibble."

The man took one look into the cavalier's eyes and commenced talking. "Monsieur le Duc has the garret suite," he said nervously. "He is not supposed to be in Paris."

Cleve lowered the point. "Thank you," he said, smiling. "The top floor, eh?"

"Oui, monsieur."

The Englishman ripped the curtains from inside the palanquin and quickly trussed the speaker. "You had best be right," he said grimly, lifting the fellow into the cab. "I'll be back."

"No need, *monsieur*. I speak the truth."

Cleve rammed an improvised gag into the lackey's mouth and slapped him cheerfully on the shoulder. "Good. Now don't go away, my friend."

IN THE REAR of the building he noticed how a huge vine climbed, in leafy fastness, all the way to the roof. He nodded and smiled. Simple as a ship's rigging. He hitched his sword around so that it hung tail-like behind him, and commenced to climb.

It wasn't easy. He was perspiring freely by the time he reached the second floor. He hung against the thick leaves outside of a large window and peeped cautiously around its edge. There were two heavily armed guards inside, posted at the foot of a sweeping staircase. Vendome was well guarded, all right.

He started climbing again. He was spent but relieved as he

finally reached the eaves. At one point, a branch had given suddenly, to let him dangle perilously for a startled moment by one hand. It had been bad; but now he hung by his fingers and sized up the situation.

Half a rod to his right a latticed window was open. Carefully he edged toward it, caught his toe on the sill, and eased himself inside. He was standing in a large room that was filled with the dull red glow of a dying fireplace.

"A fool and his luck…" he murmured, and drew his rapier.

On the opposite wall was a huge mahogany bed. In it, bed-cap and all, lay le Duc de Vendome, asleep and snoring gently. The creak of floor-boards outside the door warned Cleve that a guard stood there.

Cleve approached. He tapped Vendome gently on the end of his large nose with his blade. The duke opened his eyes and then his mouth. Cleve laid his sword-point in it before the tongue could get to work.

"Softly, *monsieur*, you may desire to use your voice in the future."

Vendome held his mouth rigid. His dark ryes promised that he'd be silent and Cleve removed the steel, but not its threat. He sat down on the foot of the bed and laid the blade carelessly on Vendome's stomach.

"This is merely a social call, Vendome," he said smoothly. "We are going to converse about our mutual friend, de Montauban."

The Duke of Vendome's eyes glittered. He didn't speak for a long moment; then he said: "You're Cleve, the Cardinal's Madman. I've heard of you."

"Interesting but inconsequential," Cleve said. "Where is de Montauban?"

Vendome's dark features frowned. In the red glowing murk there was a Satanic cast to them, "De Montauban is a guest at le Cardinal's Palace," he said.

"You're a liar!"

Vendome started forward. Cleve forced him back against the pillows with the point of his rapier. Vendome saw the cold devil in his eyes and subsided.

"You shall rue this night, Cleve," he said softly. "I'm a dangerous person to cross."

"So am I, Vendome. Who was the man you had murdered at Richelieu's Palace? He wasn't de Montauban."

Vendome's eyes widened, and then narrowed. "I don't know what you are talking about, *monsieur.*" And beneath the coverlet his hand was inching toward the knife on the table beside the bed.

"You poisoned Sarasanac to keep him from talking," Cleve said. "What were you afraid of, Vendome?"

"I do believe," Vendome replied, "that you know too much." With a sweep of his arm he swung Cleve's blade aside while his hand streaked toward the knife.

THE ENGLISHMAN didn't attempt to use the sword. He used the hilt. As Vendome's fingers curled about the dagger, Cleve struck him savagely. Once. The swarthy duke collapsed.

Cleve pulled him back on the pillow and looked quickly about for a stimulant. He didn't dare leave the bed. There was a lamp on the table so he removed the wick-holder and dashed the oil into the other's face. There was a full half a pint of it.

"Messy, but effective," he muttered as Vendome moaned softly. He lit a candle and waited. Finally the duke opened his eyes and there was black hatred crammed into them.

"You struck me," he muttered. "No man has done that and lived."

"I'm weary of this fol-de-rol." Cleve snapped. "Look, Vendome, you are drenched with oil. Lamp oil. It is very inflammable and I have a lighted candle." His eyes hardened. "Now we are going to talk."

Horror slid into the duke's eyes as he understood the significance. "All right," he said. "I'll talk. They said that you were a madman."

"I am, right now," Cleve assured him grimly. "First, we begin with the dead man in de Montauban's room at the Palace. Who is he?"

"An actor."

"Ah. Now I understand Sarasanac's connection with this. You murdered Sarasanac to prevent any possibility of his talking about the actor, didn't you? The actor was one of Sarasanac's, wasn't he?"

"Yes. Curse you."

"So far so good." Cleve said.

Suddenly he stiffened. The almost imperceptible sound of a move from behind warned him, but too late. He felt cold steel pressed against the back of his neck and a colder voice said: "Make a move, *monsieur*, and you'll fetch six inches of the knife I'm holding."

Triumph washed fear from Vendome's eyes. Cleve sat rigid, his rapier in one hand the lighted candle in the other. His mind was racing. Finally, he laughed, "Go ahead," he challenged. "Kill me and I'll drop the candle."

"*Dieu!*" groaned Vendome. "Be careful, Jacques. I'm besotted with lamp oil."

"So?" said the man behind Cleve. "Very clever." There was a quick gasp and a puff and before Cleve could prevent it, the candle wavered and flickered out. The Englishman stared numbly at the black wick. It was as if his life had gone with the flame.

"Very well." He shrugged. "I'm yours." He dropped the useless candle to the bed and waited.

CHAPTER V

KITTEN HAS TEETH

WITH THE STILETTO held firmly at the nape of his neck Cleve was forced to the far side of the room. His captor carefully deprived him of his rapier and told him to sit down. Vendome got out of bed, wiped himself free of the lamp oil and put on a blue nightrobe.

The English cavalier found his hands being bound behind him; and when the job was finished he saw his captor for the first time. Vendome had stirred up the fire.

The man was a vivid-looking person, tinseled in the height of foppishness with laces and satins of loud color. His face was sallow, scarred with arrogance, and his mouth was thin beneath a clipped blond mustache. He was of medium stature.

But it was his washed-out blue eyes that revealed the man. They were frosty eyes, glistening like ice, pitiless and hard. Cleve knew the fellow. He had seen him many times at the Court. Le Marquis Jacques de Brullier.

"You made one mistake, Cleve," de Brullier said. "You asked my lackey where *monsieur le duc* was staying, and then tied him up instead of killing him."

"I presume your method would have been murder," Cleve said dryly.

"Precisely."

"And then—"

The door burst open and the missing Duke of Montauban stepped across the threshold. He was only partially dressed. He had been preparing for bed. Behind him was the hard-faced knife-man whom Cleve had floored in Sarasanac's room.

De Montauban hesitated when he saw Cleve, a look of uncertainty clouding his handsome features, and scowled.

"What means this, Vendome?"

Staring, Cleve was shocked by the miraculous resemblance between the speaker and the corpse at the Palace. Vendome shrugged. He wore a nasty little smile on his lips.

"A visitor, Henri," he said with a nod toward Cleve. "It appears that this hideaway is known."

De Montauban faced Cleve frowning more deeply. He was a tall man, well proportioned. "How did you find me?" he snapped. "*Corbac!* I covered my tracks when I left this noon."

Cleve shrugged. "But Vendome didn't, *monsieur.* I found the bottle and its tell-tale seal in Sarasanac's room, and—"

Vendome interrupted hurriedly. He stepped between Cleve and de Montauban. "No matter how he discovered us, Henri. The fact remains that he knows now where you are."

Cleve's eyes narrowed. That interruption had been a trifle too hurried.

De Montauban said: "And who is was trying to conceal something. Why? Sarasanac?"

"A flunky of mine," Vendome said quickly. "A dead fool. No need to worry about him any more. But *sangodemi!* We must get you away from here, Henri. If Richelieu finds you—"

De Montauban nodded quickly.

"You are right. 'Tis best that I leave Paris immediately."

Cleve had a shrewd expression on his face. He suddenly concluded that it was time to attempt upsetting Vendome's little scheme, what ever it was. "If you want to know about Sarasanac and Vendome's connec—"

"Quiet, fool!" De Brullier's jeweled fist chopped cruelly into Cleve's lips. He pricked the captive just below the ear with the stiletto.

UNFORTUNATELY, de Montauban had not heard. Cleve subsided. Nevertheless, he had discovered what he'd wanted to know. De Brullier was in accord with Vendome, and de Montauban was ignorant of Sarasanac and of his dead double. He wondered exactly what sort of a game Vendome was playing.

"De Brullier's château is three leagues from Paris," Vendome was saying. "'Tis the best place to hide, Henri."

De Montauban nodded. "Very well." He started toward the door; then, hesitated as if recalling something.

"Incidentally, Vendome," he said, "tomorrow is the right time to face Richelieu with my disappearance. Do not make a flat accusation at first. Allow suspicion to grow. When the King becomes curious, accuse the Cardinal of my murder, or kidnaping. That ought to make the nobles rise and demand his death."

Vendome nodded. There was a peculiar little smirk in his eyes. "Richelieu's execution shall take place three weeks from tonight, Henri; that I promise. The nobles will be outraged if the King allows Richelieu to go free."

"I have planned it that way," De Montauban nodded. "And mark this: after Richelieu's execution, wait a week before you discover me chained in the dungeon of his château near Nantes." He laughed. "You'll probably get a reward for rescuing me."

"Undoubtedly. You have planned this well, Henri. But for the present, take de Brullier and ten of my guards and ride to his château. I'll pay a secret visit to you tomorrow night."

De Montauban stared at Cleve. "Now you know my plans," he said. "But worry not, *monsieur*. We don't want your blood; only your silence. You simply remain our prisoner until the coup is over. No harm shall come to you."

"I wish I were as sure of that, *monsieur*," Cleve said.

After de Montauban and de Brullier had gone, he stared into the dark Satanic face of Vendome, and shrugged. "Will you murder me here, or some place else?" he asked.

Vendome smiled, walked to a decanter of wine, and poured himself a drink. The knife-man, who had entered behind de Montauban, cursed fluidly. His lips were still lacerated.

"*Sacré nom*," he exclaimed. "I'm willing to make it now. I haven't forgotten our last meeting, you lousy pig."

Vendome laughed. "Tut tut, Murat. Put away your blade. I

have a few questions to ask this fool before I have you take care of him."

Cleve forced his lips into a grim smile. "What's your game, Vendome? De Montauban doesn't know about Sarasanac. He doesn't know about his dead double."

Vendome nodded. "True," he said, and sipped his wine thoughtfully. "You have remarkable perceptive powers, Cleve. Too bad you weren't perceptive enough to avoid me. I have not forgotten the blow you struck me, nor—" he inclined his head toward his hard-faced henchman—"has Murat."

CLEVE shrugged. He had to keep talking to force nerve back into his heart. It was hard just to sit there knowing that each moment might be his last. "Put your cards down, *monsieur,*" he said. "What have you to lose?"

Vendome laughed. "You are ever right, fool," he said, and commenced changing his clothes. "I have nothing to lose. In this whole affair I have nothing to lose. It is de Montauban's plan, but I am improving on it."

The flint-eyed Murat ran fingers over his bruised lips and drew his blade. "Allow me to finish him, *monsieur le duc.*"

"Silence!" The swarthy duke shrugged into his doublet and picked up his boots. "It was de Montauban's thought to disappear while under Richelieu's roof. It is mine to make him disappear for good."

"Then why go to the bother of having this Murat pig murder the double?" Cleve asked. "Frankly, it seems to be complicating the issue unnecessarily."

"It does," Vendome admitted. He was almost dressed. "But not when you consider that killing de Montauban at the Palace would be a needless waste of money.

"You see, *monsieur,* my worthy friend de Brullier is le Duc de Montauban's half-brother. Unfortunately, this relationship is not enough for de Brullier to inherit the fabulous de Montauban estates should the duke die. There are a full brother and a sister to be considered.

"Consequently, de Brullier and I have decided to mix profit with—er—treason, as you would call it."

He smiled cruelly. "De Montauban does not suspect it, but even now he is en route to his death. Of course, de Brullier will see that he signs over his estate before anything happens."

And there it was. The whole black tapestry. Never in his life had Cleve heard of a more filthy plot. There was a snakelike, unwholesome, quality to both its author and his compatriot, de Brullier.

"Well"—he sighed—"betraying a betrayal is just about your style, Vendome. I can't say that I'm surprised. Already you have killed Sarasanac and that poor fool of an actor."

"A master stroke of luck the day I noted that actor's resemblance to de Montauban." Vendome chuckled. "In death, he will be mistaken for the real duke, and Richelieu will lose his head as neatly as a wine bottle. *Sangodemi, monsieur.* I do believe I am an exceptional fellow indeed. The manner in which I cover my tracks is perfect. Sarasanac will never tell anyone that he sold me the actor."

Suddenly he frowned. "Incidentally, Cleve, how did you know that the actor was not de Montauban?"

"Simple. His rings wouldn't fit. He wore a false mole."

"*Sangodemi!* If you have wrecked my plans—"

Vendome checked himself. "What of it? So Richelieu claims that the actor is not de Montauban! Will anyone believe him? No. Not after he is unable to produce the true duke. You see, *monsieur,* I am very clever."

"And very sickening," the English rakehelly snapped. "Reptilian!"

Murat drove his fist into the captive's mouth. Cleve licked blood from his lips and laughed. "Brave man, Murat. Kill a sleeping man; strike a bound prisoner. Damme, what courage!"

Murat's thin lips writhed blasphemy. The hilt of his blade described a vicious arc. A searing pain ripped through Cleve's head; then he drifted into oblivion.

WHEN he recovered, Murat was sitting opposite him. The killer's stony features were expressionless but his eyes schemed horror. The light from the fireplace coated the side of his face in orange. He was alone.

Cleve's head had a dull throbbing ache in it; a trickle of blood had streamed over his cheek from temple to jaw. Before only his hands had been bound; now he was lashed securely to the chair. He must have remained insensible for nearly ten minutes. Vendome was gone.

"Awake, eh?" Murat said dully. "Good. Thought I might have killed you."

"Vendome?" Cleve murmured.

"Gone to safer lodgings." Murat licked his lips and smiled coldly. "He left you for me. Understand?"

"I understand," Cleve nodded. "What are you going to do?"

"Pay you back for what you did to me," Murat said. His voice had a peculiar flat quality that was chilling. There was no emotion in it. No humanity. "I wonder how loud you're going to squeal before I finish you." He raised his sword and laid its length across the fire.

"Damme," Cleve shrugged. "You'll ruin your sword."

"I can get another," said Murat. "You're a pretty cool customer. Perchance this'll warm you up."

He dropped the red hot blade carelessly on Cleve's thigh. His flinty eyes stared into Englishman's as the cloth burned away and the steel sizzled into bare flesh. Cleve forced himself to smile although the sweat was breaking out across his forehead.

He said: "Your courage grows amazing, Murat."

Fury came into Murat's eyes.

"Shut your mouth!"

The killer poked the rapier back into the coals. "We'll try your left eye next," he said.

Cleve thought: So this is it. Faith, what a rotten way to die....

His torturer raised the glowing sword-tip and his stomach lumped in protest. He wondered whether he'd scream.

Murat wore a thin smile on his lips. "Don't care for it, eh?" he asked.

He came forward slowly, still smiling, his eyes on Cleve's face.

Suddenly the door burst open. The killer whirled in surprise. He had been expecting no one.

There, striding into the room with steel leveled, was d'Entreville. His dark eyes sparked anger as he comprehended the scene: the bound Englishman, the burnt thigh, the glowing sword.

Cleve fought hard to keep the glorious relief out of his voice. "Welcome to the party, Kitten," he greeted.

D'Entreville didn't answer. His eyes were riveted on Murat's pasty face. He kicked the door closed with the heel of his foot, and started to walk across the room.

He walked on the balls of his feet, catlike, poised and ready. The glittering blade in his hand flicked, side to side, in short limbering gestures. Murat retreated. D'Entreville followed.

It was the killer who started it. He reached behind him on the table, picked up a bottle and hurled it. D'Entreville combined a leap with a ducking motion as the bottle arced over his shoulder. He sent his blade flashing for Murat's throat.

The killer parried and sidled out of the corner. D'Entreville followed, peppering his opponent with short vicious lunges and cuts.

Murat fought back with the fury of awful fear. D'Entreville gave before the attack. Suddenly he seemed to trip over a fallen chair. He went to one knee, and Cleve grinned. The Englishman knew what was coming. He had seen d'Entreville use that Italian trick before.

Murat, delirious with triumph, charged in recklessly. It was a mistake. D'Entreville's point ripped upward, beneath Murat's guard. He caught the killer just below the heart and his blade came through the back.

"And that, *mon ami,*" he said, deftly extracting the steel as Murat crumpled, "is that!"

FROM his chair Cleve chuckled. He forgot the searing pain of the burn on his thigh and the dull throbbing in his head. "Faith, Kitten," he said. "A putrid exhibition if ever I saw one. It took you almost two minutes."

"I presume," d'Entreville retorted, "that you could have done better."

"By my faith! Of course!"

The Frenchman cleaned his blade on Murat's cape and smiled. "Then why didn't you?" he inquired easily.

Cleve grinned sheepishly. He shrugged, burst into a whole-hearted laugh. "Well, Guy, you have me there. How did you locate this place, anyway?"

D'Entreville bent down and began to sever the ropes. "Cordeau," he said briefly. "*Parbleu,* why didn't you bring my attention to the seal on the bottle?"

Cleve arose, massaging his wrists. "I wasn't certain about it, Kitten. And damme, I'm not fond of being laughed at when wrong. Apparently you had no trouble in reaching this suite."

"None. I saw the light and came up. The halls were deserted."

"Hmmm. That means that Vendome has flown with every-one."

"Then you found him?"

"How do you suppose I got tied up in that chair? Of course I found him. And I found de Montauban, too."

D'Entreville's hand gripped the speaker. "You saw de Mon-tauban?"

"Yes." Cleve put on his hat and picked up his sword. "Kitten," he said, "this affair is truly amazing. If we are going to pull it out of the fire, then we're going to have to ride hell-for-leather to the château owned by de Brullier. Do you know where it is?"

"*Oui*. But I don't understand!"

"You don't have to," Cleve said, starting for the door. "Come along, Kitten."

D'Entreville looked as if he had just discovered half a worm in an apple he'd been eating. "Kitten!" he snorted. "*Corbac et sangodemi!* I should have let that fellow finish you."

CHAPTER VI

SWORDS FOR SEVEN

THE ROAD WAS a ribbon of moonlight as they pounded out of Paris. It stretched in silver ripples over the deep purple countryside, plunging through copses of wood, around farmlands, over gentle hills.

They rode close together as Cleve explained the situation above the beat of hoofs. As they topped the crest of a hill overlooking de Brullier's castle, d'Entreville reined up.

"*Pecaire!*" he exclaimed. "If what you have told me is true, we should have brought a troop."

"And waste precious time, eh?" Cleve asked. "Faith, Kitten, even now they may be killing de Montauban. It would have taken an hour to rout a company out of bed, saddle horses, and give orders. This is the only way. Besides, a troop thundering through the night would have raised the alarm."

D'Entreville cuffed back his wide hat. "I still think a troop would be the best solution. *Corbac!* Who ever heard of two men storming a castle?"

Cleve chuckled. "The idea exactly, my friend. No one! The lookout sees but two horsemen, and he is not suspicious. A whole troop and they lift the draw-bridge."

D'Entreville sighed. "Pity me, 'tis an awful fate to be saddled with a madman." And then he smiled and extended a gloved hand. "But I'm a trifle mad myself. Lead on, Richard."

They thundered down the hill. Ahead, Château de Brullier sat on the outskirts of a seven-house hamlet, looking like a battle-scarred Amazon grown old. Moonlight gleamed against the slate of her towertops; and running limply into the stagnation of her medieval moat was a trickling country stream.

The château was not large in comparison with many others, but her history was just as vivid. Here, the English Black Prince had made a headquarters. The Tenth Louis had been a constant visitor and the rebellious Duke of Burgundy had used it as a seat of war during the siege of Paris.

The gray stones were but an empty chalice now. None of the de Brulliers had bothered to keep it in repair. The castle looked decrepit and ominous. In the ghostly light of the moon death seemed to lurk in the very shadow of her mossy walls. She was a fit place for intrigue.

Riding through the hamlet, d'Entreville noticed suddenly that the draw-bridge was up. The castle seemed barred as if fearing invasion. He cursed and arrested his steed.

"Well, Cleve," he snapped, "admitting that you know all the answers, perhaps you'll tell me how we're going to get inside that stone heap?"

The Englishman cursed. "They've pulled the draw-bridge, haven't they. Well, I might have foreseen this. Naturally, de Brullier would guard against interruption."

"That doesn't answer my question," d'Entreville pointed out quietly.

Cleve bit his lip. He was still trying to find the answer when the door of a nearby house opened and a bent figure in a battered black hat stepped into the street bearing a basket. The figure saw the two horsemen and stopped.

"Eh? *Messieurs?* From the château, eh?"

"No curse it—" D'Entreville started in to say.

Cleve kicked him. "Yes, father, we're from *monsieur le marquis*," he said in a loud voice.

"Bien, monsieur. It will save me the trip." The old villager waddled over to Cleve's stirrup. He handed up the basket.

"Here's the food that *monsieur le marquis* ordered. I was just on my way. Tell him that old Jean is sorry, *monsieur,* but on such short notice he could not be quicker. Not surprised though that he's out of food. Never visits the *château* any more. Well, *bon nuit, messieurs.*"

"Good evening, father." Cleve nodded, and broke into a chuckle after the elder had disappeared. He held the basket high.

"Our key, Kitten," he said.

THEY TIED their horses in a copse of wood several yards from the moat. D'Entreville ripped the plume from his hat.

"The things I do for France," he said, eyeing it regretfully. "This cost me two hard-earned livres."

"What's the thought?" asked Cleve.

D'Entreville snorted. *"Corbac,* I'm no fool. Cleve. I know what you plan, and I've decided that I'm the best wager to put it through. Your French has too much the English accent to pass safely as old Jean from the village."

"All right," Cleve nodded. "But, I'm going with you. I can be old Jean's son. You just do the talking."

"You'll have to carry something."

"I'll carry my hat—basket-like. In the moonlight they won't know the difference. Keep your sword under cover."

D'Entreville nodded. He slouched his hat awkwardly around his head, bent down and picked up the basket. His shuffling walk gave the impression of senility.

"I hope you're correct when you say that there are only ten men there," he muttered over his shoulder.

"So am I," Cleve chuckled.

When they were on the lip of the moat across from the

draw-bridge, a lamp suddenly winked from atop the portcullis, and a harsh voice rang through the gloom.

"Who goes?"

"The food, *monsieur*," d'Entreville replied in a thin treble. "It's I, old Jean from the village. Lower the gate."

"Nice act, grandpaw," muttered Cleve.

"Close your fool mouth," the Frenchman snapped back softly.

"Against orders of *le marquis* to lower the draw," the guard on the wall said.

"Cautious rascals, aren't they," Cleve murmured. "Ask them, what you are to do with the basket. Damme, it can't fly over the wall."

A rope heaved from the top of the gate was the answer to that question. "Tie the rope to your basket," was the command.

"Why the dirty—" D'Entreville lost his temper. He stopped being old Jean from the village. He grabbed the rope with both hands and started to pull. The guard on the other end let go a startled yell; a guard beside him caught him as he started down over the edge.

The business became a tug of war. Silent, angry and determined—except for Cleve. The situation struck his sense of humor and he could hardly help d'Entreville for laughter.

"Pull, you idiot, pull," the French rakehelly exploded as his heels began furrowing toward the water. "The cursed swine are trying to drown me in the moat."

AND THEN, when Cleve lent his weight to the end of the rope, the episode ceased as suddenly as it had started. One of the men atop the wall took out his sword and severed connections. The first inkling the two cavaliers had of this strategy was when they went sprawling to the ground meshed in hemp. The wall guards hooted.

"Let that be a lesson to you country wags," they called. "We know how to handle your tricks."

Cleve wiped dust from his eyes and said: "Faith, they think we were playing."

"I'd like to play," d'Entreville snorted. "Play a tattoo on their skulls with a cane." He stood up and threw the rope from him as if it were a snake.

"No," Cleve said, picking it up again. "I think we had better keep this. I have a plan." He eyed old Jean's basket of food. "And we'd better keep that, too. I feel that we need—er—food for thought."

They retreated to the copse of wood where their horses were tethered. Cleve squatted on his heels and explained his idea. They waited half an hour and then took off their doublets, capes, and hats. The night was chill. It bit through the light linen of their shirts and raised goose-flesh on their bodies.

"*Corbac,*" d'Entreville chattered, "let's be on our way before I freeze to death."

"You'll be warm enough in a few minutes," Cleve said with a smile. He found a stout sapling and hacked it free with the edge of his blade. He trimmed it down to a section about four feet long by an inch and three quarters wide. He knotted the rope firmly about its center, and nodded to his companion.

"Ready, Guy. Let's go."

They passed stealthily around to the rear of the castle. The moon was beginning to wane. Frogs croaked in the moat; fell silent as they approached. The castle wall rose like an ominous wave over them. It stood about twenty feet high.

"I can swim if need be," Cleve whispered. "I'll go first. Follow close behind."

He stepped silently down into the water. It was painfully cold. His teeth began to chatter but he kept on. He moved forward slowly with the water rising gradually to his thighs, his waist, and finally his throat.

He kept the rope and its length of sapling firmly in his grasp. The water rose no higher and a feeling of gratitude swept through him. D'Entreville couldn't swim.

There was a mossy shelf of land at the base of the wall. The two cavaliers reached it and stood shivering as the frogs, once again secure, recommenced their music.

"Faith, this isn't going to be the easiest thing in the world," Cleve muttered, staring up at the black heights. "But we'll try. Keep the rope coiled loosely while I heave this bar of wood. And for the love of peace, catch it before it splashes into the moat, should my cast fail."

"That's about all we need," d'Entreville grunted. "A splash in the moat and half the walls guards on our necks. Proceed, *mon ami.* Let fly."

It was tedious business. Cleve cast the stick five times before it finally lodged between the stone teeth of the ancient battlements. He tested it once and relaxed panting.

"All right, Kitten," he finally said. "You're the better monkey. You go first."

"Very uncomical," the Frenchman snorted.

He slung his sword belt around and grasped the rope. By bracing his boots against the rough stone he was able to walk swiftly and silently up the side of the grim wall. His whispered: "All's well," floated down through the night. Cleve followed quickly.

THEY stood together on the wall-walk.

Cleve pulled up the rope and coiled it loosely in a dark corner. D'Entreville drew his blade.

"I wonder how many are on the wall?" he queried.

Cleve shrugged. They were at the northern corner of the wall and a huge battle turret at their backs concealed the rest of the castle. "I shall find out for you, Kitten," he said. In a raucous voice he yelled: "Heyo, to the north tower every one on the wall. À moi. In a hurry. The north—"

"*Corbac!* What the devil are you trying to do?" exploded d'Entreville. "*Mon dieu,* of all the sop-brained dolts you are the—"

Cleve said: "Not now, Kitten. Save the compliments 'til later. Take the corner over there and kick the first guard that blunders around it into the moat."

Footsteps pounded on the stone of the wall-walk. Cleve received the first visitor. Before the fellow had opportunity to yell out, he was grasped firmly by the seat of the breeches and the nape of the neck, and tossed bawling terror over the side.

Cleve grinned. D'Entreville had his hands full. Two men swept past before he had a chance to set himself. They went immediately to the parapet and stared down at their comrade howling curses in the water below. The French rakehelly threw a flying block into them and they disappeared.

"Three." Cleve laughed.

Suddenly he frowned. A man's head appeared cautiously around the corner on his side and started to draw back.

"Oh, no you don't!"

The Englishman's fingers snagged the fellow's hair. He led the captive howling to the brink and booted him over.

"Four," he shrugged. "Faith, he almost got away."

The quartet below threshed indignantly in the muddy water, bawling out curses and threats in the night. The two rakehellies paid not the slightest heed, but waited. A few moments passed before they welcomed their fifth and final customer.

Cleve held a sword to his throat. "Where is de Brullier?" he snapped.

The guard squirmed under d'Entreville's grasp. "In the dungeon," he said. *"Sandiou!* What is the meaning of—"

"How many are with him?"

"Five, and le Duc de Montauban."

"Let him go, Kitten," said Cleve.

"Merci, monsieur," the captive began to say.

"Don't mention it," d'Entreville replied and swung him lightly over the parapet. "Good evening!"

The man's curses suddenly died in a fountain of spray. Cleve eyed his companion. "Damme, Kitten. I'll wager it is the first bath they've had in weeks."

"The dungeon," d'Entreville mumbled. "*Parbleu,* Cleve, that means that they've got de Montauban under torture already. Come on, we must hurry."

FINDING the torture chamber in a medieval château is comparatively easy. It is usually beneath the keep, or owner's residence, at the strongest section of the wall.

Fortunately, the depth of the place had prevented de Brullier and his men from hearing the ruckus on the wall. Cleve and d'Entreville were able to proceed without molestation. With swords shining in the light of the scattered torches, they stalked cautiously across the inner bailey, past the dozen horses in the stable, and into the main building.

"That door." Cleve pointed as they stood in the center of a ill-kept foyer. "I think that's the staircase down to the dungeon."

"You're right."

The door opened upon a length of stairs leading down into the bowels of the château. At the bottom a glow of light was shining dully.

Softly the two cavaliers started down. D'Entreville went first, his long blade held loosely in his grasp. At the bottom was a low-ceilinged corridor, plugged at one end by a thick, iron-studded door. They approached it softly and stood listening.

A murmur of voices seeped through the wood; then a sharp though muffled cry of pain. And a brittle mocking laugh.

Cleve looked at d'Entreville. "Well, Kitten. This is the end of the trail." He tested the door lightly and it gave an inch beneath his hand. "We can get in. What are your plans?"

"There are five," Guy said, grimly stepping back. "Let's burst in and kick Hades out of them."

The Englishman nodded, placed his shoulder to the door and crashed it open. Strong light bathed them from the chamber.

Strapped to a chair in the center with his fingers in a hell machine known as the screw, was le Duc de Montauban. His face was gray, and on the table before him were a pen and a roll of manuscript paper. The surrounding figures froze in staring astonishment.

"Cleve and the Kitten!" de Brullier suddenly yelled.

His cold features contorted and he ripped his jeweled sword from its sheath. Behind Cleve, d'Entreville cursed.

"Kitten!" he muttered. "He can't call me that and live."

"He won't," Cleve promised softly. "He's mine. Take care of the rest."

"Four to one," growled d'Entreville. "What do you think I am? Split them between us and maybe we'll be lucky."

"I warn you not to pass that door," de Brullier snarled.

Cleve took a cautious step forward. The slithering sound of blades being drawn rewarded the move. The room was tight with tension. The four men with de Brullier had heard of Cleve and the Kitten and they hadn't in the least liked what they heard.

The two rakehellies carried shining steel death in their hands. Cleve took another step. His blade was slanted carelessly across his boots, but that meant nothing. It could flash into action in a split second.

"No further!" de Brullier said harshly. His cold eyes were glittering with a mixture of fear and hatred. By rights, Cleve should be dead. "We outnumber you two to one."

Cleve cocked an eyebrow. "Really!" He took another step.

D'Entreville was close behind him, crouched a little and alert.

"All right, men. Take them!" the marquis yelled.

THE TENSION snapped as cut by shears. A burly individual hurtled wildly at the Englishman. Cleve sidestepped neatly and pinked him on the arm.

D'Entreville came up from behind. An ambitious opponent

tried to circle. The Frenchman lunged accurately and the fellow tried to scream through a punctured throat. It wasn't a pretty sound.

Something licked burningly into Cleve's left shoulder. He stared through the flashing sheen into de Brullier's eager eyes. He feinted at a cautious heckler and swept toward the marquis. A man got in his path and he ran him through the stomach. The odds were more even, now. Three to two.

A chair flew out of nowhere and caught d'Entreville across the chest. He fell dizzily. The man whom he had been engaging laughed and lunged viciously.

The Frenchman rolled quickly but not quickly enough. The burning pain of a leg-wound told him that.

He struggled gamely to one knee. His enemy rushed him. D'Entreville parried weakly, but sufficiently. He was still on one knee and groggy.

Suddenly his free hand found a heavy iron mallet on the floor. As his enemy attacked again, he threw it into the man's face and broke his jaw.

De Brullier was a swordsman. Cleve kept trying to engage him, but the man was a dancing wraith, and his accomplice kept interfering. It was a stalemate until d'Entreville appeared on the scene. He drew aside the Englishman's heckler and left the marquis alone.

Cleve smiled grimly. His shoulder was throbbing dully now, and its fire seemed to give fury to his attack. For the first time, real fear glimmered in de Brullier's eyes.

"You're finished, de Brullier. Done!" Cleve said.

"Not yet!"

The marquis had been backed almost against the glowing hearth where torture instruments were heated. His free hand swept behind and came into contact with the handle of a small coal shovel. It was heaped with red, glowing ashes. He laughed and threw the flaming embers. Cleve shied away. De Brullier charged in furiously.

He was shouting:

"Now you're finished, Cleve. Finished. Finished!"

He emphasized each cry with a murderous lunge. The Englishman retreated. His shoulders and fore-arms were pitted with searing agony where the coals had struck. One of de Brullier's thrusts nipped a cut in his temple.

Suddenly, a red fury wrapped his brain in flame. He stopped moving away. With a curse, he swept aside de Brullier's blade. His blade cut hungrily into the marquis' neck; flashed away as the man started to crumple and pierced his heart before he hit the floor.

"Mon dieu!" d'Entreville exclaimed. "A slash and a thrust, almost simultaneously. How did you do it, Cleve?"

THE ENGLISHMAN looked up. He was tired suddenly. He wanted to sit down. The torture chamber was strewn with bodies. He smiled wearily. "Damme, Kitten," he said. "I don't know. I'm just good, that's—"

D'Entreville caught him as he suddenly buckled. "You've lost too much blood," he said. *"Sangodemi,* look at your shirt."

He helped, half-carried, the Englishman to a nearby bench and sat him down. From the center of the room, de Montauban stared and sighed. He had remained unscathed through the battle.

"Mordi, messieurs," he said. "I do not mind waiting, but the pain of this cursed screw on my hands is almost unbearable. Won't one of you please take it off?"

"I'm all right, Kitten," Cleve nodded, ripped his shirt off at the shoulder and stared down at the wound. It had stopped bleeding.

D'Entreville walked over and released de Montauban's fingers from the torture machine. They were ugly-looking, badly mashed and broken. The French rakehelly gave the man a look of grudging admiration. De Montauban had kept his nerve when de Brullier was applying the screw.

"I've been a fool," de Montauban said as the ropes fell from him, "a hot-headed, blind fool. It never occurred to me that Vendome would betray me. Nor had I suspicions of my half-brother de Brullier."

His handsome young face was drawn with pain and exhaustion.

"Why not?" d'Entreville snapped. "When you dabble in treachery you're bound to get a little on yourself."

De Montauban scowled. He held his mangled hand and said: "I don't consider that I was dabbling in treachery. What I planned was for France…. But you, being a Cardinalist, would not understand that."

"Mark this," d'Entreville retorted. "I hold no brief for Richelieu, although I have sworn to serve him. My distaste for you springs from the fact that you threatened France with the horror of a great civil war.

"Not only that; your methods of deposing the Cardinal were despicable. You appeared to be friendly; then attempted to knife him in the back. Fine means for a supposed honorable man! Besides, if you think that Cleve and I have enjoyed romping all over the country to save your hide, then—"

From the bench Cleve laughed. "Have pity on him, Kitten. Forget it. I've found a bottle. It has been kept down here to revive the victims, but from the label it should be excellent."

And it was.

CHAPTER VII

THE KITTEN PURRS

THE NEXT MORNING, the luxurious coach of le Duc de Vendome swung up before the gates of Le Palais de Richelieu. Resplendent in a costume of royal blue, its swarthy owner stepped out and eyed his surroundings pleasantly.

An overdose of self-esteem was causing his manner to be a

trifle more overbearing than usual and his eyes to glitter excitedly. Today was the beginning of the end—for Richelieu. And,
he, Vendome, had brought it all about where countless others
had failed. Richelieu was through! Finished!

He chuckled inwardly and addressed the *capitaine* of the
Guard.

"Tell your master that le Duc de Vendome has come from
the King with an important message for Monsieur le Duc de
Montauban!"

Of course it was a lie. But it would guarantee an audience
with the Cardinal, and after that it didn't matter. De Montauban wasn't alive to receive any sort of message, real or fancied.

He wondered vaguely how de Brullier had disposed of the
body. Weighted and thrown into the moat, undoubtedly. That
had been the original plan. Mentally he rubbed his hands together. In three weeks he would be the most famous man in
France, besides having half of the wealthy de Montauban estates
to boot.

The *capitaine* of the Guard ushered him into the grand foyer.
Vendome chuckled. "Make haste, fellow!"

The *capitaine* of the Guard scowled. "*Oui, monsieur,*" he said,
and disappeared into the library.

Vendome broke into a soft whistle and began pacing leisurely about the room. He was in excellent spirits. He wondered
what sort of subterfuge Richelieu would attempt in order to
keep him from seeing the dead duke. But no matter, he would
grow insistent.

"Waiting for somebody, Vendome?"

The voice came from the other side of the foyer. It had an
unpleasantly familiar ring to it. Vendome whirled, and a gasp
choked his speech. Finally he was able to exclaim: "*Parbleu!*
Lord Cleve!"

Cleve nodded. He wore his left arm in a sling. His lips were
smiling carelessly. "That's right," he said. "Good morning, *monsieur,* I trust you slept well."

Vendome had a sickishness in the pit of his stomach. Murat had failed. Then what could it mean? How much damage had this cursed Englishman done? He summoned all the poise at his command and shrugged. "I slept well, *monsieur*. And you?"

"Well, *monsieur*." Cleve nodded. "Incidentally, *monsieur le Cardinal* is waiting."

VENDOME glanced over his shoulder. The door to the library was open with the *capitaine* of the Guard waiting expectantly to one side.

Vendome's mind was a whirl of conjecture. He didn't know what Cleve's appearance indicated; but wishful thinking caught him in its grasp and he smiled.

So Cleve had escaped death. What of it? De Montauban was dead, and the body of his double still remained upstairs. Behind the thick walls of his castle, surely de Brullier could not have failed. Richelieu was still in the trap.

"Yes," Vendome bowed. "I must not keep His Eminence waiting."

"It *would* be bad form," Cleve agreed.

Vendome strode briskly into the library. The Cardinal regarded him enigmatically.

"You claim to have a message from the King for de Montauban?" he asked.

Vendome smirked. "Precisely, Your Eminence. It is personal, and I have been commanded to deliver it to the duke only."

"Er—do you insist upon it, *monsieur?*"

Ah. That showed how the land lay. Vendome felt the triumph swelling again inside of him. Richelieu could not produce de Montauban. Everything was all right.

"Mais oui, Monseigneur!"

The Cardinal allowed a ghost of a smile to twist his lips and tapped lightly upon a small silver bell. The doors on the far side of the room slid back. The young Duc le Montauban strode quietly into the room. One hand was bandaged, and in the other he carried a large square of manuscript.

He glanced at Vendome, but his face remained composed, and his voice was casual when he said:

"Ah. Good morning, Vendome." Then is eyes shifted to Richelieu. "I have just signed your treaty, *Monseigneur.* Here it is."

He placed the manuscript on the desk. Richelieu picked it up, scanned it, and smiled. Slowly, he was consolidating the Kingdom. Then he looked at Vendome.

"You have a message for le Duc de Montauban, *monsieur?*"

Vendome felt something shrivel up inside him. He opened his mouth but no words came forth. He stared at de Montauban as if seeing a ghost.

"Monsieur le Duc seems to have lost his tongue," de Montauban observed.

His manner was still pleasant, but his eyes were hard.

Richelieu smiled. There was no humor in it. "And his message," he added softly. "Well, *monsieur?*"

Vendome had but one idea—to get away from the library as soon as possible. His dream castles were crashing almost audibly about his ears. A great terror was icing trough his veins.

"Er—I must have misplaced it," he muttered. "Excuse me, *Monseigneur.* I feel ill…."

"Bad health," Richelieu nodded. "I know the cause of it, Vendome. I would suggest a visit to another country. Say Spain or Italy…." His eyes glinted suggestively. "For your health, of course."

"Yes, er, yes." Vendome nodded and bolted.

In the corridor he met Guy d'Entreville. The young Frenchman looked solicitous. "You look ill, *monsieur,*" he said. Then he extracted a fold of white paper from his sash and placed it in Vendome's numb fingers.

"Whenever you feel the cause of your present malady sneaking up again, *monsieur,* I suggest that you read the enclosed. Good morning, *monsieur.*"

He stood watching Vendome's hurried and stumbling progress down the hall; and on d'Entreville's face there was a look of deep satisfaction. He only wished that he could see Vendome read that message.

And, safe in the rocking confines of his coach, Vendome stared at the piece of paper he had been given, and wondered. Finally, he ripped it open. It read:

> *His mind was full of crafty thoughts,*
> *Of villainy and treason-plots.*
> *And all he did succeed in brewing*
> *Was Richelieu's gain, and his undoing.*
> *Next time he plots, perhaps he'll know,*
> *'Tis best to choose a smaller foe.*
> *Signed:*
> *Guy d'Entreville (poet)*

IV

THE SCARLET BLADE

*If Richelieu saves France from war, it will
cost him his own peace of mind; for Cleve and
d'Entreville, rakehellies of the Cardinal's Guard,
are in the saddle again. And many a Spaniard
will fall before their swords are sheathed.*

CHAPTER I

THE KING IS VEXED

AS THE PARIS clock tolled three, neither Richelieu nor Don Diego realized that their struggle had begun. Richelieu, sitting opposite the King in the Louvre, stared at the unsigned treaty between them; while a mile away, Don Diego de Isla paced before his followers and pondered ways to get it.

Of the two, Don Diego was the more perturbed. He knew of the treaty's existence, but that was all. Its content and character remained a mystery: a tantalizing mystery which threatened his temper. And Don Diego's temper had never been particularly noted for its elasticity.

As his hulking figure stomped heavily back and forth, Pizon, Castro and DuBrille cautiously held their tongues. The velvet stillness of the large room was broken by the ponderous cadence of the Don's tread and faint noises from the Rue St. Denis outside.

But finally, the Spanish ambassador turned. He fixed Du-Brille with hard eyes; eyes angry in the conviction that Richelieu's secret treaty was beyond reach, and erupted:

"*Por Dios!* Of what use is your information, *señor?* Can Spain act against France without proof? *Diablo!* Of course not! I *must* have proof!"

Jacques DuBrille shrugged. Contrasted to the speaker he appeared almost childlike. But there was nothing childlike about the expression of his face—a cunning, weasel-shaped face, with flinty eyes and twisted lips.

He countered smoothly: "I understand that, *monsieur,* and I have come to make an offer. Procuring documents is a hobby of mine. How much is it worth for me to steal a copy of this treaty?"

Don Diego stared. And then his rich voice boomed in a short, but completely unamused laugh. He knew DuBrille for a petty court leech—a cheap informer; and stealing from so brilliant a man as Cardinal Richelieu was beyond his capability.

"You pick a rotten time to jest, DuBrille," he said.

The informer flushed. He had ferreted his information about the treaty from Will Beck, personal valet to the English ambassador; and having spent an evening, as well as many livres, in getting the English lackey drunk and talkative, he meant to profit by the investment.

"I'm not jesting, *monsieur.*"

Don Diego sat down. The afternoon sun cascaded through the latticed window beside him and bathed his blubbery face in warm yellow. He regarded DuBrille pityingly; and then said with exaggerated patience: "Have you ever heard of Cleve and d'Entreville, *señor?*"

DuBrille nodded: *"Oui.* They serve in Richelieu's Guard."

The Spaniard aimed at Cleve. "One movement,
señor, and I blow a hole through you." D'Entreville
crouched in darkness against the wall.

"And you persist in your presumption to steal this rumored treaty?"

"But of course."

DIEGO sighed. "Then you are a fool! Before you take the treaty, you must first take those two fire-brands. And that is a task which even experts shun."

He leaned forward. "Mark this! Cleve and d'Entreville have thwarted every attempt my men have ever made to crack Richelieu's secret archives. They laugh at bribery. They have duped cleverer men than you; and as long as they are in the Cardinal's Guard, his secrets are safe."

DuBrille shrugged. "I know that, *monsieur,*" he said calmly. "Consequently, I have made plans to take care of them before I even start."

Don Diego laughed. "*Si.* I have tried that too. Only last month I set Pizon and Castro here out after them with muskets."

The smile on his lips died as he beckoned the shorter of his two aides forward. "Pedro, tell what happened."

Pedro Pizon, his swarthy cheeks flaming with humiliation, appeared beside the desk. "We missed," he said in a choked voice.

But Diego was not the type to ride easily on men who had betrayed him with failure. "Tell all of it, you bungler!"

Pizon licked his lips and spat the rest out as if loathing the taste of the words. "Well, after our musket-balls went wide, Cleve and d'Entreville seized us; laughingly spanked us with their swords; and then made us eat our musket powder, complete with ball."

Diego turned to the Frenchman, silken irony in his tone: "Juan and Pedro were quite ill."

But DuBrille was not impressed. Nor was he sympathetic. "A poor plan," he said. "They are fortunate to live. Now in my place I allow no possibility of mischance."

This crass display of confidence had its effect. Diego relaxed, fingering the gold medallion on his chest thoughtfully. After all, Spain had sent him to France strictly in the form of an *agent provocateur*—a creator of incidents. If DuBrille could conceivably offer a plan to dispose of Cleve and d'Entreville, he was willing to listen.

"All right, DuBrille. Get on with it."

The little adventurer produced a leather pouch from the folds of his sash. "This will eliminate failure," he said displaying it. "Tobacco, *monsieur*, ground to a very fine dust. Should it accidentally get into one's eye a painful and momentary blindness will ensue."

He replaced the pouch and gave his wisped mustache a confident tweak. "Outside are two bravos—professional swordsmen, *monsieur*—who will begin a search for Cleve and d'Entreville the moment I give the word. When they find them—Cleve and d'Entreville die very quickly."

Don Diego sat up scowling. *"Carramba!"* he exploded. "Is

that your plan? *Dios!* You are not dealing with amateurs, *señor.* Cleve is a bad man with a blade; but Guy d'Entreville is terrific!"

DuBrille laughed. He patted the place where the tobacco lay hidden. "But the best are poor when blind, *monsieur,*" he said and paused. "Understand?"

And then Don Diego saw it. He leaned forward; watched his two enemies groping defenselessly, blinded by the dust DuBrille had cast. He enjoyed the picture. His thick lips quivered, curved and then split apart. Cruel, rich laughter rang throughout the room. He slapped his portly thigh.

"*Bueno!*" he exclaimed. "*Bueno,* DuBrille! 'Tis a good plan indeed. Get on with it immediately. And here, take Pizon to add another blade...."

AND IN THE LOUVRE, Richelieu thoughtfully slid the treaty paper to one side and relaxed against the plush of his chair. A squad of Royal Guards swung by outside in the corridor. He bit gently on his lower lip and frowned across the table at Louis XIII.

The light from the high Gothic window delicately tinted the Cardinal's fine pallor. It lent his sharply chiseled features a thoughtful, profound, almost ethereal appearance.

The rhythmic tread of the Guard faded and Louis XIII looked up.

"I tell you," he said, tapping the thick document by way of emphasis, "I tell you, the risk is too great. Should Spain learn of this, she'll pour rivers of steel into France. We can ill afford a war now."

Richelieu nodded. There was no craven or shallow logic behind the other's statement. Louis XIII might be a monarch of indifferent capabilities, but he knew the state of his realm.

France was just beginning to recover from a century of sporadic civil wars. Her powerful nobles were jealous of the Crown, and internal dissension remained—although Richelieu was slowly trying to throttle it. A war of with powerful, avaricious

Spain would set history back a hundred years. And yet it had to be prepared for.

"Spain sits on the crest of the Pyrenees, Sire. She eyes our rich lands in Gascony and Foix like hungry eagle. She awaits a pretext to seize them."

The Cardinal's eyes grew hard. "Some day she'll provoke a war. But when it comes, we *must* win! The future greatness of the French nation depends on it!"

Louis frowned. Usually he trusted his brilliant advisor to the utmost. In this instance, however, the ice seemed perilously thin.

"*Monseigneur,* you must show me a way that this treaty may be signed without the slightest outside suspicion of its very existence. Otherwise, we tear it up. I'll not prepare for a war with Spain by inviting one."

The Cardinal sighed. He steepled his tapering fingers and regarded the tips thoughtfully. He cursed Louis' shortsightedness even as his keen brain began a rapid dissection of the problem.

This treaty with England was vital. It guaranteed the use of the English fleet in case of Spanish aggression. It was supposed to be secret.

Yet he realized that the moment Lord Stafford appeared in the Louvre to sign it, rumors would spread that something was afoot. And now the over-cautious Louis wanted him to stifle even them. Suddenly Richelieu smiled.

"You are giving a reception to Don Diego, the Spanish ambassador tonight, Sire," he said looking up.

The King nodded. Richelieu leaned forward, dark eyes glittering. "And among the guests will be several foreign emissaries, including Lord Stafford. *Ma foi!*" His voice softened. "Who would believe we dared? Who'd believe we had the audacity to sign a pact with England—during a reception for Spain?"

THE KING'S eyes glistened. He struck the table with the

force of pride, as if the thought had been his own. "No one, *Monseigneur!* Least of all Spain!"

"Then you consent?"

The King laughed. "Consent? Of course I consent. We shall sign it tonight beneath Don Diego's very nose!"

Richelieu stood up. He felt relieved. "We'll use this room for the signing," he decided. "I'll have two of my best men standing guard all evening."

Louis considered that inadequate. The treaty merited a regiment.

"Too many guards will arouse suspicion," the Cardinal replied. "Besides, Cleve and d'Entreville have proven worth a regiment in several instances."

"Eh? Did you say Cleve and d'Entreville, *Monseigneur?*"

Richelieu nodded. "I did."

Louis looked thoughtful. "Hmm. I have heard of those two, *Monseigneur.* In fact, I am constantly hearing of them." He eyed Richelieu accusingly. "Le Duc d'Autun is found shivering in the hall in his underpants. Who placed him there?—Cleve and d'Entreville! Last week my regiment of Musketeers marched all the way to Fontainebleau under forged orders. And who forged them? *Corbac!* Cleve and d'Entreville!"

Richelieu's features darkened. For the hundredth time he angrily considered the two rakehellies who seemed to delight in placing him in the compromising position of being protector to their roguery.

First, Comte Guy d'Entreville: satirist, poet and swordsman. He had been a gnat in the Cardinal's dignity until forced by the prelate into shifting alliance. Richelieu wondered now whether that had been a wise move. In emergencies d'Entreville was invaluable; but it was questionable at times whether that virtue outweighed his nuisance value.

Then that crazy Englishman, Lord Cleve! Cleve the curious; the tactless. The man who had been exiled from England for speaking the truth at the wrong time; especially since it concerned the King's favorite and a missing ten thousand pounds in tax-money.

Richard Cleve: brilliance of mind and wit, exceeded by its penchant for getting him into trouble. Mere consideration caused Richelieu to frown—and then to smile.

Combine Cleve's talents with d'Entreville's sensitivity and fire, and you had a Satanic pair. A partnership that argued violently with itself when not engaged in scalding others. Small wonder the King had heard of them.

"And these are the men whom you propose to use as guards, *Monseigneur?*" Louis inquired.

Richelieu withdrew from his musings. Cleve and Guy were utter rascals, but they were the most resourceful men in his service. "They are, Your Majesty," he replied.

Louis smoothed his mustache with the tip of his finger. "Well, I presume you know what you are doing," he said after a pause. Then his lips tightened. "But I must warn you that another occurrence like that of yesterday and I shall personally see that they are lodged in La Bastille. A gentleman of my bed-chamber laughed at a poem that this d'Entreville had written. Today he nurses a pierced shoulder."

The Cardinal sighed. Many times he had wished that d'Entreville would cease writing poetry. It caused too much trouble. But it was a habit which the French rakehelly had spent too long forming to be broken quickly.

Richelieu sighed again, picked up the treaty and rolled it carefully into its cylinder.

"It shan't happen again," he said. "This morning I forced both of these firebrands to promise on their honor not to draw steel unless engaged in my service. Believe me, Sire, though they be reckless rakehellies, their word is their bond."

And he formed the words with the confidence of experience.

CHAPTER II

JOIN OUR RIOT?

BUT MEANWHILE, IN the far corner of the tavern known as Les Trois Chiens, Lord Richard Cleve raised a tankard of ale to his thirsty lips and stared over its rim at the quartet of King's Pikemen sitting in the center of the crowded room.

The Pikemen were drunk—ugly drunk. As Cleve watched, one of them struck Little Jean, the spindly houseboy, savagely across the mouth. The small servant crashed to the floor, blood trickling from a small cut. Cleve put down his tankard.

His clean-shaven face did not change, although his nose, with its impudent tilt, wrinkled slightly as if suddenly itchy. He pinched it. Then he cuffed his wide-brimmed hat to the back of his head and hitched his basket-hilt rapier closer to his side.

Guy d'Entreville observed these adjustments apprehensively. When Cleve pinched his nose, fondled his sword—something was going to happen. And suddenly!

The Englishman smiled. The smile was typical: a genial, leisurely smile, personable and disarming—but, to those who knew, dangerous. There were many who believed the chestnut-haired Cleve quite mad because of this laughing prelude to peril. Perhaps he was—but merrily.

He said to nobody in particular: "I wonder if Hogsnoot over there slaps grown men as well as serving lads?"

Guy d'Entreville's dark eyes took on a definite sheen of determination. He had been writing, but now he put down his quill and picked up an ink-pot. He said softly: "Relax!"

The Englishman's eyes widened. He was perfectly aware that his close friendship with Guy had taught the Frenchman to read him like a book, but he preferred to ignore the fact by maintaining an air of injured surprise.

"But why?"

D'Entreville grinned. "You know as well as I, *mon ami*. No sword-play. You gave your word. Now relax and conduct yourself peacefully or—" He weighed the ink-pot significantly. He meant it.

In the background, Little Jean had scrambled to his feet while the Pikeman who had struck him was now engaged in a heated discussion with one of his neighbors. The episode seemed forgotten. Cleve eyed the ink-pot thoughtfully, sighed and fell back against the wall. There wasn't much sense in risking an inking for a lost cause.

"Well," he said, "'tis a bad promise that makes a man condone men like Hogsnoot."

D'Entreville replaced the ink-pot and picked up a quill. "Remember this, you hare-brained rake. Without blades we are helpless. No brawling. Understand?"

"Spoken like a little martinet." Cleve smiled. "Words of wisdom. And come to think of it, where was that wisdom this morning?"

GUY shifted uncomfortably and hunched over his manuscript. He knew what was coming. The outstanding paradox of his friendship with Cleve was the degree to which they bickered. Many at the Palace wondered how the two of them could remain so completely compatible, and at the same time carry on like a pair of ill-tempered fishwives. But they did—constantly and consistently.

In this present instance, d'Entreville's desire to escape prison had led him to promise social pacifism for them both. Cleve had agreed out of loyalty, but that didn't prevent his complaining.

"Faith, all you had to do was to remain quiet," he said. "But, not you. Ah no!" He took a draught of ale and sighed. His tone mimicked the manner Guy had used on Richelieu that morning: "I know chastising a gentleman of the King's bedchamber is bad business, *Monseigneur.* But he laughed, *Monseigneur.* An insult, *Monseigneur.…*"

Guy's neck grew red. "*Sangodemi,* Cleve! Quiet!"

The Englishman's voice trailed. He drank some more ale. "Well, you didn't have to drag me into it," he concluded.

"*Mordi!* It was either that, or land in the Bastille."

"Just you, m'lad. I didn't prick that courtier."

"Well, His Eminence demanded that we both promise not to draw steel."

"Yes. And in a moment of weakness I agreed. Now we can't use swords unless in Richelieu's service. Excellent of you, Guy. Just wait until the word spreads. Consider the number of people who don't like us. Damme! Life's going to become one long foot-race...."

D'Entreville fingered the ink-pot for a moment, and then thought better of it. He gave his companion a silent glare and bent again to work.

Cleve grinned impishly and lifted his tankard once more. It was dismally empty. He set it down and regarded it accusingly. "Hola Jean! More ale here."

His eyes swept the low-ceilinged room; probed through the murk caused by the lateness of the day and the smoky hearth, and paused at the squat door through which four men had just entered. Four hard-faced, purposeful men, carrying blades high at their sides, loose-sheathed and ready.

They stared at him, then moved apart—casually. Too casually to be natural. The English cavalier's eyes turned sharply watchful. He had seen enough danger not to recognize its coming. Those men were tensed for trouble. He inspected each carefully.

One was small, foppish, wasplike. Two were definitely professional hirelings. But it was the fourth who crystallized his intuitive suspicion and dispersed all doubt. The fourth was Pedro Pizon, the squat dark-visaged Spaniard who had attempted his life a month before.

He whistled softly. "By Gad, we're in for it." And to

d'Entreville he added, "Put aside your toys, m'lad. We have visitors."

Guy scowled. He was engrossed in rhyming sigh with goodbye, and only half heard the warning. He didn't bother looking up to see the quartet making its separate way toward the corner, intent upon his death. All were holding their hands lightly on sword-hilts with the exception of the smallest who appeared to be fondling a purse. A leather bag.

CLEVE drew his booted legs under him. Noting the way the assassins had spread themselves, he cursed. His fingers tightened on the handle of the empty tankard.

"Faith, Guy. What are we going to do about this?"

The Frenchman scowled, and continued to gnaw his quill. Cleve pulled the tankard into his lap. He alone seemed to sense the deadly purpose of the newcomers, and he dared not show it less he precipitate the crisis too soon. He needed time to think out a plan.

In other instances he wouldn't have been so uncertain. But the sick realization that he was honor-bound not to draw steel put an alien chill into the pit of his stomach. He grew tense.

"Damme, Kitten! Pay attention!"

Guy looked up, anger in his eyes. The nickname, Cardinal's Kitten, had been pinned on him several months before by Prince Conde, who considered him extremely young for his ability to claw adversaries first with verse and then with his sword. To the sensitive Frenchman it sounded faintly derisive, and he hated it for that reason.

"*Sapristi!* Don't call me Kit—"

His voice trailed off as his eyes caught the wary, premonitory look on Cleve's tense face. He froze.

Cleve acted. He sent his heavy pewter tankard spinning end-over-end directly at the back of Hogsnoot, the pikeman. Nearby two of the approaching bravos froze. The tankard struck its target squarely and caromed sharply into the open face of the drunk sitting opposite.

"*Sacré nom d'un cochon!* Who threw that? I'll tear him limb from limb. I'll skewer him."

Cleve stood up. He was quite certain that no one had seen him launch the tankard. He pointed at one of the bravos standing to the right end a trifle behind the pikeman.

"There is your man, *monsieur!*" he cried.

Hogsnoot swung around, his red wine-soaked eyes credulous and angry. Behind him, his companions rose to a man. They had all been spoiling for a brawl and now the moment seemed to have arrived. Hands fell on hilts. Furtive patrons began to inch doorward.

"*Sandiou!*" muttered d'Entreville in a startled whisper. "What in the name of a name are you trying to do, Cleve?"

The Englishman grinned, but he hadn't take his eyes from the scene. He said softly: "I'm attempting to save our necks, laddie. At the same time, I'm settling the score with Hogsnoot for clouting Jean."

"You crazy fool, do you want to—"

"Quiet!" commanded the Englishman.

THINGS were beginning to happen. The pikeman had remained in an angry stupor, and now he lurched forward and slapped the astonished bravo a vicious cut across the lips. It drew blood and the bravo responded with alacrity. He drew and lunged almost in the same motion.

The pikeman countered by lifting a chair and the thrust rasped off the rungs. It licked a small wound in the cheek of a nearby companion.

Roaring with the trifling pain, this fellow pounced into he battle with his blade singing. Somebody turned over a table. It landed athwart Pedro Pizon's toes and automatically made him a belligerent. Cleve chuckled.

"They're off!"

The grog-room suddenly churned into a seething, tumultuous riot. Laughingly the Englishman folded his arms. Little devils of delight were dancing in his eyes.

"Interesting show, isn't it, Guy?" he said.

D'Entreville glowered. He was only partially aware of Cleve's reason for starting this mix-up, but he was more concerned in trying to save his precious verse from mutilation. War holds no brief for art. A gurgling wine-bottle crashed across the table and sprinkled the manuscript with reddish-brown liquor. Rage roared to a flame in his eyes.

"*Corbac!* If I ever discover who threw that, I'll—"

"Well aimed," Cleve grinned. "'Twas probably mush, anyway." He inclined his head toward the battle-locked mob. "Now there, m'lad, is something to describe. But of course it takes an excellent poet and you're—"

D'Entreville straightened. He met the challenge before it was fully completed. "Three to one I'm good enough to do it," he said.

"Taken!"

The Frenchman stood up. He was a good two inches taller than Cleve, more raw-boned and angular. He had a trimly pointed beard; and his clipped black mustache was surrounded by a high-bridged aristocratic nose which lent a slight hawkishness to his features.

His hair was dark, like rippled pitch, and lean maroon-clad body with its belted rapier and swirling cape stood in rakish contrast to the turmoil as he thoughtfully took in the scene.

Composing in rapid, staccato burst of verse, he began to recite:

> *The Brawl is on!*
> *The clash of steel.*
> *The brawlers parry, thrust and reel.*
> *One man is down!*
> *Ah no! He stands.*
> *And now, he's hurling pots and pans!*
> *Mon Dieu! And here*

Heads up, you lout
There goes a bottle at your snout!
Too late. Oh well,
Though I must say,
Your nose was too sharp anyway....

The speaker paused and shot a glance at the door. Crowding through came the white-crossed surcoats of the Cardinal's Guard, followed discreetly by the beard and paunch of Capitaine Cordeau.

Guy swore prodigiously—under his breath. Cordeau was a pompous martinet; an unimaginative stuffed shirt.

"Well, Kitten,"—Cleve laughed—"stuck?"

D'Entreville burned him with a glare, then megaphoned his hands and finished his impromptu composition in a roar that resounded above all else:

But that is all!
Messieurs, adieu!
Here comes the GUARD!
For most of you!

Cleve looked startled, but no more than did the others who heard the words. Fighting ceased on all fronts. There was a concerted rush for doors and windows, both open and shut. In what seemed no time at all, the grog-room was deserted, except for a few unconscious ones—and Cleve and d'Entreville.

"Well, *messieurs!*"

It was Cordeau stepping heavily over the debris of battle. He stopped before them, scowling, arms akimbo.

"Quite well, *mon Capitaine.*" Cleve nodded pleasantly, stepped aside and offered his chair. "Won't you join us, *monsieur.*"

Cordeau's muddy eyes hardened. Not understanding the Englishman's whimsy, he didn't like it. "Very comical," he snapped crisply. "You two are under arrest!"

Complete surprise blanked d'Entreville's face. He had expected anything but that. "*Sangodemi!* What for?"

Cordeau pursed his lips. He made a sweeping gesture with his gauntleted hand. "Inciting a riot. Wrecking a tavern. Impertinence to your commanding officer."

Cleve swore hotly.

"But this wreckage is none of our doing," Guy protested.

Cordeau smirked. Then he beckoned his men forward. "I know what my eyes see, *monsieur.* Fall in!"

CHAPTER III

CAVALIER'S FALL

AT RICHELIEU'S PALACE they stood in the company of eight Guardmen and heard their crimes triumphantly reported.

"Cordeau is a rat," muttered Cleve as the portly *capitaine* waxed eloquent and venomous.

D'Entreville nodded. He kept his dark eyes leveled on the ornate candelabrum sitting on the edge of Richelieu's desk. "Crass understatement," he murmured. "Pole-cat."

Cleve licked his lips. He was growing tired of standing at stiff attention in the heavy confines of the Cardinal's library. He eased the hilt of his sword away from his side.

"Pole-*rat!* And that combines the foulness of both in one. A tattle-tale, too."

Richelieu heard them and glanced up. "It isn't necessary to whisper your side of this business," he said.

Cleve smiled; a look of utter deviltry twinkled in his eyes as he composed an answer. Guy caught it and shuddered. He knew that indiscretion was about to pop, and feared the worse.

"Truth *always* whispers, *Monseigneur.*"

Capitaine Cordeau grew crimson. He whirled to the Cardinal, one thick finger stabbing accusation at the two cavaliers.

"Insolence, *Monseigneur!* There you have it. It is the sort of thing I am constantly faced with."

Richelieu regarded him enigmatically. "You have presented your report, *monsieur le Capitaine*. I feel certain that no personal animosity tinged it. However, being a fair man, I must listen to Messieurs Cleve and d'Entreville before I pass judgment. Withdraw your men, and I shall listen to what they have to—er"—He smiled slightly without humor—"whisper."

Cordeau bowed. Instinctively he felt that he was being duped, but Richelieu's tone left him no alternative. With the false grace of a politician he murmured: "Ever at your service, *Monseigneur*," collected his men, and withdrew.

The Cardinal did not watch his exit. He fell back against the plush of his chair and eyed his charges over the top of his steepled fingers.

D'Entreville stood tense and apprehensive, his broad shoulders back and his chin high. He expected the worst. He was ready for it.

But, Cleve... Richelieu shifted to the Englishman and sighed. Cleve was relaxed as usual, and laughing with his eyes. The man seemed impervious to the threats of the future; perhaps because the uncertainty of his career had taught him the futility to worry.

The silence grew in weight and length until finally the Cardinal shrugged. How to make a reprimand stick to these irrepressible rakehellies was a poser. They were both born for trouble, and verbal punishment had lost potency through overuse.

"**MESSIEURS**," he said musingly, "has it ever occurred to you that I can grow sick of being constantly hung on the horns of dilemma? It seems I am habitually alternating between the decision to hang you, and the decision to honor you.

"Now in regard to this latest escapade. First: did you provoke this brawl? Second: did you break your pledge?"

Cleve shifted, "Well, yes and no, *Monseigneur*."

A thread of danger intertwined Richelieu's tone. "Now that is a definite answer, m'lord. Precisely what do you mean by it?"

"Yes to the first question, *Monseigneur.* No to the second."

The Cardinal eyed him severely, but offered no comment. He fell back into his chair and trailed a thoughtful finger along the side of his cheek.

"The fact that the both of you refrained from drawing steel may temper my punishment. But make no mistake, you shall be punished." He pursed his lips. "Punished with a terrible responsibility, *messieurs!*"

The two cavaliers exchanged glances. The Cardinal was building up to something, and they knew from past experience that it would be dangerous. Of the two, d'Entreville was the less apprehensive. He would face almost any peril rather than lose his precious liberty. Cleve was not so sure.

Richelieu got to his feet. He made a slim, dynamic figure in his trailing red robe, seeming taller because of it. He fell to pacing, hands interlocked firmly behind his back; and finally he turned.

"Yes," he continued softly, "a terrible responsibility." He frowned. "You are both rogues, *messieurs!* Reckless knaves! And yet, you possess a quality of resource and courage which I deem worth the salvage. Candidly, it is the only reason I tolerate your repeated impertinences.

"In previous instances I have tried to cleanse you of your rakehelly bent by corporal punishments. Well, *messieurs,* that has failed; therefore, a moral force seems to be demanded. We shall see whether responsibility can sweat that streak of wildness out of you, and make you true servants of France."

Cleve frowned. The Cardinal's continual reference to a heavy responsibility was beginning to irk. "You'll pardon me, *Monseigneur,*" he said carefully, "but just what is this responsibility?"

The Cardinal regarded him steadily and explained about the treaty: its necessity and its danger. Spain was seeking a pretext to involve France in war. The treaty with England would do that, if it ever fell into unfriendly hands.

"And it must not fall into unfriendly hands, *messieurs*," he concluded crisply. "It will be your duty to see that it doesn't. When you stand before the door to that little room in the Louvre tonight, you will not be guarding a mere document of State. You will be guarding the future of French security; the lives of thousands!"

The Cardinal's slim hands folded.

Cleve smiled faintly. "A nice thought," he said. "Frankly, *Monseigneur*, if you had given us an alternative I should have preferred the Bastille."

AND THAT night he paced irresolutely before the innocent-looking door to the treaty room and cursed. He and Guy were in a deserted second-floor corridor of the Louvre; but even so, the gay noise of the glittering assemblage down-stairs could be heard. The Spanish reception was in full swing, and non-participation made the English cavalier feel itchy.

He paused before a full-length mirror. There was a gay restlessness in his eye. The black doublet he wore was slashed with silver; his short military cape was faced with *fleurs de lis,* and his black thigh-high boots fitted without a crease.

"*Sangodemi,*" grunted d'Entreville from his chair. "You are very pretty, *mon ami.* But relax. You're not going anywhere."

Cleve sighed; eyed his companion. Guy was sitting easily asprawl with his hands locket comfortably behind his head. He was garbed in military court dress—white and gold, with brass buckles on his gray boots and a lane of diamonds running the length of his sword-sheath.

"A fine fop you make, Kitten," the Englishman said. "Mind you don't fall asleep."

D'Entreville sat up. "*Corbac!* Don't call me Kitten! I've fought duels for less."

Cleve didn't comment. He walked over to a chair and sat down with a frown. They had been on duty for thirty minutes.

It was beginning to rag his nerves. The sweet strains of music and laughter lifted from below.

"Wish I had a drink," he said.

Guy shook his head. "No. We're on duty. A soldier's responsibility is not to be taken lightly. Remember it."

Cleve shrugged and polished his nails on the shoulder of his doublet. "Consider it this way, Kitten. Our orders state that we're not to appear to be guarding that room. Faith! A bottle will only strengthen the illusion. It is almost a duty!"

An expression of longing surfaced the Frenchman's hawkish features; but his sense of decorum doused it. "*Corbac!* No! And stop foisting illogical logic on me!"

"By Gad! What's illogical about it?"

"You have me there! It just doesn't ring true."

"Now there's reasoning! It doesn't ring true; therefore it isn't—"

He broke off. Coming up the corridor was a man. A man who strode at a leisure pace with his hand negligently on the hilt of a long rapier. He was tall, olive-skinned, dressed foppishly in green; he wore a half-spade beard after the Spanish fashion.

CLEVE scowled. The corridor had two staircases, one at either end, but he had supposed the end from which the stranger was coming, closed.

"Your pardon, *messieurs*," said the man arrogantly. "Who occupies that room?" He jerked his thumb at the door of the treaty chamber.

D'Entreville looked up. He wasn't used to being addressed as if he was a lackey. He didn't like the newcomer's manner.

"I do," he said deliberately. "Why?"

The stranger eyed him coldly. "*Why?* Now here's a rude question. And rudely put, I think!"

Guy straightened. He made no attempt to get up. There was

something about this fellow that rubbed the prickles of dislike into his throat.

"Candidly, monsieur, I don't particularly care whether it's rude or not. But, since you have inquired about my room—"

"I doubt that it is your room, *monsieur!*"

Guy stood up slowly. "You do, eh?" he said softly.

The tautness of his tone warned Cleve that now was the time to intercede. He stood up too. "It is his room, true enough," he told the man. Then he caught the jutting line of Guy's jaw and added hurriedly: "I believe it would be to everyone's interest if you take your leave, *monsieur.*"

The stranger offered him a twisted smile. His fingers were now tight on the hilt of his rapier; white-capped and strained.

"I appreciate your efforts, *monsieur.* But it would hardly befit a man of my stature to turn tail from a"—he toyed with the word—"*Kitten!*"

And that did it! Guy would take that from Cleve but from no one else. His arm licked out. Hard fingers whipped into the stranger's mouth. The soggy smack of them under-emphasized the force of the blow.

"*Dieu!*"

The stranger recoiled. His face was a white mask and the marks of Guy's fingers stood in scarlet contrast to the pallor. He put tracing fingers to them and bowed.

"There is a garden outside, *monsieur.* I'll be waiting!"

When he had gone, Cleve stared at his companion. "Neatly done, Kitten. Now what are you going to do?"

"*Corbac!* Make a pin-cushion of him!"

"Yes. I presume that would be in order. Of course, we both know that a—er—soldier's responsibility is not to be taken lightly, and that we have a room to protect. But that applies only to me, doesn't it? Me and wine."

Guy hitched up his rapier. The full fire of his blood had been aroused. Reason melted beneath it. But even so, Cleve's irony was beginning to raise his innate sense of duty—and he didn't want it, now.

"I shan't take long!" he snapped.

"Ah now, I'm not so sure. Duelling with a man without drawing steel will take a bit of doing. You promised to use your blade only in Richelieu's service. Remember?"

Guy felt his hot resolves crumbling inside of him and he fought against it with the stubbornness of pride. "You're a fine one to preach, Cleve! *Sangodemi!* Who are you to—"

Cleve chuckled. "Temper, Kitten!"

Sheer recklessness leaped into d'Entreville's eyes. "All right," he said gently. "I promise you I'll not draw my blade. But, I must keep my appointment. This is a question of honor. I'll find a way to satisfy it."

"That'll be a neat trick if you can—Hey! Wait, Guy! What are you going to do?"

But d'Entreville was half-way down the corridor, walking doggedly. He didn't turn his head; merely tossed the words ahead and let them drift back. Quickly he said:

"You'll find out later. No man can insult me and—"

But that was all....

Cleve heard a faint step from behind and started to turn. A heavy hand clogged his mouth; a sickening blow thundered against his head. For a brief flashing instant he saw the dizzying sweep of the floor rushing up to meet him and he knew that he was falling.

Then a cloak of sable seemed to drop over everything to blot out vision. It closed in, tighter, tighter. Faintly he heard a chuckle. A voice said:

" 'Tis done, DuBrille!"

And he knew no more.

CHAPTER IV

MARCH, KITTEN!

HOW LONG HE remained senseless Cleve never knew. He seemed to be struggling on hands and knees in a cramped world stuffed with feathery blackness. He heard faint voices and groped mentally toward them.

The voices grew louder; more distinct. He opened his eyes and light cascaded through, clearing the soot that had been encrusting everything.

"How do you feel, m'Lord?"

He struggled to a sitting posture. He felt weak and faintly nauseated, but that was leaving. He was on a divan in the corridor and there were people all around. Bending near was Lord Stafford, a glistening wet goblet in his hand. Cleve remembered him from childhood.

"Are you all right, Cleve?"

"Yes."

Stafford straightened. He put the goblet on a nearby table and frowned. He was a slim, long-faced man with gray eyes and thin lips. "This is bad business," he said. "What happened?"

Cleve put his hand to his head. It was wet from the water Stafford had used to arouse him. It was beginning to ache in thick, bulging throbs.

"I don't know precisely. I heard a noise. Turned. And—and, that was all. Silly of me. I should have been prepared."

Some of the men who had ringed him turned away.

"The treaty's gone," Stafford said.

That didn't mean much at first. Cleve sat there on the divan and fought against the urge to lie down again. "Gone?" he said blankly. The significance suddenly struck like a cudgel, but all he said was: "Not very good, is it?"

"No. It isn't."

Then Stafford sat down beside him. He seemed nervous and he kept jerking at the little goatee on his chin. He added: "Somebody has talked."

Cleve smiled wanly. He was beginning to feel better; more like himself. "Obviously."

"But who? Damme, there's the question. Never was there a more astonished man than I when I arrived with His Eminence, found you asprawl and the door wrenched open. Count d'Entreville was just coming up the hall."

"D'Entreville!"

Cleve stood up. It seemed the wrong thing to do at first, for an intense wave of dizzying sensations rocked him. Then it passed and he felt better.

"I fear the Count is in some difficulty," Stafford volunteered.

A LACKEY offered Cleve a glass of brandy. He accepted it and stood sipping slowly. "About the treaty," he said. "Who is suspected? The Spanish, of course."

Stafford shrugged and shook his head. "No. Not exactly. Don Diego and his retinue have been under close surveillance all evening. Not one of them left the ballroom. As a matter of fact, they appeared eager to be watched."

Cleve finished his liquor and set the empty glass down. "Really," he said. His mind, with its almost feline curiosity, was beginning to play with a lot of questions. "Tell me, m'Lord, did you notice a gentleman in green near Don Diego at any time?"

Before Stafford could reply, Richelieu stepped through the press of courtiers and Royal Guards. The Cardinal's face was a waxen mask. His dark eyes were snapping. He jabbed Cleve with a glance and said to the English ambassador: "Does Cleve throw any light on this, Stafford?"

"No, M'Lord. Cleve was struck from behind."

The Cardinal frowned. "So. From behind, eh? Then, if le comte d'Entreville had been with him it never could have happened." He regarded Cleve without much harshness. "Apparently, *monsieur,* this is not your blame. You have not eyes in the rear of your head. No, there is only one culprit...."

He turned deliberately. Cleve hadn't noticed before, but d'Entreville was standing beside the door, pale-faced; strained. The Cardinal's chill gaze swept him and returned to the Englishman.

"Monsieur le comte d'Entreville is under arrest for treasonable neglect of duty," he said quietly. "It will please me if you take his sword, *monsieur.* Confine him to his quarters. He is your prisoner."

D'Entreville's sword came out slowly, reluctantly. And when he spoke, his tones were imbued with the deep sincerity of the friendship which had been born of action and forged in the fires of mutual peril.

"Rather you, Cleve, than any living man!"

There was drama here; but as Cleve accepted the blade, his feelings for burlesque crept to the surface. That impish perversity which had so often dropped him into hot water suddenly became manifest.

"Kitten," he said slowly and with a faintly traced grin that belied paternalism, "Kitten, you are a *bad, bad* boy!"

... And a block below the Louvre, a man entered a dingy, half-lit room. He was tall, olive-skinned, and dressed in green. The side of his face was streaked with two painful-looking red welts. His sword-sheath dangled limply without its sword. He looked tired, disheveled. But his eyes were snapping curses.

Another man, deep in the shadows, looked up. "What happened?"

The olive-skinned individual slumped into a chair and poured himself a drink. "Dieu! What didn't happen? 'Tis only by the grace of fate and a madman's whim that I am alive!"

"Then you picked the quarrel?"

The man in green took a gulp of liquor and nodded. His companion stared for a moment, then commenced to laugh.

"*Pecaire!* You look badly mauled, *mon ami.* Badly mauled!"

The other cursed. "Mauled by a crazy mad kitten," he erupted savagely. "Do you know what that man d'Entreville did?"

"No, of course not."

"He didn't take his blade from its sheath! He attacked with the scabbard and all! *Mordi!* God save me from ever again fighting that sort of a madman!"

GUY D'ENTREVILLE paced the floor of his quarters and fought the curse of an over-vivid imagination. With each step his mood grew darker: He was disgraced! Blackened! Unredeemable!

He visualized France wracked and smoking as the blood-smeared armies of Spain marched and counter-marched over her prostrate body. And it was his fault—his fault alone!

"I think it was a mistake to give you back your sword, Kitten. You look nigh ready to use it—on yourself."

Cleve spoke from his comfortable position atop the bed. He chuckled and untied the cords holding the portieres near his head.

"I fear you're not to be trusted with ropes either."

Guy didn't answer. A candle guttered uncertainly from its bottle-based position on the table. It sent weirdly dancing shadows along the walls. Somewhere outside a clock tolled twelve. A distant dog barked.

The Englishman threw his legs over the side of the bed and sat up. He had been trying vainly to arrive at some solution to the treaty's disappearance. There was a tantalizing fact dancing in the dim borderlands of memory, but it had eluded him. He gave it up.

"Damme Kitten, do we turn in? Or, are you prepared to brood 'til dawn?"

D'Entreville cast him a searching glance. There were times when Cleve's apparent inability to accept serious things seriously baffled him. The Englishman had once said: "Never do anything about anything until it happens—and then, do plenty!"

Guy frowned. *Corbac!* Something had happened all right!

He walked over to the wall; unhooked a pistol from its peg and rammed it into his sash; then jerked on his gauntlets and reached for his plumed hat. Polite interest glimmered in Cleve's eyes.

"Going somewhere?"

Guy paused. He was under arrest and the thought put a defiant jut to his chin. "That's right," he said.

Cleve arose leisurely. He grinned. "You forget one thing, Kitten. You're my prisoner."

"Well?"

The Englishman shrugged. He reached for his hat. "Damme, do you think I allow my prisoners to run willy nilly where they choose? Don't forget, *monsieur,* a soldier's responsibility is not to be taken lightly."

"Corbac! I've heard about enough of that phrase."

"You coined it, m'lad."

"That's beside the point. What do you intend doing about this arrest business?"

"Why, to accompany you, of course." Cleve tipped his hat at a rakish angle and placed gloved hands on his hips.

"Faith, whose prisoner are you anyway? If you venture out alone, then you are escaping. Breaking arrest. Really, Kitten, don't you think you've enough counts against you without asking more.

"Now, they'll hang you only once. Escape, and they'll probably hang you twice. Two hangings in one day is rather hard on the neck. No. I'll go with you."

D'Entreville grinned. *Sandiou!* What could one do with a man like Cleve? Besides, although it was against his principles to admit it, the irrepressible Englishman was as necessary to him as his right arm.

"Very well," he shrugged. "You win. But, 'tis on your own initiative, remember."

The other nodded. "That's better," he said.

THEY stole furtively down the hall and into the rear courtyard. The night was silver-touched by a moon that drenched the earth with brilliance, made the street-cobbles resemble great deep-set sapphires.

A Guard challenged them sleepily. Cleve drew his blade and grasped Guy firmly by the arm.

"Taking the prisoner for an airing," he said crisply.

"Pass," replied the Guard.

Outside in the street, they walked smartly toward le Quai de l'Ecole. The city was still in the translucence of blue that filled the night, and its stillness made their footsteps ring where they should have clacked faintly. Ahead the waters of the Seine moved, silent and white through the shadows.

"Where away, Kitten?" Cleve asked.

D'Entreville's lips were thinned; determined. He had soaked his mind in the facts of the case, hoping against hope to uncover a thread—a single lead on which to proceed. There was none.

Of course, he realized now that the man in green had been purposely sent to distract him. But no one had seen the man in green. He had disappeared as suddenly and as unexpectedly as he had appeared. As for the rest… an open door; Cleve sprawled unconscious on the floor; the treaty gone.

But through the misery of his own conscience, one fact had been looming in size and substance; and it was upon this that the cavalier had decided to act. Only one man in Paris would benefit appreciably by the seizure of the Treaty.

"I believe a visit to Don Diego seems in order," he said.

"Perhaps." Cleve nodded.

They continued their way for a brief moment. Cleve stared thoughtfully into the night, once again probing for some-thing…. And suddenly that dancing secret at the back of his memory grew unwary and stepped into his trap.

"Who is DuBrille?" he asked quietly.

D'Entreville came to a sudden stop and eyed Cleve piercingly. From the past he had learned the deductive powers of the Englishman. Whatever Cleve's seeming recklessness, there was a razor-sharp intelligence inside.

On more than one occasion that intelligence had sliced through the dark cloak of mystery; and although Cleve rarely used it—because as he often said: "thinking deprives a man of so many senseless pleasures"—it was there. Guy was grateful for it.

"DuBrille's a petty informer, a blackmailer," he said. "What of him?"

"Nothing. But I'll wager ten to one that he knows more concerning the treaty's disappearance than does Don Diego. Furthermore, I'll double the stakes on the possibility of his having it in his possession now."

"Pecaire! But why?"

"Because I have a bump on my head," said Cleve and chuckled. "DuBrille's name was the last thing I heard before losing consciousness. Faith! We've been so engrossed about Spain in this affair that we've completely forgotten that some ambitious adventurer might have lifted the treaty to sell it on an open mart."

D'Entreville snapped his fingers. *"Sangodemi!* Why didn't you speak of this in the first place, you lout?"

Cleve chuckled through the shadows. "Perchance because I didn't think of it in the first place," he said; and took Guy by the elbow. "Come on."

CHAPTER V

DEAD MAN'S INN

DUBRILLE LIVED IN a ramshackle hostelry that traced its beginnings back to the days of the eighth Charles. Located in an obscure alley near the foot of le Pont Neuf, it combined the fine assets of being both unknown and unnoticeable. A wretched, weed-grown, inner court guarded its front entrance, and the waters of the Seine its rear.

As d'Entreville led the way up to it, Cleve noticed that except for the lawful night-light, the building was to all intents and purposes deserted.

"Fine burrow for a rat," he remarked softly.

Guy chuckled. "And when you've said that, you've said all. DuBrille is a rat if ever there was one. The only reason I know of his whereabouts is that he sold Richelieu some information a year ago, and I acted as emissary."

A light twinkled in Cleve's eyes. "Sort of a cat and mouse arrangement, eh?"

The shaft bit deep. D'Entreville stopped in mid-stride and glared. "*Sangodemi*, Cleve! You've gone too far! I'll tolerate your calling me Kitten, but when you commence concocting rancid puns, I'll take no more. Come on! Draw!"

Tears appeared as the English rakehelly sought to restrain his laughter. "I—I can't," he finally gasped. "And don't roar so loud. You'll have the house down on us."

"*Pecaire!* I'll have more than that down on you," growled the Frenchman. "*Peste!* You're crazy anyway. Come along."

The knocker made a hollow sound against the ancient oak of the door. Almost immediately a night-capped head poked itself from a side window. A peevish challenge: "What do you want?"

"To get in, of course," Cleve said. "Open up!"

The head disappeared and they could hear the pad of slippered feet approaching. Then the door swung inward and they were staring down at a night-shirted midget with the face of a patriarch gone to seed. He held a candle high and squinted at them.

"Well?"

Cleve cast an amused glance at Guy. "Did you ever say that good things come in small packages?" he asked.

D'Entreville shook his head impatiently. "No." Then he looked at the midget. "We desire to see DuBrille."

"Monsieur DuBrille," the little man corrected harshly. *"Mordi!* They all want to see Monsieur DuBrille. Foreigners! Bah!"

Cleve's eyebrow arched. "Foreigners, *mon petit?*"

"Sangodemi! Don't refer to my size! Yes, foreigners. Cursed Spaniards, and an English sot."

Guy looked at Cleve and drew his blade. The little innkeeper darted back.

"No violence! No violence!"

"Silence, squirt! Take us to DuBrille and quietly!"

"Murderers! Help! Help!"

With a sweep Cleve bent down and picked up the midget. He clamped a gloved hand over the writhing mouth and nodded to Guy.

"Damme. Let's get inside before this town crier raises the Watch."

THE TAVERN'S interior was no great improvement over its outside. The walls were cracked and smoke-stained and great rolls of dirt clotted the corners. Cleve deposited the innkeeper on the floor.

"And now, laddie, where is DuBrille?"

The innkeeper glowered and said nothing. D'Entreville cursed.

"Well," Cleve said, "we'll have to find him ourselves."

He tucked the midget under one arm and mounted the rickety stair-case. Guy brought up the rear, sword gleaming in the wavering light of the candle.

They paced along a narrow corridor, dingy, with warped doors lining either side. The sound of their feet reverberated hollowly on the bare boards of the floor. Then, turning the corner, they were confronted by a veritable cascade of yellow light. DuBrille's door was open, hanging on its hinges.

Cleve shifted the now passive midget and drew his sword. Guy's pistol came out silently. Thus prepared, they trooped into the well-lit room.

There was a tarnished candelabrum on the mantle with seven candles burning, the fire in the hearth glowed dully, the blinds had been drawn tightly across the sole window—but Cleve noticed none of these things. His halt was so sudden and horrified that Guy bumped into him from behind.

"Good Heavens!"

There was DuBrille—or rather, what was left of DuBrille. He had been stripped and spread-eagled on the table, a thick gag rammed into his mouth. Sickening burns told what had been happening: torture, silent and cruel.

The room was a turmoil. Cleve sheathed his blade with a snap and set the innkeeper down.

"Faith, there's one rat who's been well trapped," he said, indicating the corpse.

The innkeeper began to snivel. He swore he knew nothing; he had been asleep. Guy brushed past him and walked to the table. A finely wrought stiletto was buried to the hilt in Du-Brille's throat. He drew it forth and stared at it.

"They must have been in a hurry to leave so valuable a weapon," he said.

Cleve nodded. He eyed the wrecked room; the ripped bedding, the gutted cabinet-drawers, the gaping closet. A huge coffin-like chest in the corner attracted his attention. It was closed; and that was an anomaly in such fiercely searched quarters.

D'Entreville said: "Spanish steel."

Cleve shrugged. "What did you expect? Of course it's Spanish. The whole story is written so plainly that it's well nigh audible. Mark the confusion of this room. Apparently DuBrille possessed something that he refused to give up. Undoubtedly the treaty. His greed for gold probably overcame his prudence.

"Those Spanish gentlemen, of whom our host spoke so highly, came to collect it. DuBrille tried to bargain. They searched the room, and failed." His eyes grew grim. "And then they went to work on him, with full success."

"What makes you think that?" asked Guy.

Cleve indicated the stiletto he held. "They used that, didn't they?" he said. "If they hadn't known DuBrille's secret they wouldn't have killed him."

Guy stared moodily at the figure on the bed and nodded.

D'ENTREVILLE frowned and lifted a torn blanket and threw it over the body. "Doesn't the fact that the Spanish knew that he had the treaty preclude that he was working for them?" he said. "Why should they kill their own man?"

"Ah me," Cleve sighed, shook his head and regarded the other tolerantly. "Faith, Kitten, you said yourself that DuBrille was a rat. Once he had his fingers on the treaty he probably sought to cross the men who had hired him originally."

Cleve bit thoughtfully on his lower lip. "But it isn't the obvious I'm interested in now, Guy. DuBrille stole the treaty, true enough, but—"

He looked up. "Damme! How did he find out about it in the first place? It was supposed to be a secret. Only the King, Lord Stafford, Richelieu and ourselves knew of it."

Guy shrugged. Causes weren't his immediate worry—consequences were. *"Pecaire!* What difference? The deed's been done." He stared at the Spanish stiletto. "The important fact remains that Don Diego now has the treaty. No one else would be interested enough to torture and kill DuBrille and ransack his room this thoroughly. *Bien!* Let's go after Diego. We waste time loitering here."

Cleve walked over to the chest that had originally piqued his curiosity. His fingers curled under the lid's edge; it lifted easily and fell back with a crash against the wall. He bent over its contents, and straightened abruptly.

"Damme!" he muttered. "Is this a tavern or a morgue?"

Inside the chest was a body: a corpse garbed in the livery of a house-lackey, blue and silver. Its face was round with a lumpish red nose, and a brace of blue eyes that looked merry even in death. Beneath the chubby chin was a small round hole—the sort caused by a rapier blade. The sour odor of stale ale wafted out of the impromptu coffin.

"Dieu, they *are* thorough!"

"Well," said Cleve, "he died drunk. He'd have liked that."

D'Entreville bend over his shoulder. "*Corbac!* You know him?"

"Yes. Name was Will Beck. He was the personal valet to Lord Stafford. Been in the family for years." Cleve let the lid fall into position again gently. He had liked Will Beck in the old days.

Now he frowned. "And that," he concluded, "solves DuBrille's source of information. Beck talked a lot when besotted. He was close enough to Stafford to hear much. The ambassador probably let something slip, unconsciously of course, and Beck spilled it to Du Brille after getting drunk."

"Then Beck was the English sot that our host mentioned. I was beginning to wonder."

"Speaking of our host," Cleve said looking up, "just where is he?"

D'Entreville looked quickly toward the door, where the little man had been standing. It was deserted, gaping; the midget gone.

Cleve blew out all of the candles in the candelabrum and

plunged the room into a brooding gloom; then stepped to the window and parted the thick drapes.

"I'd have liked to ask that little imp a few questions," he murmured. Then he stiffened. "Damme! We've got to leave this place, Kitten."

D'Entreville moved up beside him. Below in the moon-drenched courtyard was the missing innkeeper. The little man was headed hurriedly toward the street, casting nervous glances back over his shoulder and acting generally terrified. Even as they stared, he broke into a shrill, bleating, yell.

"Ho the Watch! Murder! Murder!"

Guy took a deep breath. He had been carrying his blade bared, but now he snapped it into its sheath to get it out of the way. The Watch! *Sandiou!* All he needed was to be arrested on the scene of a double murder and the headsman's block would become a certainty.

He darted for the door.

"*Pecaire!* Cleve!" he exclaimed. "If we're leaving—what are we just standing here for?"

CHAPTER VI

THE NIMBLE SPANIARD

CLOUDS WERE BEGINNING to clot the moon as they walked up to Don Diego's residence on the Rue St. Denis. They paused in the blue black shadows to inspect the place.

The house stared back ominously, its windows like great dead eyes. Brooding silence prevailed. The place seemed asleep.

Guy didn't like it. Don Diego's position demanded an armed retinue. It was certain that there were guards somewhere inside that silent edifice, but whether asleep or alert was a question.

The Frenchman allowed his fingers to caress the reassuring coolness of his rapier hilt. No longer did he feel honor bound not to draw. If nothing else, this was the Cardinal's business! He tapped Cleve on the shoulder.

"Watch yourself, *mon ami.*"

The Englishman nodded. He tugged his hat more firmly on the side of his head. Then, like gliding wraiths, they slipped across the street.

Naturally, the steel-banded door was closed. Guy tested the small casement beside it, and surprisingly the window gave easily under his hand. Cleve chuckled.

"Amazing efficiency, eh?"

He waited while D'Entreville hitched up his blade and disappeared silently into the black rectangle; then followed.

They were in a small foyer with dark stairs leading into the blackness above. The very air felt as if it had been steeped in heavy, brooding, silence.

Guy, standing tense and listening, let his eyes become accustomed to the murk; then motioned Cleve forward. He heard the sibilant slither of the Englishman's blade leaving its sheath.

The archway to a large room gaped to their right. The room was heavily carpeted, had a sunken floor and a high ceiling. At one end Guy could make out the vague lines of a huge desk.

"This was first," he breathed. "That desk pleads to be searched. And move quietly, Cleve. No noise!"

The Englishman nodded. But his incongruous fancy was beginning to grow restless. It rebelled against the tenseness of the situation, demanding action or some form of relief.

At that moment his toe discovered a heavy foot-stool. It caught and pitched him headlong, with a startled yell and a crash. The flimsy end-table that was in his line of fall toppled aside, the candle-holder and vase atop it clattering.

Then came a thick silence; the tense breathless silence that inevitably seems to post-script bedlam.

"My nose," muttered Cleve.

"Quiet!"

There was movement from above, and a voice sent a challenge ringing down the staircase. A Spanish voice.

"Who goes?"

Guy muttered a curse. He froze, teeth clamped on his lower lip.

"*Por Dios!* Who is there?"

The voice was insistent, demanding of an answer. D'Entreville took a deep breath, flexed his sword-arm. He lifted his voice in delicate modulation.

"*Meeeoow!*" he said.

IT WAS perfectly executed, but therein lay its flaw. Cleve couldn't take it—not from the man known as the Kitten. From his position on the floor his mad humor bubbled over and he giggled.

The voice from above lost some of the alarm which had charged it. "Felipe? Here puss, puss, puss...."

"*Meeoow!*" said Guy.

He kicked Cleve in the vain hope that the pain would sober him. But the English rakehelly was beyond pain. Silent throbs of laughter convulsed him. Guy's kick, abetted by the second *meeooww*, only added fire to the flame. It cracked restraint into audibility. Cleve rolled on the floor and roared.

"*Dios y Diablo!*" exclaimed the voice from above. "Who is down there!"

The challenge restored Cleve's sense of reality, but not for long. The game was over. "Who?" he roared back. "Damme! Nobody but us Kittens."

Guy threw up his hands. "*Sacré nom!*" he sighed. "That caps it!"

Feet thumped their way down the staircase. D'Entreville faded as the saffron of a lantern filled the foyer. Cleve stood up. He was still chuckling softly, but his eyes were alert. He held his blade slanted across his boots.

A slim silhouette stepped into the arch.

The man held a large lantern in one hand and a pistol in the other. It was aimed at Cleve. Unnoticed, Guy stood against the wall near the arch.

"One movement, *señor,* and I blow a hole through you."

Cleve allowed his rapier to drop. It clattered loudly against the shattered end-table. "I shan't move," he promised.

"*Por Dios!* I don't think you will either."

He stepped down into the room, past Guy's motionless figure. "Bent on private business, eh *señor,*" he said to Cleve and placed the lantern on the desk.

The Englishman shrugged. "Something like that," he admitted. In the background he saw Guy slowly draw his pistol. Apparently the Spaniard was alone. "Business concerning Don Diego," he finished. "I have come to see him."

The Spaniard's mocking smile built itself into a jarring, sarcastic giggle. "Really, *señor!* Ha! Even if I believed you, that would be impossible. The Don has left Paris."

Cleve bit his lip. "Sudden wasn't it? When did he leave?"

The Spaniard was still smiling. The pistol he held came to a focus on the Englishman's heart. For the first time Cleve noticed that while the speaker's lips were smiling, the beady black eyes glittered with the chill sheen of a killer.

"That, *señor,* is none of your affair. Besides, I shall not waste time. The fact that you have stolen furtively into this room proves you a spy."

The trigger-finger tightened. Cleve's stomach tried to escape via his back-bone. "You see, *señor,* we Spanish do not trifle with spies. Ah no, *señor.* We shoot them!"

Guy broke the tension. He had crept on cat-feet up behind the speaker. He placed his pistol coldly on the man's neck, just under the ear.

"You won't live that long, *monsieur.* Drop that weapon. Be quick!"

THE SPANIARD stiffened. His pistol jackknifed from his fingers and landed with a dull bump atop Cleve's toe.

"Damme!" the Englishman yelped. "*Not* that quick!" He retrieved his rapier and arose eyeing Guy ruefully. "Faith, next time a man thinks to invest lead in me, don't diddle about in the background so cursed along."

D'Entreville chuckled. "Had I obeyed my impulse, I'd have let him shoot. Remember, he arrived down here only at your insistence." He nudged the captive gently. "Sit in that chair over there."

The Spaniard obeyed and they bound him quickly, silently, with the drape-cords from the windows. He made no comment, submitting to the action sullenly.

"Post yourself by the archway, Cleve," d'Entreville said. "If Don Diego has left Paris, I desire to know where. When my friend here commences to tell, I don't want to be disturbed."

The Spaniard's lips curled. "You'll learn nothing from me," he said.

D'Entreville shrugged. "I'm not trifling. There is too much at stake. You say Don Diego has left the city. Very well. It couldn't have been more than an hour ago. We have just come from DuBrille."

The other smiled enigmatically and stared straight ahead. Guy looked over to where Cleve had been standing. He was a trifle nonplussed at first. Cleve was missing. And then he heard the sound of the Englishman's boots softly climbing the stairs.

With that he returned hotly to the adamant prisoner. Somehow he must make the man talk. The mere fact that Diego had fled so unexpectedly proved that he possessed the treaty. Time was valuable.

"I'll give you one more opportunity, *monsieur*," he snapped. "Where is your master?"

The Spaniard smiled again, insolently. Guy pursed his lips. There was an ornate green flask on the table. He picked it up thoughtfully; shattered it on the edge. Then he approached his prisoner.

The jagged glass presaged horror. The transparent teeth were cruel, hungry. Instinctively the Spaniard flinched. He had a fair face and an imagination.

"When did Diego leave Paris?"

Sweat began to bead in globules on the captive's forehead. The broken glass was only scant inches from his eyes—too close for human flesh to stand. The words seemed to wrench themselves involuntarily from his lips. "An hour past," he gasped.

D'Entreville pressed forward. He had made a breach in the man's silence. He meant to widen it. Questions beat in sharp staccato.

"Was he on horseback, or in a coach?"

"A coach."

"Describe it. Speak out, curse you!"

"His official coach. The green one."

"How many horses?"

"Six."

"How many men?"

"Ten."

"Has he the treaty?"

"I don't know what you speak of."

"*Sandiou!* Yes you do. Shall I give you this glass? Now tell me: has Diego got the treaty?"

"*Si.*"

"That's better. Now, where is he going? What road? Tell me his destination."

"I—I…. *Por el amor del cielo, señor!* Take it away. I shall speak no more. Cut my face to ribbons; gouge out my eyes; my voice is still."

GUY STEPPED back. He was beaten. No matter how much the end justified it, an innate decency prevented him from using the glass. With a sobbed curse, he threw it away.

He looked up to see Cleve casually stroll back into the room. The Englishman's blade was in its sheath, his tongue in his cheek, a small black vial in his gloved hand.

"How's the party going?" he inquired.

Frustration lent fire to d'Entreville's words. *"Corbac,* Cleve! Where have you been?"

Cleve nodded toward the archway. "Exploring," he said easily. "Nobody home except our friend here."

The prisoner cursed. Cleve regarded him cheerfully. Then he walked over and handed d'Entreville the small vial he'd been fondling.

"Candidly, Kitten, I felt that we would waste too much time in making our friend here talkative. So I wandered. And now I know where Don Diego has gone."

Guy had started to inspect the vial, but at the words he looked up. "Where? *Sapristi!* If this is a prank...."

"I don't think so, except possibly a prank of Fate. At any rate, ask our friend whether the Don hasn't left for a sea voyage."

The Spaniard exploded. *"Diablo!* How did you find out? There is no one left to tell, except myself and—"

"Trifle inaccurate," Cleve corrected. He plucked the vial from Guy's fingers and held it up. "Found this upstairs. It had evidently been lost during the rush of departures. But, if one has an intelligent eye, it tells quite a bit concerning the worthy Don."

He chuckled and read the white label affixed to the vial: *Prescribed for Don Diego de Isla. One tablet after meals. A positive remedy for sea-sickness. Compounded by the learned Doctor and Alchemist, Jean Calapso.*

He looked up with a smile. "The fact that a man does not order tablets for sea-sickness unless he intends to take a sea voyage, abetted by the informative reaction of our guest, seems to prove my point, don't you think?"

D'Entreville nodded wisely. "Perfectly, *mon ami,*" he said.

"Well, what are we waiting for?"

They left the Spaniard howling curses and repaired to the stables behind the house. Fortunately, Don Diego had been in too much haste to dispose of his fine collection of blooded horses. They selected two of the best and swung quickly into the saddles.

"Now mark this, Guy," Cleve said, reining in his mount. "We can only hazard as to which port Don Diego is headed for."

D'Entreville nodded. He was perfectly aware of the nebulous quality of their information. "The fact that he is going by sea precludes the possibility of his heading for the border," he said.

"In fact, it seems to establish in my mind that he seeks to shake French soil from his heels as quickly as possible. One does not have to cross water to reach the Spanish border, and the roads are good."

Cleve pulled his plumed hat more firmly over one eye. "I reason the same way," he admitted. "Diego is devious. Mark the way he stole the treaty. If you were he, where would you go?"

"Le Havre. It is the closest port, a route hardly to be suspected in event of an alarm. It lies northwest while the Spanish Border is due south. And as you say, Diego is devious."

The Englishman nodded. "Then it's Le Havre." He shot his companion a meaning glance. "Faith, Guy! We're gambling as if we were gods. If we're wrong about Le Havre…." He let his voice trail.

And then the whir of wings attracted them, and a trio of white dove-shapes burst from the garret window.

"*Mordi!*" Guy exploded. "The Spaniard has freed himself."

"And three carrier pigeons. Damme, Kitten, look! They are heading northwest. Let's away. Those birds are being sent to warn Diego, and if we're right concerning Le Havre—there'll be trouble!"

CHAPTER VII

RIDE, KITTEN, RIDE

CAPITAINE CORDEAU WAS out of temper, for tucked in the folds of his white sash was an order demanding the arrest of Cleve and d'Entreville, and apparently he was not going to have the pleasure of serving it. For over an hour he had led his stumbling squad through the dark streets of Paris; for over an hour, he had suffered one frustration after another. With each passing minute his face grew longer.

Having discovered the unofficial absence of the two fugitives, he had felt triumphant. He had, of course, reported it to Riche-lieu. But now, he was beginning to regret the action.

Richelieu, had been in a towering rage. *"Monsieur le Capit-aine,"* he had said testily, "collect a squad. Bring those trouble-some rogues to me or—don't return yourself!"

Cordeau was beginning to suspect that, as far as his career in the Cardinal's Guard was concerned, he was through. It wasn't a nice feeling and he blamed it all on Cleve and d'Entreville.

The squad marched on. Boots cracked against rough cobbles; rapiers tinkled rhythmically; the torches in the van thrust back the black velvet of the night. They high-lighted the angry, worried flush on Cordeau's cheek. And then, the Western Gate hove into view.

It was open as usual, the soldiers of the watch standing idly around, but upon the appearance of Cordeau's weary squad, they stiffened. A man went into the wall-house to summon the officer in charge. This worthy appeared, sleepy-eyed and curious.

"Oui, Monsieur Cordeau. What brings you here at this hour?"

Cordeau whipped the document of arrest from his sash. It was a precise gesture, made expert by repetition. He was thumb-ing it open when a warning shout shattered the night, to be followed by the wild pound of horses' hoofs.

Then, careening madly around the corner, hunched low in the saddle, came two riders. Two rakish riders who demanded a clear away. Cordeau recognized them instantly—Cleve and d'Entreville! He ran toward them waving his documents of arrest. Cleve was nearest.

"Halt, Stop. Stop in the name of the Cardinal!"

Cleve waved, a laugh on his lips. Cordeau twisted aside just in time to prevent being ridden down. His hand, with the orders for arrest, was still upraised. Cleve's hand licked out and plucked the papers from it.

"Can't stop now, old boy. Thanks."

And then, he was gone, thundering with Guy through the

Gate. Cordeau felt that he had just missed being hit by two lusty cyclones.

"*Sacré nom! Corbac! Sangodemi!*" He whirled, glaring at his men still standing agape at the unexpected rush of the two. "*Parbleu!* Louts! To horse! After them!"

Sergeant Burdet stepped forward. "But, *mon Capitaine,* we have no mounts—"

But Cordeau wasn't reasoning. "What of it? Into your saddles and after them! Come! To horse—er, I mean...." He heard the sergeant's words for the first time. "Well, find some horses. We must pursue!"

But an hour passed before his men were mounted and ready to ride.

DAWN found the two fugitives halfway to their goal. They had been riding like twin furies; pounding recklessly, pausing only long enough to stretch saddle-weary legs and to ask questions. At first, they had been worried. Had they chosen the right road? Was Don Diego actually ahead?

The first stop out of Paris relieved that. The innkeeper said: "A six-horsed green coach, *messieurs? Mais oui.* It passed this tavern. Stopped to change, and then it rolled—rolled like a thunderbolt. You will have to ride if you desire to overtake it. It wasn't idling. I should say it preceded you by almost an hour and a half, *messieurs.* Perchance more."

Cleve flipped the man a coin. The thrill of the huntsman stirred him. They thundered on through the night, and each stop brought fresh encouragement. A coach cannot outrun two glory-bent riders. Now they trailed by an hour... three-quarters of an hour... a half. And then, Guy's horse went lame. That cost them thirty valuable minutes.

Outside of Rouen they slowed a trifle. Cleve looked across at Guy. He pointed a travel-grimed glove.

"Tavern ahead. Do we pass it?"

D'Entreville shook his head. His mount was tiring. He could feel the animal fade beneath his knees.

Cleve nodded. His horse was still strong and seemingly in-exhaustible, but so close was his bond with Guy that it never occurred to him that he should push on alone. Furthermore, recapture of the Treaty was hardly a job for a single man.

They pounded into the court of the tavern as the bright chin of the sun was freeing itself from the eastern horizon The tavern consisted of two stories, fronted by a deserted court. It looked neat and trim and inoffensive. Guy put his hand to his mouth.

"*Hola* the inn!"

Nothing happened. With a curse he slid from his horse and made his way stiffly toward the door. It burst open and a man stepped out. He had a musket leveled. D'Entreville froze and in the background Richard Cleve gave vent to a silent curse. Those pigeons had had time to warn Diego. This was a trap.

"Watch it, Kitten!"

But Guy didn't need the warning. He had recognized the situation. However, Cleve's sudden yell distracted the man with the musket long enough for d'Entreville to make a sudden catlike bound to one side. His fingers snatched for his pistol. The man saw the action from the corner of his eye and pivoted. The musket belched orange flame and Guy felt something tug faintly at his hat.

Then his pistol was free. He fired cross-armed as he turned for his horse. It was a lucky shot. The man dropped the musket and seemed to fold slowly in the middle. He seemed to topple in sections to the ground; first his knees, then his hips, his shoulders and head.

BUT THE shot was a signal, apparently, for a full dozen cut-throats poured into the yard. Guy hurled his empty weapon at the foremost and got one foot in the stirrup.

"*Sangodemi!* A hornet's nest!"

Somebody grabbed his boot. He kicked the man in the face and swung astride. Another bravo sprang forward with a raised blade. There wasn't time to draw and fend off the blow.

D'Entreville set himself. And then, Cleve loomed out of the turmoil. A dazzling flash of steel—and the man went down.

"Let that be a lesson, laddie. Never draw on a defenseless man."

Guy dug his spurs deep. *"Corbac!* Cleve, cease playing and come on!"

Then they were spurring hell-for-leather down the road, leaving the ambushers howling. As they met the base of a gentle hillock, Cleve twisted and looked back. He began to laugh. Guy reined up and regarded him with a frown.

"Pecaire! We elude that trap by the flick of an eyelash! In fact, we're not out of it yet. They'll pursue, and they have fresh horses. What is there to laugh at?"

Cleve pointed back toward the inn. The place had suddenly taken on the aspect of a small battlefield. A stream of eight horsemen had appeared out of the east. As the two cavaliers stared, the first of these engaged Don Diego's hirelings. Guy watched incredulously.

"Sangodemi, Cleve! What's going on back there?"

Cleve laughed again. "Cordeau!" he announced triumphantly. "Old pot-belly himself. Apparently our assassins have jumped him, believing that he's been sent to aid us!"

"Parbleu! Well, I'll be—" Guy roared. He matched Cleve's laughter with his own.

They rode on, after that, feeling almost triumphant. At Quilleboeuf they picked up fresh horses and the information that Don Diego had preceded them by a trifle more than a half-hour. Cleve grinned through the road dust that powdered his face.

"Ten to one we enter Le Havre on his heels, Kitten!"

Guy laughed. The pounding pace had driven nails of fatigue into his joints. He was weary, unutterably tired. And yet, the Englishman's light-hearted challenge seemed to give him fresh strength.

"Taken."

He lifted a flask of spiced wine to his lips; drank deep, thirstily; then, flipped the empty bottle to the waiting groom. "Let's be off!"

But Cleve was destined to lose the jesting wager. They did not enter Le Havre's on Diego's heels. Even as the church spires of that town appeared on the horizon, they were stopped.

IT HAPPENED without warning. A small detachment of soldiers appeared on the highway. Troopers from the fort. The cavaliers slowed their mounts to allow the cavalcade to pass, little dreaming what would happen. The troopers reined up and their officer motioned Cleve and d'Entreville to do likewise.

"Damme! What's this?"

D'Entreville shrugged. "I don't know," he said. "I don't like it."

The officer was very young and inclined toward pompousness. "You ride from Paris, *messieurs?*" he asked.

"Yes."

"And one of you is English and you both serve in the Cardinal's Guard?"

"*Oui.* What of it?"

The officer drew a slip of paper from his glove, consulted it thoughtfully; then motioned his men forward. Cleve frowned.

"Well?" he said.

The officer stared at him. "You are under arrest."

"What?"

The officer moistened his lips. "You are under arrest," he repeated. "In making your escape you forgot that the Cardinal has a carrier-station in Rouen. Orders have just arrived by pigeon to hold two Cardinal's Guardsmen, one an Englishman. You admit to that; therefore I feel safe in assuming that you are Cleve and d'Entreville."

"Let me see that order," Cleve said.

The officer passed it over with a faint smile. The English cavalier scanned it briefly.

"Faith! It's signed by Cordeau. Damme! Old pot-belly is becoming amusingly resourceful."

But d'Entreville wasn't that charitable. "*Sandiou!*" he erupted. "The bungler! Cordeau betrays France! Diego cannot be far ahead and we can stop him." He whirled on the officer. "*Monsieur,* there was been a mistake. We ride on the King's business. The Spanish Ambassador is fleeing the country with vital papers. *Mordi!* You *must* aid us!"

"Sorry, *monsieur le Comte.* My orders are to arrest Lord Cleve and Comte d'Entreville."

"*Sangodemi!* You young fool! There has been a mistake!"

"I doubt it. Capitaine Cordeau's signature is well known at the Fortress of Le Havre. He once held a command here. Present your sword, please."

Guy paused. Then his fingers shot to his hilt, but the trooper behind him understood the intent, and was quicker. His ready blade lifted and settled coldly against the rakehelly's neck. Cleve made no move, for a slight pressure warned him against resistance. There was a trooper behind him also. Guy sat still and cursed. The officer shrugged.

"Must you force me to bind you, *messieurs?*"

There was nothing else to do and Cleve accepted it. He shook his head. "No," he said. "We are very peaceful men." He smiled crookedly. "Especially when there are blades at our backs."

"*Bien,* I felt that you might be impressed by such an argument. Shall we go now?"

CHAPTER VIII

PRISON IS A QUIET PLACE

THE SHORT RIDE to the military prison at Le Havre was accomplished in silence. A listless silence on Guy's part. Coming when their success seemed assured, the sudden dark turn of events had instilled a numb hopelessness in him.

Cleve felt somewhat the same way. But his silence was more thoughtful than despairing. The issue was not settled until Don Diego had left France and as long as he could think, the Englishman was hopeful. Of course, Cordeau's unexpected stratagem of sending pigeons from Rouen had been a heavy blow, but Cleve wasn't through. In his mind there persisted a nebulous, indefinable hope. There was a way to wiggle free of this situation—there had to be.

At the fort the officer ordered them to dismount and led them smartly across the bailey, into the dimness of the prison block.

"Colonel de Chais, the *commandant,* is not here right now, *messieurs,*" he explained, leading them into an iron-bound cell. "I fear you'll be forced to wait a while."

Guy stared dully through the bars as he clanged shut the metal-studded door. He said: "You're acting the fool. This is a mistake."

The officer smiled wisely and shrugged. He went away. They heard the crisp cadence of his heels fading down the corridor—and then, silence.

Guy sighed. He turned from the heavy door and walked over to the room's lone window. He felt tired and sick. But he refused to relax on one of the two wooden cots provided. If he relaxed, his vivid imagination might plummet him further into despair. Cleve suffered none of this disinclination. He collapsed and lay staring face upward.

"Cordeau must be in a devil's frenzy," he mused aloud. "First he rides after us. Then he sends pigeons." He rolled over and propped his head up on the palm of his hand. "Damme! His Eminence must have scared the liver out of him."

But Guy wasn't listening. He stood wearily before the bar-striped window, staring at the many quays of Le Havre spread below in panoramic completeness. The cell was on the second floor near the western bastion. He could see a good distance in either direction. Gradually his eyes lost their listlessness and became probing, inquisitive.

The harbor was a clutter of shipping. Vessels of various nationalities were moored in democratic order. Holland, England, Portugal, France, Sweden. He studied each; then passed on. It was an excellent game, shifting attention from himself and his worries to something more abstract. And then, suddenly, he was staring—trembling like a hunting dog come to point.

A hundred rods or so down the waterfront, moored beside a French ship of war, was a barque. An ill-kept black barque, yellow-trimmed, bearing twenty guns and flying the arrogant gold banner of Spain. But that wasn't what held him.

Parked on the dock beside the vessel was a large green coach. A travel-stained coach with six drooping horses and two attendants garbed in the garish livery of the Spanish ambassador!

HE STEPPED back, his mouth dry, his hands clenched in bitter, impotent anger. Not satisfied with denying him the right to pursuit, Fate seemed bent upon torturing him with the sight of the quarry—from behind bars. He choked back a curse.

On the cot, Cleve frowned. He regarded his tall companion curiously. Then he arose with a sigh and trudged over to the window.

"What's the fuss, Kitten?"

Guy didn't speak. He pointed, his finger trembling slightly as he did so.

Cleve followed the line of the finger and frowned. At first he saw nothing. Then his eyes picked out the Spanish barque, the green coach, and he understood the significance of each.

"Well," he said slowly, thoughtfully, "it seems that we have found Don Diego."

D'Entreville's eyes were bleak, "What of it?"

The Englishman shrugged. "Well, it *should* save us a bit of time once we get out of here."

Guy laughed bitterly. "*Mais oui.* All we have to do is summon that young fool of an officer and say: '*Monsieur,* we have a vital errand to perform. Do you mind freeing us?'" He moved moodily away from the window and sat down. "*Corbac!* Let's not be silly!"

"Faith, Kitten," Cleve said. "We've been in tighter pinches than this." He spoke without shifting his gaze from the barque. "At least, we're not manacled. We have our hands and our wits." His eyes narrowed. "And about two hours in which to use them. Undoubtedly the captain of Diego's ship plans to sail with the tide. By the looks of the water-marks on the jetty it is just coming in."

From the cot Guy said: "*Corbac!* Why speculate. We'll be here to watch him sail. Even free hands and wits aren't breaking the walls of this nest."

"Kitten," said Cleve slowly, "you're a fatalist." He hooked a thoughtful thumb into the folds of his sash and bit his lip. The thumb pressed against something that crackled faintly. And suddenly Cleve's lean face was alight with excitement. "And, by Jupiter! I'm an absent-minded dolt!" he concluded and pulled the paper forth.

It was the document of arrest that he had lifted from Cordeau. There wasn't much to it. Merely a blanket warrant for the joint arrest of Lord Richard Cleve and Guy, le Comte d'Entreville on charges of treason, signed by Cardinal Richelieu and emblazoned with the seal of France. However, it had fanned a plan into flame. A plan so simple and obvious that it was laughable.

CLEVE picked up a tin cup lying atop a stand between the cots, and went to the door. "*Hola!*" he cried. "Hey, jailor! Jailor! Fetch the officer of the guard!"

Guy looked up. "*Parbleu!* What are you bent upon now?"

"Wait and see." Cleve banged the tin cup smartly on the bars. "*Hola* the Jailor! *Hola* the guard! *Hola* anybody!"

"Mad!" d'Entreville muttered and shook his head regretfully. Then suddenly he jumped up, stung by quick realization. "*Sangodemi*, Cleve! You've thought of a ruse, haven't you?"

"That's right." Cleve swept the cup along the door-bars in a clattering crescendo.

"What is it?"

"It's a good plan," Cleve admitted. He chuckled and addressed himself further to the corridor. "Come on, out there! Wake up!"

"Now see here, Cleve! I'm in this as deeply as—"

"All you have to do," said Cleve, "is to follow my lead. We are not ourselves. We are two other fellows. Understand?"

"No."

"Good." He turned back to the door. "Where the devil is the officer of the guard? Oh, there you are. Damme! 'Tis about time. All of you needn't have come."

The young officer, six soldiers and the jailor had arrived simultaneously. The officer was quite red in the face.

"Monsieur Cleve! What is the meaning of this?"

Cleve scowled. "Much! In the first place, I am not Monsieur Cleve. In the second, my comrade is not le Comte d'Entreville. And in the third, you've made an outrageous mistake! Now open up, and let us out!"

The officers trembled with indignation. "*Mordi!* I'll do no such thing!"

Cleve nodded grimly. "I think you will," he said. "Mark me, you've bungled this business from the onset. Without heeding our objections, you have kidnapped us and held us against our will. Damme! *Monseigneur le Cardinal* will be quite interested in learning how his secret agents are treated."

"Secret agents?" blurted the officer.

"Yes. I am Robert de Grisson."

The officer pointed to Guy. "And he?"

Cleve's mouth was thin, but his eyes began to dance. "He is Anastasius Pooh," he replied.

"Who?"

"Pooh," said Cleve. "Anastasius Pooh."

In the background d'Entreville squirmed.

"Ridiculous," said the officer.

"He is, rather." Cleve admitted. "But, make no mistake, *monsieur,* he is very important."

"I don't believe you, *monsieur,*" snapped the officer. "You are Cleve and d'Entreville."

"Really? Have we ever in so many words admitted that?"

"Well—er...."

The officer chewed his lip. "Well—no."

"Of course, we haven't. And why? Because we aren't. That was a conclusion to which you leaped, *monsieur.* You dismissed our protests as ridiculous. We had hoped to present our true credentials to Colonel de Chais, but because he is not here, we have been treated as felons."

"But...." There was a thread of uncertainty in the officer's tone. "But both of you were coming from Paris. It stood to reason that you were the fugitives. In fact, I still think you are."

CLEVE'S voice was soft. He acted the part of a man controlling a deep indignation. In the background Guy stared and tried to figure out how Cleve was going to prove all of this nonsense.

"Mark this, my fine popinjay," snapped the Englishman. "We are not Cleve and d'Entreville!"

"You will have to prove that, *monsieur.*"

"Very well. I shall."

"You have credentials?"

"Of course. But they are of a secret nature and not to be exposed to every subaltern we run up against."

"Then, I am sorry, *monsieur,* but—"

"Now hold on a moment," Cleve said. "I want to ask you one question."

"Very well. What is it?"

"Would Cleve and d'Entreville be carrying the orders for their own arrest?"

"Why of course not," retorted the officer. *"Corbac!* How would they get them in the first place?"

Cleve nodded. "Precisely," he said. Then he produced the papers he had purloined from Cordeau. "Read these, and then open up. We have an important mission to perform and if, through your stupidity, it has been ruined, I can assure you that you won't get off with less than three years imprisonment! "

One glance at the important looking arrest orders was all that the officer needed. His face went completely white. He had made a terrible mistake. The two men in the cell couldn't be Cleve and d'Entreville. The mere fact that they carried the arrest orders for those two proved that. He licked his lips and returned them. He motioned the jailor to open the door.

"This has been a tragic misadventure, *messieurs,*" he said. "If you had mentioned those orders before, this never would have occurred. I did not know that you were secret agents. I trust that you won't be hard, Monsieur de Grisson. I sought only to do my duty."

"We shall see," Cleve said uncompromisingly and stepped out. Behind him, d'Entreville whispered: "Cleve, I could kiss you."

"Try it," the English rakehelly grinned, "and there'll be one less Frenchman."

CHAPTER IX

NO SWORDS FOR STOWAWAYS

THE CHASTENED OFFICER returned their swords and escorted them personally to the gate. He was frightened. He showed it. As they waited for horses to be brought from the stables, he said:

"Messieurs, if there is anything I can do to rectify this embarrassment, please command it!"

D'Entreville grinned crookedly. Here was an unparalleled opportunity to bag Diego. A groom led a horse up to him and he swung lightly into the saddle.

"I desire that you lend me twenty men," he said.

"But of course."

The officer turned to give the necessary orders. Cleve stopped him.

"I doubt that it's necessary," the Englishman said.

Guy's mouth fell open with astonishment. *Sandiou!* Did that crazy Englishman believe that they could tackle Diego and a whole boatload of men—alone? Cleve seemed to sense the undeclared question.

"I fear we'll have to accomplish our mission without official help," he said calmly.

He inclined his head toward the end of the street. A small troop of eight horsemen had just rounded the bend. In the lead was the rotund figure of Monsieur le Capitaine Cordeau.

D'Entreville understood. They had to leave quickly. "You're right, *mon ami,*" he said and touched spurs to his mount.

They left the gate casually, so as not to attract attention, but at the first corner, they increased the gait to a sharp canter. It wouldn't take Cordeau long to set the officer straight about them; and then the whole town would be searching.

"*Corbac!* We must get off the streets," Guy said. "We need a refuge, a place to think."

Cleve nodded. But he didn't answer. His mind was already on the future. Two men pitted against Diego's crew, with Cordeau's soldiers in close pursuit—the odds seemed impossible. Yet that was the way the game had to be played.

"We've played it before," he muttered. "We've—" Suddenly he looked up. "Kitten, do you remember the way we stole into the fortified castle of le Marquis de Beaucaire?"

Guy nodded. *"Oui."*

"Well, we'll try the same scheme on Diego and see what happens. Damme! It has to—"

The dull booming of a cannon interrupted him. It sounded from behind, from the fort. D'Entreville twisted in his saddle.

"Pecaire! The news is out! They'll be swarming after us in a moment."

Cleve frowned. They needed a refuge, a place where they could disguise themselves. They were marked men. He stared up the twisted street and nodded.

"If memory serves me correctly, Kitten, there is a den of iniquity further up this avenue called La Malle. I put up there when I first arrived from England. Papa Renault is accommodating to fugitives and he knows how to keep his mouth closed."

"Bien!" said Guy. "Let's go."

ABOARD the black barque, Don Diego heard the boom of the fortress cannon and frowned. He lumbered across the quarterdeck and stood against the railing.

Since arrival in Le Havre he had been constantly apprehensive. First there was that stupid business with DuBrille. He should have had the body disposed of instead of allowing it to remain as evidence of his visit.

Then there were the pigeons from Paris—Juan Castro's warning concerning Cleve and d'Entreville. He hadn't liked that. Those two rakehellies had tossed dead cats into his plans before. But he had quelled his unease. Now the cannon brought everything to the surface.

"Por Dios," he said to the man beside him, "why can't we up anchor and away? This suspense is torture. That cannon may be a signal."

The ship's captain, Filipe Ariza, shrugged. He was a black-bearded man, garbed for utility rather than display, and possessing the calm confidence of one who knows his business.

He bad been in the harbor of Le Havre for three long weeks waiting for Diego to appear, and it had been a stay not without benefit. He knew the manners and customs of the fort, as though it were his own.

"Be at ease, Excellency. That cannon signifies the escape of a prisoner, a signal for soldiers to return to the fort, and nothing more. As for setting sail immediately, I fear that it is quite impossible. Le Havre is a shallow harbor. To cast off before full tide is to invite running aground. Furthermore, we are not provisioned. Observe the men at work in the waist."

Diego scowled. "This vessel was supposed to be ready to sail at a moment's notice," he snapped. "It was supposed to be provisioned."

"But it was provisioned, Excellency. But you took so unexpectedly long. My men had to eat, and I dared not give them shore leave. Had your warning pigeons arrived a day ago instead of last evening everything would have been ready." He shrugged. "Except the tide."

Diego flushed. Ariza was one of the few who refused to be bullied by him. This, plus the fact that the stocky captain was right, shook the Don with fury. His thick fingers pressed the hilt of his rapier. And then he relaxed. After all, he needed Ariza.

"You are impudent, *señor*," he said harshly. "But I'll let it pass. We are all nervous. Double the porters loading the cargo. Have this tub fit for sea in an hour, and sail at the first opportunity."

Ariza nodded weekly. He had seen the Don's fingers on that swordhilt and had trembled inwardly. "*Si,* Excellency," he said.

Diego was mollified somewhat. He sighed dismally and walked, a vast hulk of a man, down the break in the poop, and into his ornate cabin below. Ariza stared after him bitterly, and then called his first officer and ordered the man to go ashore and pick up more porters.

"Go to the taverns, the pot-houses," he said. "There are always idlers about. Hire ten or fifteen of the husky ones, and bring them back at once. *El Conquistador* must be provisioned fully within the hour."

The first nodded. He had overheard Don Diego's command. "*Si, señor, el Capitan,*" he said.

ARIZA turned to find Pedro Pizon standing next to him. The swarthy aide had just come on deck.

"His Excellency Don Diego commands me to take charge of things, *capitan,*" he said. "What were the orders you gave that man?"

Ariza glowered. If he disliked Don Diego, he loathed his thin-lipped aide. Pizon was arrogant, incompetent, and yet dangerous. Besides that, he was a dandy. A long velvet cape hung from his shoulders, his hat was white with a blue-green plume; his red doublet was studded with seed pearls. Ariza hated dandies instinctively.

"My first officer has gone ashore to hire more porters, Señor Pizon," he snapped. "Would you have rather gone?"

Pizon regarded him sharply; saw the danger in his eyes and transferred his gaze to the yellow sides of the forty-gun frigate moored at the adjacent pier.

The frigate bore the name *La Gloire.* She was a king's ship, flying the white and gold ensign of the budding French navy at her peak, and her clean sharpness of line that bespoke newness and speed. There was a hard, watchful air about her that nettled Pizon.

He turned to mention it to Ariza, but the stocky little master had walked away and was now standing at the far side of the quarterdeck, staring out to sea. Pizon shrugged and dismissed the forebodings that the proximity of the French man-o'-war had inspired.

A quarter of an hour passed. The first officer returned. He brought with him a motley collection of men who stood clustered in the waist staring uneasily at others engaged in stowing cargo. Ariza eyed them disgustedly.

"Por Dios!" he snorted. "I said ten or fifteen men, *señor.* The huskiest."

The first shrugged. "Eight were all that I could gather, *capitan.* In this port the busy people are all busy, and the idlers seem to prefer idleness."

Ariza cursed. He told the first to put the newcomers to work and walked away. But Pizon remained. He found pleasure in watching other men labor.

Two ragamuffins in particular attracted his attention. At first he thought that there was something familiar about them, but closer inspection proved him wrong. *Diablo!* After all, did a gentleman of his station know knaves at sight? Especially, two such utterly disreputable looking knaves as these. No! Of course, not! Nevertheless, they fascinated him.

He watched them idly as they stood at the end of a chain of men engaged in passing articles, hand to hand, from the pier to the hold. Each time a fresh bag or keg was dropped into their arms, their bodies seemed to sag wearily. Strange that men who spent the day in idleness could appear so tired, so seemingly near exhaustion. The Spaniard stared with increasing interest at the two. Labor was torture to them.

Down in the waist, the slighter of the two porters, a brown-eyed man garbed in a seaman's costume that appeared to have been stolen from some hulk's slop-chest, said: "Come on, Pooh. Look alive."

The other gave him a bleak glare. He shifted a ragged boot; crushed it down hard on the other's bare toe.

"Yip!" exclaimed the first.

"Don't call me by that ridiculous name," Guy snapped.

"All right, Kitten."

"Not that, either!"

"Anastasius?"

"Corbac! Take this bag of grain and cease gibbering. *Sandiou,* you and your plans!"

Cleve lowered the grain into the hold. The weight of it

seemed to tear his arms from the sockets. He was dead for sleep. The all-night ride from Paris was exacting a toll. But he smiled.

"Well," he said, straightening, "we're on the ship, aren't we?"

"*Oui.* As miserable, lice-filled porters. *Corbac!* If my revered father could see his son now!"

"He probably wouldn't know you," Cleve replied. His forehead creased. "And I hope no one else will."

CHAPTER X

SEÑOR ENEMY

THEY WORKED STEADILY for another quarter of an hour. Conversation was brief because they needed their breath. There were twenty men engaged in loading and the deck was a clutter of gear and stores.

Occasionally Cleve would dart a glance about and remark some aspect of the scene that would be worth remembering. Back at La Malle Tavern they hadn't had time to formulate a set plan of action. The ship's first officer had appeared with his call for porters even as they had finished donning the ragged disguises Papa Renault had dumped at their feet. Now it was a question of first finding and then taking the treaty. After that, nothing mattered much.

Guy ran the back of his hand across his sweaty forehead. The last cask had been lowered into the hold and the chain of porters broke ranks and stood panting, awaiting new orders. Guy caught Cleve's eye and nodded. In the milling throng two individual's wouldn't be noticed and now was the time to act. The treaty could only be in one place—the master's cabin in the stern.

Cleve gave no indication that he had seen the other's imperceptible nod. He sauntered over to the water-keg lashed to the dock-side bulwark and took a deep draught. Other porters, seeing him, followed suit. He allowed them to elbow him aside;

let them push him toward the mizzen, near the cabin-door. There wasn't a guard posted in sight. He smiled, satisfied.

D'Entreville wandered aft. He stood nearly opposite Cleve, staring idly out to sea, a nondescript figure in striped jersey and baggy sea-breeches.

The bosun piped his whistle to call the porters for their wage. Men tumbled from all sides to fight for a place in line. They attracted the attention of everyone, except the garish figure on the quarterdeck who watched narrowly the two ragamuffins who apparently disdained money.

The two had glided toward the master's cabin. Guy shot a hurried glance over his shoulder. So far they hadn't been noticed. He didn't see Pedro Pizon staring down from above. The French rakehelly grasped the doorknob and pressed it around and the door to the cabin swung inward on silent hinges. They stepped inside.

THE CABIN'S wooden ceiling was low. Its varnished surface caught the reflections of the sunlit wavelets outside and cast rippling radiance over the scene. Silhouetted in stark relief against the afterports lay Don Diego. He was stretched upon the red-cushioned seat which ran the length of *El Conquistador's* stern, snoring loudly with his mouth open.

The cabin was beautifully furnished. There was a thick carpet on the floor, a canopied bed on one side, a table and chairs on the other. Racked beside the door were a brace of pistols, two cutlasses and a musket. Guy unpegged a cutlass. Cleve followed suit. The feel of the heavy weapon in his hand gave him new confidence. They tip-toed across the room and stood looking down on the Spanish noble.

"Beautiful, isn't he?" said Cleve.

Guy nodded. "Like a pig." He placed his cutlass coldly on the Don's fatty throat. "Come come, *mon beau cochon!* Wake up!"

Diego let out a series of short snores which sounded like a ten-gun broadside, smacked his lips and continued to slumber. Cleve slapped him lightly on the stomach. The Spaniard grunted and opened his little eyes. Incomprehension misted them at first; and then he sensed the wrongness of the setting. Two lean-jawed, begrimed faces staring down at him. He started to raise his head, felt the chill edge of Guy's blade, and fell back.

"One chirp, m'lad," said Cleve, "and we'll cut a new mouth in your throat."

Diego frowned. He did not know what this was about, but he did know that he didn't like it. Especially the blade at his throat.

"Dios y Diablo!" he exclaimed. "What is this? Who are you?"

"Two old friends, fatty," said Cleve.

"Mais oui," Guy nodded. "Two old friends who have come all the way from Paris to wish you a fond farewell." His cutlass pressed significantly on the Don's Adam's apple. "A fond farewell, *monsieur*. One way or another. *Comprenez?*"

Recognition widened the other's eyes. He looked first at Cleve and then at Guy. His thick lips formed the word almost silently: "You!"

D'Entreville didn't bother admitting his identity. There was only one thing he wanted. He meant to get it; and then leave as quickly as possible.

"The treaty, *monsieur*. Where have you secreted it?"

Diego's eyes were furious, and he attempted to sit up again. Guy's steady blade deterred him.

Suddenly a voice behind rasped: *"Por Dios!* That applies to you also! Drop those weapons!"

THE TWO cavaliers whirled. Framed in the doorway, backed by a dozen armed seamen, stood Pizon. His blade glinted sharply in the dancing light. Cleve felt his stomach constrict. He shot a quick aside to d'Entreville and advanced.

"Keep the Don entertained, Kitten. I think I'm going to be busy."

Guy nodded silently. He shifted to face the door, but his blade never left Diego's blubbery neck. "Stay your distance, *monsieur,"* he told Pizon. "One move and I'll slice your master's threat like bacon."

Pizon paused uncertainly. Diego cursed him.

"Diablo! Take them, Pizon! They dare not harm me. They seek the treaty and only I know where it is. They have to keep me alive. Come on, you fool!"

Cleve laughed softly. "Damme, yes," he said. "Come on. I have a score to settle with you, laddie."

The door was narrow, and Cleve had counted on that. He tossed aside the besmudged gray cap he'd been wearing; pinched his nose slightly and grinned. Then he advanced further, his blade held carelessly aslant across his thighs.

Pizon licked his lips. He saw the mistake immediately. He should have brought his men into the cabin before challenging. This way he could only bring his blade, and that of the sailor's beside him, against the Englishman. With a curse he tried to rectify the error.

Too late! Cleve met him with a chuckle and a catlike bound! Their steel met in a jarring metallic clash and the Spaniard's slender rapier shattered close to the hilt. He had made the mistake of trying to parry strongly against the solid weight of a cutlass. With a yelp of terror, he bolted back between the two burly seamen.

Cleve kicked at the door to shut it, and failed. The sailors surged forward. He engaged the foremost and slashed the fellow's arm open. Another took his place. After that it was touch and go.

The English rakehelly was unused to the weight of his curved blade. He found it awkward at times. Especially when his rapier-trained reflexes attempted whip-like ripostes or feints. A quick *binde* was likewise hampered. He found it safer to play with the cutlass' basic advantages. The jabbing thrust, the slash, the chopping parry. But those tactics were draining his scanty reserve. Tiring rapidly, he retreated and more sailors poured through the door.

"Shouldn't stay up so late of nights," he reprimanded himself hoarsely. He wore a ghastly grin.

Then Pizon reappeared. He hadn't had time to fetch a new blade, but there was a thick belaying pin in his fist. Cleve tried to duck as it spun suddenly toward him. Fatigue slowed his reactions. The pin struck, and he pitched forward, senseless.

IT ACTUALLY seemed as though he had blinked his eyes, so fast did time fly in the pit of unconsciousness. Later d'Entreville told him that he'd been out for the best part of twenty minutes. It didn't seem so.

He came to with amazing suddenness. All at once everything seemed to clear and he was lying on the floor, tightly bound and staring at the sun-patched ceiling. Overhead on the quarter he heard the tramp of men's feet and the faint sound of cheering. The floor seemed to be canted slightly. He was still in the master's cabin.

With a faint frown he tried lifting his head. A stab of pain behind his ear reminded him where the pin had struck. The pain subsided and became a dull ache, and now it didn't bother him. Paradoxically he felt rested.

He discovered Guy kneeling on the rug a few paces away, pouring liquor out of a bottle. Cleve rolled over on his side. He found that they had bound him with three separate ropes. One held his hands locked flat to his stomach; another drew his elbows tight against his sides—he could feel the tautness of it across the small of his back—and the third held his bare ankles together. D'Entreville was trussed in a similar fashion. Cleve sighed.

"Faith, Kitten," he muttered, "you're wasting good liquor pouring it out that way. What do you think you're doing?"

The Frenchman looked up. He was sweating. Getting to his feet and then to the sideboard where the bottle had stood, had been strenuous work.

"How do you feel, Cleve?" he asked.

"All right." He frowned as the floor rose and fell under him. "What's happened?"

D'Entreville nodded toward the afterports. "We're under way," he replied. "Everyone is up on deck waving goodbye. They bound us and left us here for future reference."

"Considerate of them. Did Pizon crown you with a belaying pin, too?"

Guy scowled. "No. When you went down, I left Diego to keep the vermin from pinning you to the floor. Diego threw that beef of his at me from behind and knocked the legs from under me. After that I didn't stand a chance. Ten men were on my body before I could swear."

"Hmmm. Damme, I fear we botched this enterprise beautifully. I still can't understand how Pizon appeared so opportunely."

Guy cursed fluently for a moment. "The pig was watching us from the poop," he finally concluded.

THEN he placed the empty liquor bottle between his knees and strained toward the piece of paper on the floor beside him. Cleve sat up with an effort.

"Faith, Kitten, what are you trying to do?"

"Pecaire! The only thing that is left to do," the Frenchman gasped. He finally succeeded in grasping the fold of paper with the tips of his fingers and straightened with a sigh. "I took this paper from you while you lay unconscious."

"Ah. So it's robbery now, eh?"

Guy ignored him. He stuffed the paper into the neck of the bottle.

"So that's what you're about," the English cavalier exclaimed suddenly. "That paper is the document for our arrest. You plan to use the sea as a messenger,"

D'Entreville nodded. *"Oui.* I understand that it is a law that bottles containing messages must be picked up and delivered. Well, I consider a slim chance better than none. We aren't out of the harbor yet. The chances of this message being picked up are excellent. The mere fact that it is official-looking should bring it before the proper authorities; and if Cordeau reads it—"

"Faith, that's giving Cordeau the benefit of the doubt," interposed Cleve. Then he struggled to his knees. "We ought to put something in it to identify this vessel. Damme! Even if Cordeau does understand that we're at sea, he won't know where to look."

His eye caught the table standing across the cabin from him. Then he grinned, dropped to his side, and rolled heavily across the floor. He brought up against the foremost table-leg with a jarring crash. A silver spoon tinkled to the rug. He stared at it and sighed with relief.

"It bears the ship's monogram," he said. *"El Conquistador—* Cadiz." He inched his way around to seize the spoon and sat up, sweating, the silver implement firmly in his grip. "Kick the bottle over here," he panted.

D'Entreville complied. The Englishman rammed the spoon down the thick glass neck and reinserted the cork firmly. He banged it twice, awkwardly, against the floor. Then he tucked the container hard against his body and commenced to roll toward the afterports in the stern.

"Sangodemi, Cleve!" Guy suddenly blurted. "Make haste! They're leaving the quarterdeck. Coming back!"

Cleve reached the seat under the after-ports. He could hear the thud of feet approaching. He felt bruised and winded.

"Feel like a damned bowling ball," he gasped.

With a superhuman effort, he got his legs beneath him and surged to the red-cushioned window seat. The cabin door rattled. He rolled over; the bottle cracked through the glass of the ornate port and dropped free. The splash of its landing was faint. He turned and found Don Diego eying him suspiciously from the doorway.

"You English swine! What are you doing beside that port?"

Cleve grinned. The pent up energy went out of him. "Resting," he said easily. "Merely resting, old boy."

Diego advanced. *"Por Dios!"* he snapped. "Then you'll rest where you belong—in the hold!" He beckoned to the seamen behind him. "Get these pigs out of here."

CHAPTER XI

DINNER FOR THOSE WHO DIE

THE WHINING CREAK of *El Conquistador's* timbers was the only sound that reached Cleve as he lay sprawled in the dark depths of the ship's afterhold. Through the lifted hatch he could discern the first bright gems of the coming night. Stars distant—distant as freedom. He considered them bleakly.

D'Entreville cursed. He sat up and mashed a cockroach which had somehow wiggled inside the leg of his baggy pants, and scratched. In the dim light his lean features were darkened by a week's beard. He was scowling. His despondency was deeper than Cleve's because he had given up hope sooner.

If that bottle—their slender chance of success—had been picked up, *El Conquistador* would have been stopped before this. *Sandiou!* That was the only way to look at it. As for escape, well, what could two men do, chained to the wall and far at sea.

"Well, Cleve?"

The Englishman shrugged. He didn't feel like talking. In fact, he no longer felt like thinking. He plucked a straw from the crude mattress upon which they were lying and inserted it between his lips. Of course, when they landed in Spain there was a possibility of ransom or escape, but until that time they could do nothing.

D'Entreville stood up. The long chain that manacled his wrist clanked faintly. He stared longingly up at the hatch.

"Mordi! Diego's a monster. A week we've been in this stinking hole! A week! *Le bon Dieu!* I feel like a mud-slimed pig!"

Cleve nodded. "I too feel like something one finds under rocks," he admitted. "But, damme, Kitten, it can't last much longer. This infernal voyage has to end somewhere."

D'Entreville sat down again. Three days ago he had offered Don Diego his parole to be allowed to walk the decks and breathe in the cool sweet air of the day. The fat Don had laughed and kicked him brutally.

"Mais oui," d'Entreville said now. "This voyage will end, true enough. And then what? *Corbac!* I'll tell you, Cleve! Spain will send her bloody armies into—"

"One moment, Kitten. We've suffered that once today."

Guy sagged. "Sorry, Cleve, I'm overwrought."

A smoking yellow lantern appeared in the hatchway. Guy looked up. It was probably the beetle-browed bosun bringing their supper.

"Tonight I'll have filet mignon and nothing less," he called.

"Bueno, señor. Perhaps I can do even better than that by you."

IT WAS Pedro Pizon, smiling evilly and walking toward them. He was dressed loudly in yellow—yellow breeches and thigh-high Cordovan boots. He had five men with him.

"Parbleu! If it isn't the fop in person."

Cleve sat up and grinned. "That color suits your temperament, Pizon."

The Spaniard's boot dropped back for a vicious kick. Then he seemed to catch himself. He shrugged and turned to his men.

"You know what to do," he said. "Get on with it."

Cleve braced himself, not knowing what to expect. For some reason, Pizon had singled him out in previous instances to vent his cruelty upon. Was this another? Apparently not. The five men converged. One drew forth a large key and unlocked the manacle that held his wrist. Another tugged at his filthy shirt. Cleve arose struggling.

"Damme! What is this? What's coming off here?"

"Your clothes," Pizon said. "Tonight Don Diego has decided to dine with swine. But you must be clean first. Your present condition would turn any gentleman's stomach."

Dinner with Diego! *Pecaire!* That didn't sound right, and yet he seemed to mean it. D'Entreville chuckled bitterly. "Is this a joke?" he asked.

"No, *señor*. You have my word that it isn't."

"Well, I'll be damned," said Cleve.

The rough but efficient toilet took nearly a half-hour. The clothes which Pizon had brought were not fine, but they were clean. The feel of them was good. Breeches, a linen shirt open at the throat, and a pair of worn sea-boots. By good luck more than good management, Guy received a wide leather belt. Cleve had to be satisfied with a twist of rope.

Pizon approached as they stood adjusting their new garments. The swarthy Spaniard patted the silvered pistol that snuggled in his sash.

"Mark this, *señors*. I am armed. Every man aboard *El Conquistador* is armed. We are far at sea. There is no possibility of escape. I tell you these things so that you'll not attempt tricks when you join Don Diego. Understand?"

Cleve nodded. He had been trying to puzzle out the situation without much success. This business didn't add up. "I understand," he said.

But Guy refused to recognize the futility of questions. He said: "Why does Diego suddenly thirst for our company, Pizon? He seems to have fared well enough without it until now."

The Spaniard chuckled. "You'll see, *señor. Por Dios!* You'll see!" And that was all that he'd say.

THEY were sent up out of the hold under watchful eyes and made stand against the bulwarks while the hatchway was being closed.

The sea was a carpet of sable, and overhead the sky was glittering with stars. The first wind of the evening had died, and

El Conquistador barely rippled ahead. Gone was the forward surge that had marked its earlier passage.

D'Entreville took a heady lungful of air and looked at Cleve closely. "I don't understand this," he muttered. "I don't trust it."

"Faith, and that makes two of us. But whatever the game, Kitten, we'll play. Maybe something will happen."

The speaker looked down at his boots. One toe was touching a yellow coil of rope. The coil had one end looped firmly around a cleat and lay but scant inches from the open slot of a deck-drain. He acted without thinking. His toe moved slightly and the rope snaked through the drain to trail softly in the water. Then Pizon came up and ordered them to precede him to the master's cabin in the stern.

The table was set for five, garish with ornamentation and foodstuffs. It was dazzling to the two half-starved wretches who saw it. Don Diego was already seated, his bloated face smiling in the saffron wash of the lanterns. He didn't bother to arise.

"Ah! The guests of honor," he greeted them. "Enter, *señors.*"

They stood blinking on the door-sill, unused to the lights; and then the sailors behind gave them a brutal shove and they staggered forward. Guy turned hotly. Cleve gripped his arm.

"Temper, m'lad. Temper."

Guy relaxed. He glared hard at Diego. "*Sangodemi!* So this is the way a Spanish noble treats his prisoners, eh?"

Don Diego lifted a wineglass in his jeweled fingers. He had already spilled a few drops on the froth of lace of his collar, and it was apparent by his careful deliberation that he was more than a trifle drunk.

"I don't know what you are talking about, *señor,*" he replied with a shrug. "After all, I am giving you a banquet. What more could you ask. *Por Dios!* 'Tis a great deal more than you deserve."

Cleve sat down. The week in the hold hadn't left much patience in him, but his face didn't betray it. He said: "Let's put out cards down, Diego. What's the purpose of this?" He gestured to include the heavily ladened table.

THE SPANIARD drained his wineglass and patted his sensual mouth daintily with his handkerchief. Pizon had taken up a position beside him; two armed ship's officers lounged alertly against the latticed afterports, and near the door, so far unnoticed, stood Capitan Ariza. The Don's little eyes were taunting.

"Tonight," he said slowly. "Tonight, *señors*, you will be amused by us. Tomorrow, we shall be amused by you."

"A neat play on words," Cleve nodded. "What does it mean?"

Diego laughed thickly. "Mean? *Diablo, señor.* It means that I'm giving you a farewell banquet. I am a man of whims, you see. Tomorrow you hang! *Si.* Both of you—from the highest yardarm. Did you think for a moment that you could cross me and live? Ah no, I'm not that sort. My father used to say: 'Be generous to your enemies, but always kill them!'" He nodded his great head soberly. *"Bueno.* Tonight I am generous."

"Why you—" With a strangled cry d'Entreville surged forward. Behind him Ariza jerked out a pistol. The *capitan's* arm flashed up, then down. He struck with the thick barrel of the weapon. Guy collapsed over a chair.

"Pick up your friend," Diego directed Cleve. "Mayhap that will teach him manners. Carry him to the window seat and revive him."

Cleve had gone tense, but upon the words he relaxed and nodded. There wasn't much else he could do. He hooked his arms under Guy's limp form and carried it aft. The two men standing there drew aside. There was a faint trickle of blood near the temple where Ariza's pistol had struck. Cleve blotted it with the cuff of his sleeve. He patted Guy's cheeks, massaged his wrists.

D'Entreville stirred slightly. The blow had been more efficient than vicious. Cleve darted a hurried glance over his shoulder. Their captors were ignoring them. A new wine bottle had been broken and a toast was being given to Ariza for his quick act.

The Englishman was thinking fast. Diego had a subtle cruelty that could become fiendish. Undoubtedly it would make the banquet a ghastly business as the evening wore on. Cleve knew that he couldn't take much more and remain rational. He had to get out—now. They weren't taking him back to that foul hold to wait death in the morning.

D'ENTREVILLE moaned slightly. Cleve clamped a cautious hand over his mouth. From the time he had slyly kicked that coil of rope overboard, the mad plan which had unconsciously inspired it, had gradually been taking form. It was a chance—a long, desperate chance. But, it was better than nothing.

"Kitten?"

D'Entreville's eyes opened. They were clear. He frowned slightly at Cleve's hand.

"Listen, Guy," the Englishman said. "They aren't watching now. They don't think we'll try anything." He took his hand away.

D'Entreville said, *"Pecaire,* my head." Then, he nodded. "Go ahead, *mon ami.* What is it?"

There wasn't much time and Cleve realized it. "Look, Guy, I know you can't swim. But I can. We're going over the side, right now. There's a rope trailing in the water. The port behind you is open. We hit through it together, and hold tight to me. If we miss that rope we're fish-food. Understand."

"Oui. It's better to be fish-food than rope-bait anyway."

"Good."

Don Diego's rich voice called, "Is that cursed friend of yours awake?"

Cleve straightened. He turned leisurely and regarded his captor. A good ten paces separated him from the nearest of the Spaniards. With a faintly traced smile he nodded and pinched his nose lightly. Behind he could feel Guy sitting up; growing tense. The Kitten was deathly afraid of the water, and he knew it. He was well named, Cleve thought.

He said to Diego, "He is awake, fatty, I just want to take this opportunity to bid you a fond adieu. Your food would probably be lousy anyway."

And then, with a laugh, he whirled. "Better to drown than hang!"

They seemed to go through the latticed port as one man; locked firmly together. They left a stunned tableau behind. But Diego reacted instantly. To have his prey escape vengeance so quickly, so bravely, enraged him.

He dashed for the afterport roaring curses. He pulled two pistols from his sash and sent bullets down into the stygian waters. Pizon came up beside him and followed suit. But it was a futile gesture. The prisoners were gone, swallowed up by the deep. Diego threw his pistols away. He felt cheated.

CHAPTER XII

MADMEN DON'T DROWN

"DON'T STRUGGLE! RELAX!" Somehow Cleve managed to gasp those words before he and Guy dented the black surface. And then they were plunging into it. Down, down, deeper into the chill depths with the pressure roaring in their ears.

Cleve's grip did not lessen. When he felt d'Entreville stiffen with fear, he jerked once, commandingly, and the Frenchman subsided.

They came to the surface. For Guy it was like coming back to life. The ornate stern of *El Conquistador* towered castlelike over them, spotting blobs of yellow on the water with her lights. They could hear voices calling questions from her quarter. Then the afterports burst open and Don Diego's pistols began to spout. Pizon followed with his. The balls went wide.

The towering ship began to glide away and terror crowded into Cleve's throat. The rope—where was the rope? With Guy clutching firmly to his neck, his movements seemed leaden.

Then he felt the rope rasping wetly alongside his cheek. Faith! What luck! He had gauged the direction of their plunge almost to the inch. They had landed almost atop it. Blessing the ship for making such slow headway, he gripped the slender line, and d'Entreville did the same.

Through the blackness they heard Ariza say: "Shall I come about, Excellency, and lower a boat?"

"Dios y Diablo! Of what use would that be? In this pitchy night it would be difficult to locate a full-rigged ship, much less two suicidal fools. No. They are lost. Let them drown."

Cleve breathed a sigh of relief. Then, with d'Entreville following close behind, he pulled himself hand over hand through the water until Diego's cabin hung like a balcony overhead.

"Corbac!" chattered Guy close by his ear, "this is a stupid time for me to learn how to swim." He chuckled quietly. *"Sandiou,* it isn't bad, though. Not bad at all. What next, Cleve?"

The Englishman frowned. It was certain that they couldn't hang on the rope forever. The water-pressure caused by the ship's passage would soon weary them into letting go. Already his arms were beginning to feel the strain. He cast about him desperately.

The ship's rudder loomed on his right. Looped midway and running from it to the black hawse-hole above him were the thick links of the rudder chain. From his position it was hopelessly out of reach. But wait!

FILLED suddenly with an idea, he looked over his shoulder at Guy. First they had to get their arms free for work, and that couldn't be accomplished as long as they were forced to cling to the rope.

"Look, Kitten," he said softly, "reach behind you with one hand and give me that part of the rope which trails."

Without a word the Frenchman obeyed. He handed Cleve a sodden loop.

The Englishman said, "Now hold me while I tie a noose under our shoulders."

"Parbleu! Why?"

"To take the drag off of our arms. Here, one moment. Ha! That does it. You can relax now, Kitten, but keep your arms lapped over the rim."

"Sandiou! Don't call me Kitten. What next?"

"Well, we'll kick off our boots, then take our shirts and belts and knot them together into a crude rope. Then, we'll try to loop them around the rudder chain overhead."

"And then what?"

"And then, we'll steer the ship back to France," Cleve snapped peevishly. "Don't ask so many fool questions and let's get busy."

It took nearly a half-hour. The drag of the line and the weight of the water hampered their movements. Cleve was almost about to give up, when d'Entreville surged half his length out of the sea and looped the improvised line over the chain. Now came the devilish part of the business. Would the damn thing hold?

Above they could hear the noise of Diego's party. In a sense it was a blessing, for it had muffled the sounds of their struggle. But it was nearing an end. Too much liquor was beginning to thicken voices into incoherency. Eventually there would be snores and then silence.

"You had best try it first, Cleve," Guy muttered. "You are lighter."

The Englishman nodded. But he considered it wiser to wait a bit. The ship was beginning to settle down for the night and the fewer people astir the better. Besides that, they both needed a rest. They lay back against the pull of the encircling noose and trailed comfortably. Fortunately the water wasn't cold.

"It has occurred to me," d'Entreville said after a pause, "that the moment we put our weight on the rudder chain, the helmsman will become aware of it. He'll feel it through the wheel and raise an alarm."

Cleve frowned and bit his lip. He had noticed that the wind was freshening. The pull of their towline was increasing. In one way that was good. The pressure of water against the rudder would counteract any strain they might throw on the chain when they clung to it. But, by the same token, the pressure would hold them more tightly, hinder their movements.

"It's a chance we'll have to take, Guy," he said. "If you will notice, we don't have to perch on the chain long."

"*Mordi!* What do you mean?"

"Look above the rudder chain's hawse-hole, a trifle to port. What do you see?"

D'ENTREVILLE craned his neck. He frowned. Above the hawse-hole, dim in the night, was the vague outline of a closed gun port; a stern-chaser gun on the low deck beneath the master's cabin.

"*Pecaire!* Is it open?"

"I think so. It juts out along the base; doesn't lay flush to the stern. Damme! 'Tis worth trying anyway."

D'Entreville grabbed him as he reached for their improvised rope. "Look, Cleve, you do it alone. I'll hang here on the end of this towline. No sense in alarming the helmsman too much. If you make it, toss down a line and I'll come up without touching the rudder chain."

Cleve nodded. "Agreed." Then, he gripped their line of shirts and belts. The quickening rush of the sea sucked hungrily at his body as he pulled himself upward. The makeshift rope stretched sickeningly. His shoulder muscles ached with the strain and the breath grew hot in his throat. But finally his dripping fingers closed around the cold links of the anchor chain, to send a thrill of triumph through him.

From the quarterdeck faint voices drifted down to him. "*Por Dios!* We've struck something there with the rudder!"

"How so?"

"It jerked suddenly to port beneath my hand, *señor.* Ah! There she has become free again."

Cleve, working quickly, had whipped his body across the

The roar was deafening,
and Cleve felt himself
lifted from the deck
and flung out to sea.

chain, placed steadying fingers against the stern and had taken his weight from the links by placing one foot on a large iron stud in the sternpost and the other against the outer lip of the hawse-hole. He stood astraddle in this delicate position while his eager fingers stretched for the gun port further to the left.

As he had suspected, it was loose, having become warped slightly. But it was difficult to open. He stood there, quivering with the strain of his position, while he fought to work the obstinate thing free. Below Guy watched with his heart pounding thunderously in his throat. Should Cleve slip now, it would be all over.

But Cleve didn't slip. Almost sobbing, he worked at the stiff gun port. And then it gave suddenly and his bleeding fingers curled tightly around the sill.

After that there wasn't much trouble. By inching his grip, moving first one arm and then the other, he managed to wedge the port open further. The gaping muzzle of the stern-chaser complicated things slightly, but with a dextrous twist of his body he slid in past it and slumped secure on the floor.

When he had regained his breath, he stared around him. It was dark, but as his eyes became used to it, he could make out objects. The room in which he found himself seemed to serve a multiple purpose. A lazarette, a gun cabin and a powder room. Roundshot were racked around the wall and three great hogsheads of powder were set about the steering drum. He didn't pause to investigate further, because his fingers had brushed that which he had been instinctively searching for—a coil of rope.

"Pssst! Here you are, Kitten!"

Guy's white fate peered up from the black background of the sea. He caught the rope which Cleve cast him and hauled himself up it with quick business-like heaves of his arms.

CHAPTER XIII

GHOSTS IN VELVET

FOR THE BETTER part of ten minutes they lay beside the stern-chaser, two bedraggled figures, glistening, half-naked, and too weary to speak or even congratulate each other.

The cant of the flooring told of a freshening breeze; the earlier calm had ended. Except for the increasing creak of the rigging and timbers, the barque made headway in silence. In the cluttered gun room nothing but the rasp of their breathing disturbed the stillness.

Finally, Guy sat up. He was cold, shivering. His voice came shakily between chattering teeth.

"*Sangodemi!* The first thing we do is find some clothes. I don't know how you are, Cleve, but I'm practically naked."

Cleve spoke without moving, without even opening his eyes. A great lassitude seemed weighted on him. But there was no suggestion of it in his tone.

"Damme," he snorted. "You learn to swim, avoid a disagreeable banquet, and still complain. Faith, next time I decide to leap off ship-sterns, you stay home."

Guy crossed arms over his bare chest and massaged his biceps vigorously. "Very funny," he grunted. Warm blood began to circulate through his shoulders. He stood up. "I wonder if they keep clothes down here? *Parbleu!* It's so black I can scarce see my hand in front of my nose."

"*Your* eyes should be excellent in the dark," Cleve sighed. He rolled over. "Kitten."

A wet palm reached out of the darkness and clipped the speaker smartly on the stomach.

"Ouch! That hurt!"

"*Pecaire!* 'Twas supposed to."

"Well, where are you going now?"

The Frenchman had stepped around the breech of the stern-chaser and was now groping blindly through the cabin. He didn't answer Cleve's question. A dull thud and a stream of subdued blasphemies were the result of his stubbing a toe against a large sea-chest. Then there came an exclamation of triumph, followed by the glint of flint on steel, a puff of flame, and wavering light. He'd chanced upon a box of candles and a tinder-box.

"*Corbac!*" he exclaimed. "That is much better."

"Especially for your toes," Cleve said.

He sat up, rubbed his eyes. The parts of the cabin which had been previously obscured became apparent. He noted with satisfaction the single door up forward; its reassuring thickness and its heavy lock. Besides being a gun and powder room, the cabin appeared also to be a luggage compartment. The trunks of Diego, Pizon and retinue were piled neatly in a corner.

"Faith! Besides offering their hospitality, Diego and Pizon now offer us their wardrobes. You know, Kitten, perhaps we've been doing an injustice to those rats."

D'Entreville frowned slightly. Although they were safe

enough for the nonce, their hoarse whispers resounded hollowly through the silence of the room. It was dangerous.

"Speak more softly, Cleve." He regarded the pieces of baggage and smiled. *"Pecaire!* We may die before the night is out, but by the Devil, we'll die in style!"

WITH the efficiency of professional thieves they looted the trunks. They hauled an impressive display of finery from the chests. Cordovan boots of softest leather, plumed hats, collars of Venetian lace, silver-slashed doublets, velvet capes, jeweled rapiers, daggers, and even breastplates and morions. They pawed through the mass, cheerfully making their selections.

Finally arrayed in a costume of forest-green, d'Entreville stepped back. There were buckles of silver on his russet-colored boots. The sword that hung at his hip was silver-hilted and his broad-brimmed hat was gray with a yellow plume.

"Cleve," he said, grinning, "as one fop to another, how do I look?"

The Englishman studied him critically. "Too conservative," he decided shortly. "Now take me for example. Blue cape, scarlet doublet and breeches, white boots. Frankly, you can't really look at me without holding your ears."

" 'Tis rather loud," Guy agreed.

"Understatement. This costume shrieks. It's one of Pizon's, I'll warrant. Ah, here's the prescription." The speaker bent down and plucked a gold medallion from one of the gaping chests. He strung it on his chest.

"What's that for?" d'Entreville wanted to know.

"Bravery, Kitten. It takes courage to appear in these clothes. Dammc! I feel like a blasted butterfly."

… They hadn't a set plan as they stole softly out of the gun room and down the slanted corridor toward the mizzen companionway. At the foot of it, Cleve gripped d'Entreville's arm tightly and murmured: "Faith, Kitten! Are we just going to walk up to Don Diego's cabin and request the Treaty and our liberty?"

In the starlight that sifted down through the deadlights above, Guy's face was hard. There was a challenge in his eyes. He nodded.

"Something like that," he replied softly. "I have a sword now. I can get him before he gets me with his crew. The Treaty will be destroyed by then." He shrugged. "Dying won't be so difficult." Then he smiled faintly. "As for you, *mon ami*—stay here. I'm a Frenchman, this is for France."

Cleve's lips were twisted sarcastically, but his eyes displayed open admiration. "And you're just enough of a fool to go out that way! A damned show-off."

Guy shrugged. "If I destroy the Treaty, I've served my purpose. *Pecaire!* Have you a better plan?"

The Englishman nodded. "Certainly. Let's take the ship!"

"*What?*"

"Let's take the ship. Damme! I'm in the mood for exercise anyway."

"*Sangodemi,* Cleve! Have you lost your sense entirely? I know that you have always been touched with madness, but think, man! There are only two of us."

Cleve grinned.

"You've been counting, I see. Of course, there's only two of us. But, we're such exceptional fellows, Kitten!"

"Nonsense. *Mordi!* Such insanity! Two men capturing a fully manned barque."

Cleve's voice came soft through the murk. "Want to wager, Kitten?"

"*Parbleu!* The odds are a thousand to one."

"I'll take them. Mark this, the crew is asleep. The Watch will expect nothing." He paused. "Well, Guy. What do you say?"

"I say it's utterly mad," d'Entreville muttered; and then he chuckled. "But, *mordi!* I'm a trifle mad myself. Let's be about it, Cleve. I'll take the starboard and you the port, we'll meet on the quarterdeck." He paused uncertainly and added: "I hope!"

AS THEY went out on deck, they met an ear-ringed seaman, who upon seeing Cleve's gaudy costume, tugged respectfully at his forelock and bowed.

"Good evening, Senor Pizon."

Cleve's fist flashed briefly, descending on the nape of the man's neck. "Good evening my man," he said, and caught the sailor's limp body. He looked up at Guy. "First come, first served, Kitten. Pull the fellow into the shadow of the companion and bind and gag him,"

Then he strolled leisurely down the deck. D'Entreville stared after him and cursed. He jerked the sailor down the companion, cut a length of rope into segments and tied him securely. After a hurried check, he looped the rest of the line around his waist and returned to deck.

He found Cleve leaning nonchalantly against the starboard bulwark, staring idly out to sea.

"There were only two watches forward," he said. "As an added precaution I bolted the forecastle companionway from the outside."

"What did you do with the watches?"

"Dragged them here. There at my feet. Care to truss them up, Kitten? I believe I'll go aft and have a talk with the helmsman."

"Ah, no!" D'Entreville disengaged himself from the rope and handed it to the Englishman. "Tie them yourself. Do you want to hog all of the fun? Besides, we agreed on a plan of action. I was to take the starboard and you the port. What happened?"

"There wasn't anyone on the port," Cleve muttered.

He bent down and began binding his victims. Guy walked away. A thick, threatening silence lay over the ship. Suddenly, from the quarter came a short cry, and then an indistant thud. Cleve, his fingers darting through a series of intricate knots, stared apprehensively over his shoulder. Had that stifled outburst been noticed, or had the men below slept through it undisturbed? Then he stiffened.

"Egad! I had forgotten you!"

There was a dark figure cautiously descending the forward rat-lines, moving stealthily against the lift and sway of the rigging. The lookout from the tops! Apparently, the fellow had watched the slugging from his perch, and having decided that silence was the better part of valor, was now attempting to sneak an alarm to his sleeping comrades below.

"But I don't think we shall allow you that privilege," the English rakehelly breathed.

He fondled the belaying-pin he had been using with note-worthy results and slunk along the bulwarks. He met the man as he landed. Straightening swiftly, Cleve said: "Let's be star-gazers, m'lad," and swung. The lookout suddenly lost his ambition.

THREE minutes later Guy stood beside him, panting slightly. "I lashed the wheel," he reported. "*Sandiou!* It was a close call, though."

Cleve rose from the tightly bound lookout. "What happened?"

"*Mordi!* There were two of them on the poop—the helmsman and the first officer. The First was in a chair. I thought he was asleep, but as I bludgeoned the helmsman, the villain jumped me. I feared he would raise the ship before I silenced him."

"You silenced him, and that is the important business, Kitten."

"*Oui*, I suppose so. Look, Cleve, as I stood there on the quarter an idea struck me. Why not load these wretches into the long-boat and set them adrift. We can throw them a poniard and a few provisions. It will take them off our hands."

Cleve nodded. That would be the safe way to play it. "All right," he agreed. "Take care of that, Guy, while I set to work insuring our conquest of the deck."

"What do you mean?"

Cleve smiled in the starlight. He had been acting on impulse as he went along, but now he had a plan clearly in mind.

"Merely this," he said, "there are two light carronades up in the bow, and I think they'd look much handsomer set in the poop. You can sweep the whole ship from the poop."

D'Entreville chuckled as he saw the other's intent. *"Bien,"* he said. "As soon as I'm finished here, I'll help you. There is a demi-culverin on the quarterdeck already."

"Faith! Now *that* was very kind of the ship's designer," said Cleve, and glided away.

It took them three-quarters of an hour to accomplish their respective missions. Three quarters of an hour in which the sweat of labor and growing apprehension drenched their bodies and their clothes. D'Entreville found that lifting squirming men over the side and into the davited longboat on the poop was strenuous exercise. Added to this, on two occasions, he had been forced to leave the task to stalk sailors who had appeared unexpectedly to stand watches.

"Pecaire! Never saw so many cases of insomnia," he complained.

And Cleve—Faith! The bow-carronades belied their classification as light guns; they were anything but that. Short, squat little weapons with large bores and heavy bases, they could not be lifted by one man. He was forced to take them apart, lug them to the quarterdeck, and reassemble them again.

He was completing the job as d'Entreville cautiously lowered the longboat and cut the lines. Then they met for a short conference. A council of war.

"We need powder and ball," Cleve said. "I'll like to turn that culverin behind us, but the noise would wake Diego."

D'Entreville nodded. *"Oui.* We've been uncommonly lucky until now. It's best not to press it. Are the carronades loaded?"

"About two charges apiece."

"Peste! That isn't sufficient. Wait here, I'll see if we can't remedy it."

He turned without giving Cleve opportunity to protest and glided down the break in the poop and across the deserted decks. Amidships he paused before a dark companionway, drew his rapier and disappeared from the Englishman's view.

Perhaps five minutes elapsed before he emerged. During that time Cleve stood gripping the pooprail, straining his ears to catch any sound besides the sail-whispers of the sleeping barque, and praying.

D'Entreville had found the ship's magazine. He staggered to the quarterdeck, bent beneath the weight of a canvas bag crammed with powder, ball and muskets.

"Parbleu!" he gasped lowering the load. "I feel like a cursed Atlas." He smiled grimly and pointed to the munitions, then to the carronades placed on the port and starboard sides of the quarter. "But, I also feel safer. We control the poop. Let them come!"

CHAPTER XIV

THE SLEEPING BEAR AWAKES

BUT CLEVE WASN'T satisfied. It was true, that for the first time in over a week, fortune had smiled. But how long would that smile last? Suddenly the futility of their position struck him. What was the next move? Where did they go from here? They were two against four-score men. Anything could happen.

"Faith," he murmured softly. "I feel like the man who has grabbed a sleeping bear by the tail. There remains nothing else than to hold on." He paused. "And pray."

Guy had overheard. *"Sangodemi,* Cleve, let's put the future aside. It's not like you to brood."

They stood for a moment in silence, staring absently at the deserted, star-washed, decks. The barque seemed barely to keep headway under a fragile breeze from the northeast. She had been partially becalmed all night. The peace of the night seemed to have settled over her. The lull before the storm, Cleve thought, and looked up with a frown.

"Damme! Who's brooding, Kitten?"

"*Corbac!* You are."

"I am not. I've been thinking. Do you realize that if we hold the quarterdeck for any length of time, we're going to get hungry, and thirsty?"

Guy nodded quickly. "*Pecaire!* That's right. One moment I'll go and fetch—"

Cleve grabbed his arm. "I'll go," he said. "You stay here and see if you can't fix some sort of barricade. There are several small kegs lashed to the base of the mizzenmast."

"Oh, very well."

But Cleve never reached the ship's galley. As he stepped quietly across the waist, a faint noise from the bow attracted him. He froze. The noise came again: a soft, clinking sound that might have been unheard under other circumstances. With a cold feeling in the pit of his stomach he drew his blade and began to move forward.

He heard voices as he neared the forecastle. Muttered commands in Spanish followed by the soft pad of feet. Something was happening. He shrank against the mast and peered cautiously around.

Dimly, in the night, he made out two shadowy figures hunched in front of the companionway to the crew's quarters. He had locked that companion after he'd taken care of the forward watches. The two figures were joined by a third—and then a fourth. A fifth!

"Well, so that's it, eh?" he muttered.

The men climbing stealthily over the bow were the watches whom he and Guy had cast adrift a half hour before. They had used the poinard the French cavalier had cast them to cut their bonds. The barque had been moving so slowly that they had managed to row back to her. They had circled the stern carefully so as to come up under her anchor chains. Now they were using the links to steal aboard.

Cleve stepped out from behind the mast. He meant to stop this business quickly and efficiently. The watches weren't armed; he was.

"All right, m'lads," he said softly, "Relax!"

BUT the sailors had other ideas. Disregarding the rapier Cleve held, they whirled as one man and charged. He got one of them through the chest, before they bore him down. And then he was fighting for his life.

A hobbled boot smashed the sword free of his fingers. A pair of hands crushed his throat. He lay on his back, kicking indiscriminately in all directions. A cursing, yelling, seaman held one of his arms. He wheezed in Cleve's ear as he attempted to break the arm.

Somehow the Englishman managed to draw his legs up to his chest. He did it fast enough to crash one knee into the face of the man choking him. The grip on his throat lessened and he gulped in air gratefully. Then he shot his legs hard into the massed bodies overhead. Men catapulted off of him. He jabbed a fist into the throat of the wheezer, and rolled to his knees.

"By Gad! That's better," he panted.

There was a pause, caused by the fury of his counter-attack, and he made use of it. He saw his rapier lying a few feet to the right. With a cat-like bound he threw his weight against an on-coming sailor and scooped the light weapon up. Somebody was clawing his face from the side. He flung his arm back, his elbow striking brutally into the fellow's nose, and whipped the sword upward into the groin of another assailant charging at him from the starboard. A scream of agony rent the night. Cleve jumped to his feet.

He had to get out of here. The companion to the crew's quarters was open and sleepy-eyed men were pouring through it, brandishing knives, cutlasses and pistols. Cleve sent his blade darting into the ring of bodies surging in on him. It drove them back. He retreated.

But now the forward part of the boat was black with men. A pistol roared in the night and the ball smacked viciously into the bulwark beside him. It seemed as though he were fighting a million men. Cutlasses chopped at him from three sides. One nipped him in the arm. He laughed, but the pain of that wound enraged him.

His blade became a viper's tongue, licking quickly in and out among the clumsy cutlasses. A man crumpled, stung through the throat. Another reeled back clutching his side. For one furious moment the Englishman's cautious retreat halted.

"*Sacré bleu,* Cleve! Down! Get down! Hit the deck!"

Dimly Cleve heard d'Entreville shouting these instructions. He gave a panting yell and fell back. The rapidity with which he sent himself sprawling to the boards knocked the wind out of him.

A fraction of a second crawled by; and then, from the quarterdeck, came a frightful crash. He heard the grape-shot scream a few inches over his head, and heard the agonized chorus of groans, curses and screams which rose from the gory heap in the waist. The crew had been riddled horribly by that rain of death from the carronade.

Then he was on his feet again and pounding toward the poop. His breath came in great gasping sobs. He felt hot and sick with the effort of it.

THE DOOR of the master's cabin burst open, and Don Diego appeared, fully dressed and clutching a sword uncertainly. Cleve bowled into him before the Spaniard had a chance to use it. The door loomed in welcome. Hurdling the prostrate Don, Cleve sped through and slammed it shut behind him. He shot the bolts, and sagged for a moment in panting relief.

On the quarterdeck, Guy crouched behind his smoking gun and eyed the carnage he had wrought. Fifteen bodies littered the forward decks, some mangled horribly. He licked his lips.

The rest of the crew had scattered. He could distinguish the black bulk of them clotted in the bow. Directly below him Don Diego was crawling to his feet, cursing monotonously. The Spaniard looked up, saw Guy, and stopped. D'Entreville picked up a musket.

"Get up forward with the rest of the scum," he said. "Go on! Run, before I put a ball through you!"

Diego's fat face was ludicrously amazed. "*Dios!*" he exclaimed. "You're dead. You're drowned. I saw you—"

"*Corbac!* On your way, *señor!*"

"But how? What—"

The French rakehelly planted a ball directly between the speaker's feet. He picked up another musket.

"*Allez!*"

Diego left. He lumbered across the decks toward the others.

Below, Cleve suddenly found himself in more trouble. With his back against the door he stared across the lantern lit confines of the master's cabin into the beady black eyes of Pedro Pizon.

Pizon had been sleeping on the window seat. Upon the Englishman's crashing entrance, he had looked up in startled confusion. Now recognition was followed by incredulity. "*Diablo!* You!"

Gasping, Cleve could do little else than nod. A minute crawled by as they faced each other. And then Pizon acted. He rolled off of the window seat and came up with a pistol. Cleve rammed his body to one side, and the murderous-looking pistol went *click*. Nothing happened.

"Empty!"

The word came like a snarl from deep in the Spaniard's throat. He surged forward, drawing his rapier.

"*Por Dios!* I've attempted to finish you three times, Cleve. But now I shan't fail. How did you escape drowning? How come you here?"

The Englishman shook his head. He was almost done in. He

needed his breath for other things besides talking. So he lounged there against the door, blade slanted wearily across his boot. Pizon paused beside the table.

"Tired, aren't you. Well, *señor*, we shall make you a trifle more tired before the end."

Cleve didn't say anything. He watched the other alertly and waited. Pizon was fresh; he wasn't. From above Guy's voice boomed:

"And mark this, Diego; I have another carronade waiting up here, besides two muskets. Send your men aft and I'll blow them back into your fat face. Stay where you are. Understand?"

"Fool! Do you think you can take this ship?" Diego's rich voice returned. "Best surrender now, and you'll have a quick death. Later...." He laughed cruelly. "I am a man of whims, *señor*. I know several amusing tricks."

THEN Pizon charged. Cleve was barely prepared for it. He had been listening to the voices outside. The swarthy aide's blade leaped viciously at his throat. He caught it on his hilt, deflected it past his cheek. Pizon leered.

"I'll play with you a while, swine!"

Cleve met his next thrust with a ready blade and a quick riposte. "Play lightly, laddie. I'm wearing your clothes. It would be a shame to ruin such fine cloth."

"Diablo!"

"Ah, now, temper, old man. Temper."

The Englishman laughed. He felt fresh vigor pouring into his body. For the first time he began to carry the play toward the Spaniard. His blade knitted a circle of peril around Pizon, driving him back —back in increasing disorder.

In the center of the saffron-washed cabin, the dark aide made a stand. He somehow managed a quick binde that momentarily stopped the waspish offensive; drove Cleve to a loss of balance, and allowed two murderous thrusts in sixte. The English rakehelly parried one miraculously and felt the sting of the other lightly. No damage!

But Pizon pressed on, fighting with the savagery of desperation. He fought with his blade low, an Italian crouch which he had adapted for his own requirements.

"Why don't you sit down?" Cleve panted. "It would be easier."

Pizon's lips writhed, but no sound came from them. His high forehead glistened with sweat. And then he made his first and only mistake. He attempted a double feint at the stomach, but Cleve broke it up with a flashing seconde that jerked the Spaniard off balance. There was a quick opening and the Englishman found it. His steel rasped over the other's hilt and slip deep into Pizon's side. The Spaniard staggered back clutching the wound.

His rapier clattered to the floor and his eyes were big, amazed.

"You did it," he accused stupidly. "You did this to me. *Dios!* It burns. It burns!"

He felt the window seat against his calves and sat down. Crimson leaked between his clutching fingers. He sprawled wearily against the ports and lay there staring at Cleve and wheezing harshly.

"You'll live," Cleve said. He knew that he was lying, but a plan had struck him. "You'll live, Pizon, but not if you don't talk."

There was hope in Pizon's eyes now. "What do you mean? I am wounded, *señor*. You wouldn't slay a wounded man."

Cleve lifted his blade. "Damme! Why wouldn't I?"

The Spaniard writhed in a spasm of agony. "You devil," he gasped.

"Where is the Treaty? Where does Diego keep the Treaty?"

The Spaniard was growing weak; he was dying; and yet no recognition of the fact showed in his eyes.

"If I tell," he sobbed painfully. "If I show you, you'll let me live, *señor*."

Cleve nodded. He felt dirty doing this. Why couldn't he let the man die in peace; allow him the dignity of a quiet death?

Pizon pointed weakly toward a small writing desk on the starboard side of the room. "In a black dispatch case you'll find—"

A streak of pain seemed to stiffen his body. It choked short the words he was uttering and held his lips stiffly agape. By the time Cleve reached him, he was dead.

The cavalier lifted the Spaniard's limp legs to the window seat, threw his ragged cape over the corpse; and then turned to the desk.

Now that he was close to the thing, he moved fast.

He was forced to open three drawers before he found the case. It was lying partially concealed beneath a litter of correspondence and pen-quills. Trembling slightly, he fumbled with the brassy clasp, opened it and thrust his hand inside. The case was empty. The Treaty was gone.

CHAPTER XV

AND DOWN WE GO

ON THE POOP, Guy placed a musket conveniently at his knee and fumbled hurriedly among his store of munitions. The portside carronade needed to be reloaded—and reloaded quickly, A brooding silence hung over the wallowing barque, and he realized that it was but a prelude to danger. Don Diego was not the type to give up his ship to two men.

Shortly after their bellowed conversation, the Spanish noble had collected the frightened crew and sent them down into the forecastle. Even now a council of war was being held. Both carronades had to be ready!

Swiftly he selected a fresh powder charge and rammed it home. He found a package of thick brown wads lying beside the squat base and crammed one hard against the powder. He heard a noise and grabbed up his musket. Then he saw the slim outlines of Cleve against the mast-light on the mizzen, and he put the gun down again.

The Englishman bent down beside him. He was laden with three bandoleers, a brace of pistols, two muskets and a half-keg of ball.

"Pizon disputed my right to be in the cabin," he said and shrugged. He put the arms and munitions near at hand and picked up a handful of grape. He poured it down the hungry muzzle and followed it with several more. D'Entreville sprinkled black powder into the touch-hole and picked up one of the pistols Cleve had brought.

"Where did you get this, *mon ami?*"

"From the arms rack beside the door. I stripped it of everything. I suppose I should have—"

A shout arose from the forward hatch.

"*Corbac!*" Guy exclaimed. "Diego's ordered them to rush us!"

THEN like a bellowing herd of cattle men swept along the decks from the darkness of the bow. They surged toward the silent quarter, fierce in their intent to take it by sheer weight.

Cleve half-rose. D'Entreville yanked him down. Musket fire began to wink from the shadowy companions, from behind masts.

"*Sangodemi!* Keep down, Cleve. We have the better elevation. The lip of the deck flooring protects us from low shots."

Cleve nodded. He scuttled crab-fashion across the deck to the other carronade. Between the balustrades of the poop-railing he saw how close the attackers were. Diego must have fired them with a patriotic fervor.

They kept yelling: "*Viva* Philip! *Viva Hispania! Viva Hispania!*" Ugly pikes, cutlasses and knives glittered.

"Let them come close," Guy roared above the bedlam. "Mark me, Cleve. Let them come up to the muzzles. *Pardieu!* I told Diego I'd blast them to—"

He touched his match to the breech. The flame was sudden and terrible, lighting the faces of the swarming crew. A great invisible hand seemed to strike them down; to bowl them into ghastly bleeding heaps. D'Entreville turned away from the slaughter.

"Dios y Diablo! Go on, you swine! Don't allow them time to reload that gun!"

It was Diego howling orders from the bow; sending a new wave of seamen against the smoke-cloaked quarterdeck. Brave Diego! D'Entreville cursed him for a monster.

Then he felt suddenly numb. The crew was obeying. More men were rushing down through that crimson waist, rushing desperately over the riddled bodies of their comrades! They were coming, and he had nothing but an empty cannon with which to stop them.

Even as he sponged out for reloading, he realized the futility of it. The defense of the poop was over. Finished! They'd be on him before he could ram home the first charge.

And then once more the quarter was wreathed by flame-pierced smoke. The assault party melted under a hail of grape; dropped to the decks like so many stringless puppets. Guy stared in unbelief through the gun-haze, and Cleve patted the carronade in front of him and grinned.

"Forgot to fire last time, Kitten!" he said.

After that there were no more senseless charges against the poop. The fifty bodies littering the waist argued mutely against it. A tribute to Don Diego's stupidity.

But it did not mean a cessation of hostilities. Having learned a bitter lesson, the Spanish Don attempted other tactics.

HIS FIRST proved more annoying than dangerous. By sending musketeers beneath the decks and then up through the hatches and companionways, he attempted to pick off the defenders. Shadowy figures would flit suddenly from hatch to a mast; always advancing; firing alternately; seeking to filter aft, one by one, until they could rush. None ever penetrated further than the mizzen.

The cavaliers met the move, lying flat on the quarterdeck and poking flaming musket-mouths between the rail balustrades. They offered practically no target and their elevated position gave them a definite fire-advantage. After an hour of desultory fire, the snipers were withdrawn.

Then Don Diego had ten or twelve sharp-shooters climb the shrouds. If height was an advantage he meant to have it. From the tops the musketeers poured a dangerous fire down upon the cavaliers. And there was no defense against it. No place to take cover. The hot balls slapped viciously into the flooring all around them. Cleve was grazed painfully before d'Entreville solved the problem.

Working with desperate swiftness, the French rakehelly extracted all of the quoins from the breech of the starboard carronade. Gradually the muzzle tipped back until it was staring belligerently at the ghostly sails above. A musket-ball hissed through the dark and splattered against the rail.

Guy added a handful of grape-shot for good luck and fired. The carronade heeled madly back against its base. She roared up into the night. And the snipers came down, but only three of them on their own volition. The other eight made ugly squashing sounds as they thudded limply to deck.

Cleve sighed. "Damme! Give it up, Diego," he called. "We're on this quarterdeck to stay. Keep feeding us men and you soon shan't have any left. Disarm and perchance we can get this hulk to a port. A *French* port, incidently."

There was a moment's stillness; and then, a volley of pungent curses and threats fouled the air as Don Diego made reply to the terms. *Por Dios!* The ship was nearing Spanish waters! The proud vessels of King Philip were all over these waters.

He concluded: "And if we can't capture you, then we'll lay siege until you drop from exhaustion. Two men can't take a ship this size, mark me, *señors.*"

"*Sangodemi!* But we're doing it," d'Entreville roared back.

But Cleve licked his dry lips and shrugged. What Diego said was true. If, in the dawning, the barque should come within hailing distance of a Spanish boat, the game would be over. From his position in the bow, Diego would be able to yell explanations across the sea and the other ship would make short work of the two men holding the poop.

Cleve sighed.

"Faith! We fight a losing battle, I'm afraid, Kitten," the English cavalier told his companion. "Even if we're not stopped by another ship in the morning, there remains the fact that we are but two against a possible twenty. Already, I'm about done. How long can we hold out without collapsing over our guns?"

"*Corbac!* Long enough to sink the ship! A ball from the demi-culverin behind us, and we start down. There'll be no surrender, Cleve!"

"Damme! Who said anything about surrender?"

"Well, you inferred as much."

Cleve smiled tiredly. He repeated a line from an old pirate chanty:

> *And when we can't give blow for blow,*
> *Then scuttle the vessel, and down we go.*

D'Entreville nodded agreement.

CHAPTER XVI

HIS SWORD IS FIRE

THE MORNING FOUND their position still unchanged. Diego had decided to watch and wait. He kept musketeers posted at strategic points to prevent their securing food or water from the deck larder amidships.

The two defenders lay sprawled on the sun-swept quarterdeck and licked their drying lips. Thirst was beginning to torture them. Added to this, they were sodden with fatigue. The snipers and the sudden alarms that were cruelly devised to keep them awake, had been all too successful.

"Sail ho!"

The cry came from up forward, from the lips of a seaman squatting behind an improvised barricade beside the leeward bulwarks. D'Entreville sat up with a curse. He craned his neck and saw nothing.

"It's behind us," Cleve explained. "Coming over the northern rim. That small patch of white. See it?"

Then the Frenchman saw the square topsails of a ship, stark white against the glimmering blue of the horizon. A sensation of utter futility went through him. That boat was coming fast, rising slowly out of the sea.

It was only a question of time. Previously, he and Cleve had fixed the wheel so that the long black barque had come about into what little breeze there was. To get back on a decent tack, without the aid of a crew to handle the sails, was out of the question.

"We can't outrun him, Cleve. *Pecaire!* I guess this is the beginning of the end, eh?"

The Englishman frowned, never taking his eyes from the growing sail at the stern. "Maybe," he said slowly.

D'Entreville stood up. An ambitious sniper sent a ball screaming off the pooprail beside him. He ignored it, his lean face tense and white.

"Before we get the culverin ready," he said, "I'm going to swing down the stern and through the windows into Don Diego's cabin. *Mordi!* When we go down, I want to make certain that the Treaty goes with us."

Cleve shook his head. Another musket ball hammered into the rail. With an almost leisurely motion he raised a pistol and returned the fire.

"Don't bother," he said carefully. "The Treaty isn't there. I searched for it."

"Thoroughly?"

"Yes. I feel certain that Diego carries it with him."

"But—"

"Say, is there a glass up here on the poop, somewhere. I'd like to have a better look at that ship."

D'Entreville picked up a heavy brass spyglass from beside the wheel-post and handed it to him. He did it automatically, while his mind digested the other's disheartening news.

Cleve crawled to the after-rail and clapped the glass to one eye. He remained a long while, peering over the sparkling wavelets of the sea. So intent was he that d'Entreville frowned.

"What is she, Cleve?"

"A damned big frigate," the other replied. "She's fast, too. She is fairly leaping along with a bone in her teeth."

Guy cast a nervous glance forward along the decks. They were deserted clear to the rough barricade the Spanish had thrown athwart the bows. Men were half-standing, shading their eyes and staring at the oncoming frigate.

"How long before she catches us?" he asked.

And then, Cleve gave vent to an excited curse. "Damme!" he erupted. "Damme! She's not Spanish. No, by Gad! She's French!"

"**FRENCH!**" The word burst from Guy's throat. He leaped toward the stern and stood beside Cleve staring incredulously out to sea.

"*Parbleu!* Give me that glass!"

Cleve turned and handed it to him. Then he saw that the forward part of the poop was unguarded and crossed it swiftly. It was well he did. An enterprising sailor, envisioning praise and gold from his portly master, was crawling stealthily along the decks. The English cavalier sighted carefully along the barrel of a musket and pulled the trigger. The sailor stood up and flopped clumsily to his face.

"And let that be a lesson to you," Cleve muttered and picked up another musket.

Don Diego's rich voice floated back from the forecastle: "You'll pay for that man's death, *señors*. Pay by lingering longer on the rack. When that distant ship of Spain arrives, it will be my turn." He laughed. "My turn, do you hear?"

Without a spyglass, he was still unaware of the frigate's nationality. From the stern, d'Entreville yelled: "Oh no, *monsieur*. Look again. 'Tis not one of your cursed Spanish ships that comes, but a Frenchman. The game is done. Diego! That Treaty you have stolen will never reach Madrid. We've won, *monsieur!*"

From the forecastle came the murmur of speculation. And then one sharp-eyed man unleashed a cry of anger.

"*Diablo*, Excellency! The swine speaks the truth. That ship is flying the lily-banner. She's French!"

"*What!*"

"*Por el amor del cielo*, Excellency! Don't hit me! I am not lying!"

"Fool! You *must* be. These are Spanish waters."

Ariza broke through the wrangle of voices. "*Por Dios*, Excellency. He is right! She is not built after the Spanish fashion. Her free-board is much lower in the stern. And that banner at her peak is white and gold."

Veins stood out on Diego's forehead. His little eyes were snapping. But he controlled the awful anger that welled up inside of him. His thick fingers touched his doublet, beneath which the vital document was concealed.

"How long will it take the French to overhaul us?" he asked Ariza.

The *capitan* frowned thoughtfully and stared hard at the distant frigate. "Two hours, Excellency, if the wind holds. Maybe more."

A crafty glitter replaced the anger in the don's eyes. He said: "How far are we from the Spanish Coast?"

"About sixty leagues."

"Near enough to make it in the longboat?"

The don's idea was plain and Ariza smiled slightly. "*Si*, if the weather remains as it is."

Diego chuckled. "*Bueno.* The longboat is riding at the bow beneath the anchor chains. Provision it, while I rob Cleve and d'Entreville of their triumph. *Por Dios!* I am too quick for them, *señor.* Too clever! And I always have been. They have met their match."

He arose from his crouched position. They had been conversing, in safety, behind the foremast. He peered cautiously around it.

THE BULLET-SCARRED poop was framed by ragged sails, red-splotched decks, the crisp blue and gold of the day on either side. There seemed to be no life on it, but Diego was not deluded.

Two firebrands lay concealed back there; two devils who had returned miraculously from a watery grave to take the barque and the lives of two-thirds of its crew. The Spaniard was vaguely aware of how they had accomplished the last two things, but their return from certain death remained a riddle.

"So you dogs think you have won?" he cried. "Ah no! The Treaty for which you have worked miracles is still in my hands. Before this week is out, His Gracious Majesty Philip of Spain will have it in his hands to show the world the treachery of France. He will have the proof necessary for a declaration of war. Our all conquering armies will march. *Adios, señors!*"

D'Entreville frowned. He was lying against the stern-rail with the spyglass against his eye. His lean face was smudged and powder-grimed; his fine clothes torn. He had just ascertained the name of the pursuing ship. *La Gloire.* But Diego's words held his attention now.

"What does he mean?"

Cleve shrugged and fondled his musket. "Damme, I don't know. But I don't like it much. Fatty has something brewing."

Musketry broke out forward and they ducked against the flooring, only to sit up again in surprise. No bullets hissed through the air. The fire was not directed at them.

Cleve said, "Well, I'll be damned!"

He peered through the thick balustrades. Stacked amidships and lashed firmly behind the main hold were three inverted dories. A withering fire was being poured into them, sending long splinters of black and yellow into the air. It continued until the small boats were sieves. And then the firing stopped. Silence fell.

But not for long. Two heavy hogsheads were lifted to the rim of the barricade and sent crashing across the deck. From them a yellowish liquid gushed, soaking deep into the wood. D'Entreville caught the lettering on the side of one almost immediately.

"Lamp oil!"

"Lamp—"

Cleve leaped to his feet. Suddenly he knew what was going to happen. But even as he cried out, a hand hurled a flaring torch down from the bow into the pooling oil. An indistinct plop… a puff of lambent flame… and the decks swirled into a small inferno that grew and grew.

High yellow flames licked the lower sails and ran up them quickly. Black smoke arose in a swelling column. The bows were partially obliterated by it. And through it all came the mocking laughter of Don Diego. D'Entreville cursed.

"*Sangodemi!* He's fired the ship! He's gone mad!"

"Don't be a fool! He's escaping. The longboat is tied forward. That's why they wrecked those lifeboats. We're being left here to roast while he rides safely to Spain with the Treaty. A neat trick, Kitten, and well worthy of the cunning devil."

"So now," said Guy quietly, "this *is* the end of our voyage."

CHAPTER XVII

ARREST THESE HEROES!

A CURTAIN OF fire raged upward, totally obscuring the port side of the bows. But through flame-gaps to the leeward could be seen the flitting figures of the crew, swarming over the bowsprit base and down the anchor chains.

D'Entreville bent over, swearing inarticulately, and touched off the port carronade. A few screams rewarded the effort. Then he hurdled the railing, blade in hand, and charged.

Cleve let him go. He had other plans. Because of the slant of the waist, the fire was eating aft toward the main hatch. If it ever reached the powder magazine....

He tore over the rail and across the deck. He saw Guy leap dextrously through a curling hole in the flames; and then Cleve was plunging down the after-companion.

There was a heavy sledge hanging from pegs on the wall of the corridor. He snatched it up and continued his way. Acrid smoke was seeping down from above. It caught in his throat, set him coughing. He held his breath and raced on, down another staircase until he was standing in the cool dim depths of the bilge-deck where the air was damp and clear of smoke.

A sea-cock bulged to the left. He slammed the heavy sledge against it and a spray of sea water leaped upward to drench him. But he didn't pause. He ran along the length of the ship, moving forward, cracking open one valve after another until he was wading knee deep in chill, brackish water.

Then he regarded the job, satisfied. With luck the sea would reach the powder magazine before the fire. At least there was a chance now that they wouldn't be blasted into eternity.

When he reached the deck again, through the forward companion, *El Conquistador* was already beginning to settle. Heat blistered him. The mainsails were sheets of flame. Suddenly from the bow came a roaring boom—the thunder of a cannon.

"Good Lord! Has the fire reached the guns already?" Then he saw the cause and laughed. "Damme, Kitten. Giving a celebration?"

D'Entreville, wreathed in powder-smoke, was bending near a huge black bow-chaser, a long eighteen. He didn't answer Cleve; he was too busy spitting wild, furious curses. He leaped over the gun-tackles suddenly, to sponge out the iron monster.

"Corbac et sangodemi! Missed! I missed the swine!"

Cleve slapped out a star-shaped spark that had fallen on his shoulder, and went to the bow. A glance over the bulwarks told him d'Entreville's target.

The longboat lay dead ahead, heavy with men, its oars moving desperately. It looked like an oblong spider. White strained faces stared back at the doomed barque. The gross frame of Don Diego could be distinguished in the stern.

His heavy voice could be heard above the crackling flames, urging the sweating oarsmen to row, and there was a thread of terror in his voice. He had never expected the two men on the barque to reach the bows. He had forgotten the long-range bow-chaser.

WITHOUT a word, Cleve leaped back to the breech. His practiced eye followed the length of the barrel, sighted along it carefully. He jerked a quoin from its place to elevate the muzzle slightly. Guy's shot had been high, he could see the white patch of it in the sea, but by now Diego's straining craft was abreast it and passing.

Guy rammed the powder home with a flip of the rammer. Both men were working furiously and efficiently, without a word. They knew the importance of this business. It was their last chance, after many failures. Guy crammed in the wadding and lifted the heavy ball to the lip and sent it rolling down the gaping maw. He set his weight to the rammer again and rammed the charge firm.

"Ready!"

Cleve inserted a quill of black powder. He checked his aim.

Fortunately there was practically no sea-swell. The weight of water pouring through the sea-cocks held the ship steady as a stone fort. Breathing a prayer, he set the match to the touch-hole.

The report crashed with a swirl of choking smoke, to roll out across the water. Like a thing alive, the bow-chaser reared insanely against the stout manila of its breech-ropes. The target was obliterated by a cloud of smoke. A stunned, tense, silence. There would be no third try. Diego would be out of range before they could reload again.

And then a sob broke from d'Entreville's throat—a sob of relief and thanksgiving.

The boat had been literally blown out of the sea. A few bobbing heads and splinters marked the spot where it had been, where before it had been surging desperately away.

Diego was finished. They saw his bloody head for a flashing instant, and then he sank out of sight, carrying with him the stolen Treaty. A few bits of bloodstained wreckage, and that was all. One by one the heads disappeared, and so the peril of a Spanish war was ended.

Cleve opened his mouth to say something, but the words wouldn't come. He could find no words for the surge of triumph in him, none that would pay full tribute to his victory. Finally he exploded: "Damme! Well, *damme!*"

And then something behind him unleashed all of the thunders of heaven. He felt his body clutched, pygmy-like, in an irresistible grip and lifted out over the rippling sea. The thunder deafened him, and he fell in silence. His consciousness was fast draining away. His mind seemed to have room for only one thought, and that kept repeating crazily:

"By Gad! By Gad! The fire won the powder magazine after all. Shouldn't have wasted my time."

HE WAS barely aware of things after he struck. He felt the cool quiet of the sea close over him, heard the soothing ripples of his passage, and tasted brine. Then he was on the surface again, treading weakly, too stunned to fear the heavy bits of debris that plummeted into the water all about him. A fragment of wood crashed against his shoulder and sent a streak of agony through his body. He fainted.

It must have been only a moment later that he recovered consciousness, then Guy's white face swam into vision. There was a ragged red wound from temple to jaw. Cleve, hardly able to move, reached for him and sank into the sea again. Firm fingers gripped him, dragged him back into the air by the nape of the neck. He felt air flood into his lungs and the mist cleared a trifle.

Something nudged his shoulder. It was the charred butt of a mast. Ropes were trailing from it.

Guy said, "Hold on to it, Cleve. I'll lash you to it. *Corbac!* You're in bad shape. One moment."

He felt the other tie a rope under his arms, and the pain of it made his mind fade into oblivion. He kept shuttling back and forth, after that. Back and forth between consciousness and darkness. They must have hung to that bobbing mast for hours, but he couldn't rightly remember.

Then there was a brief moment of clarity. He saw the glistening yellow sides of *La Gloire* looming over him. Cordeau's bushy red face was glaring down at him.

"You two knaves are under arrest," Cordeau said. "What happened to that barque?"

"I've wondered for a long time, Cordeau. What *did* happen to it?" Cleve laughed in a whisper. It hurt too much to laugh louder. "Suddenly, I turned around and there was no ship. No ship...."

The pain struck again when they lifted him aboard and he fainted. After that, his mind recorded a sequence of blurred pictures, cloudy, distant, and fading quickly. He had a vision of a deck with many people cluttering it and everyone talking. He heard Guy croaking hoarsely.

Next he was in a room. Comfortable. A man leaned over

him and worked with something on his shoulder. From the conversation he learned that he was suffering from shock, exposure and a broken shoulder bone. But he'd live. In a few days he'd be able to take to the deck.

"That's important," he thought. "Always be able to walk."

Time was a swift-flying streamer, but his half-conscious mind managed to pick up scraps of information. The bottle had been picked up, its meaning deciphered by Colonel de Chais in Le Havre.

"Might have known Cordeau wouldn't have the wit," Cleve thought. The frigate had been following *El Conquistador* for days, and Cordeau had been prepared to follow them to Africa, if need be.

It seemed that their escape from Paris had put the pompous captain in a bad light. Their recapture, at all costs, had been imperative—to Cordeau. No man could tell what Richelieu might have done if he had failed. The Cardinal wasn't very lenient with bunglers.

"But now I've got you, my precious rogues," Cordeau was saying. "I've broken rules, exceeded my authority and commandeered a warship without orders. But the sight of you two dogs languishing in La Bastille, where you belong, will be more than ample pay for the trouble!

"Parbleu! The man aboard that ill-fated black barque— whoever he was, *messieurs,* he betrayed you. He dropped a flask with your arrest orders in it, and an identifying spoon to mark the ship upon which you had fled. *Sandiou.* If that man were but here, I would feel honored to throw my arms about him and kiss him respectfully on both cheeks!"

Slowly Cleve opened his eyes. He found himself, on a cot in the polished wardroom of the frigate. Sitting in a chair nearby was d'Entreville, his face swathed in a white bandage, his left arm in a sling. At the foot of the bed stood Cordeau. Cleve regarded him steadily.

"You try it, *monsieur le Capitaine*," he said evenly. "You try it, and I'll kick you into the middle of next week!"

THE PALACE of the Cardinal was *en fête*.

The men of the Guard were gathered in groups, filling the entire area of the main court. Capitaine Cordeau appeared from his headquarters and strode stiffly toward the dias at the far end. A silvery blast brought the guardsmen to order.

"Attendez!"

Without another word the men slipped into disciplined formation. Their white surcoats, emblazoned with the embroidered hooped cross of the regiment, were dazzling in the sun. Tasseled pikes glittered, plumes fluttered, swordhilts twinkled. In silence Cordeau stepped to the dias and pulled a be-ribboned document from his sash.

In the front ranks, one Guardsman slyly nudged another. "What's biting Cordeau?" he whispered. *"Corbac!* He looks as though he has just swallowed a lemon."

The other man shrugged. "I don't know," he replied. "One moment, he's going to read."

Cordeau held the paper at arm's length and squinted at it distastefully. He was quite red in the face. The regiment awaited him in patient silence. Almost furtively, he cast an eye up to the balcony where the Cardinal and the King were standing. He shrugged hopelessly, and loudly cleared his throat.

" 'Be it known, on this the second day of August, the year of Our Lord 1630, that Coronets Monsieur M'Lord Richard Cleve and Monsieur le Comte Guy d'Entreville'"—he paused, lips sagging—" 'be elevated to the rank of lieutenant, in *Monseigneur le Cardinal's* Regiment of Guards.'"

The speaker's fat face was beet-red, but he continued doggedly. " 'That they be cited by me, their *commandante*, as brave, resourceful men, who have won their new ranks by deeds far outside the line of duty, inasmuch as by the gallantry of their actions they have saved France. This bravery in....'"

Up in another balcony, a bit above the one occupied by

Richelieu and the King, two bandaged men listened to the hesitant words of the *capitaine,* grinned as the voice rose in their praise, and slowly shook hands, well satisfied.

ABOUT THE AUTHOR

THOSE RAKEHELLIES CLEVE and d'Entreville cover a lot of ground; but in comparison to their creator they're a couple of old mossbacks. Murray Montgomery has been so many places and tried his hand at so many things that he sounds slightly confused by it all.

Maybe that's because he was born in Winnipeg, Canada, on the day Great Britain declared war on Imperial Germany. He says, a little wonderingly, "It was a case of enter Montgomery and commence firing!" During adolescence in New York and on Long Island, he tells us, "I developed a six-foot-one frame; a distaste for polo—the result of a lack of compromise between myself and the horse; and a positive lust for yachting.

"Books had always interested me, so I read prodigiously and after consuming such teen-age tomes as Nietzsche's *On the Genealogy of Morality*, Kant's *Critique of Pure Reason*, Plato's *Republic*, etc., etc., I decided to write something of equal importance. I gave my all to the literary world—and the literary world promptly gave it all back. I decided to become an artist."

At this point the record becomes a little breathless. From ten easy lessons in art he proceeded to trap-drumming "in a snappy little aggregation known as Kings of Rhythm." This particular brand of royalty appears to have been out of fashion at the time, for Murray quickly makes his second appearance as a writer (selling two stories out of twenty), then decides to become an actor.

Follow closely now. He gets a part in a play—and the play closes after a brisk two-day run. He becomes a salesman for the Royal typewriter company. Then he decides to write a play, but first becomes an actor again (the part he gets is in another turkey); takes a fling at producing for the Flushing Summer Theater; and goes barnstorming with a road company of "Let Freedom Ring."

"I lost ten pounds," he comments ruefully, "and a lot of enthusiasm. Returning to New York, I wrote my play. Because the Broadway producers seemed to regret that very much, I got a job as a reporter until the thing blew over."

Still with us? We're almost through. Watching corpses dragged out of the river wasn't quite to Murray's taste, so he gave up police-reporting and went to work for the scenario department of Twentieth Century-Fox.

"They had gotten hold of the play I had written and felt obliged to pay hush-money," he blushes. "Even so, I felt encouraged, so I tried my hand at writing again—and wonder of wonders, sold everything I wrote, with the result that I am still writing."

We like happy endings, and we like Mr. Montgomery and all his works—so there remains only to add a few hearty cheers and the statement that the Rakehellies' papa is now a full-fledged American citizen, resident in Great Neck, Long Island. No puns, please.

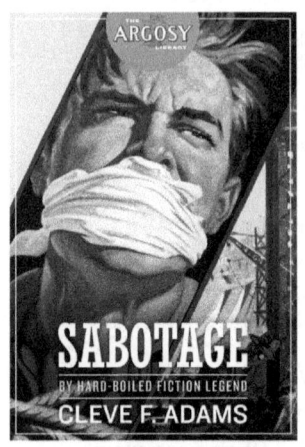

SABOTAGE
BY HARD-BOILED FICTION LEGEND
CLEVE F. ADAMS

CHAMPION OF LOST CAUSES
BY WILLIAM F. NOLAN
MAX BRAND

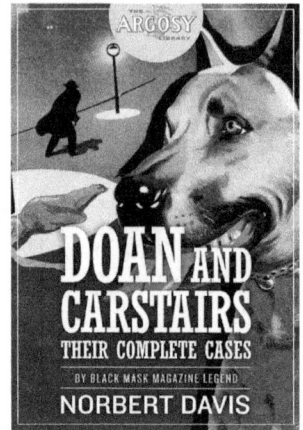

DOAN AND CARSTAIRS
THEIR COMPLETE CASES
BY BLACK MASK MAGAZINE LEGEND
NORBERT DAVIS

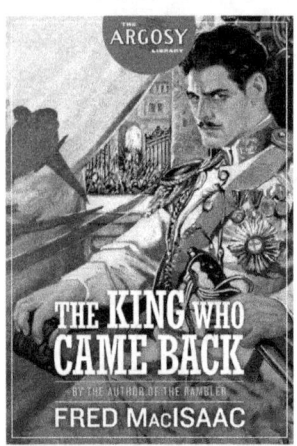

THE KING WHO CAME BACK
BY THE AUTHOR OF THE RAMBLER
FRED MacISAAC

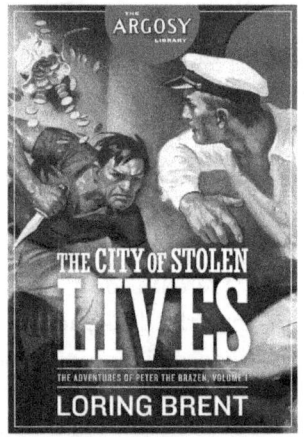

THE CITY OF STOLEN LIVES
THE ADVENTURES OF PETER THE BRAZEN, VOLUME 1
LORING BRENT

THE RADIO GUN-RUNNERS
BY SCIENCE FICTION LEGEND
RALPH MILNE FARLEY

BLOOD RITUAL
THE ADVENTURES OF SCARLET AND BRADSHAW, VOLUME 1
THEODORE ROSCOE

THE SCARLET BLADE
THE RAKEHELLY ADVENTURES OF CLEVE AND O'ENTREVILLE, VOLUME 1
MURRAY R. MONTGOMERY

SEMI DUAL
THE COMPLETE CABALISTIC CASES OF
THE OCCULT DETECTOR, VOLUME 2: 1912-13
J.U. GIESY AND JUNIUS B. SMITH

SOUTH OF FIFTY-THREE
BY THE AUTHOR OF THE TORCH
JACK BECHDOLT

SERIES 2 • AVAILABLE SPRING 2015

THE ARGOSY LIBRARY ™

SERIES 2 INCLUDES:

* BRAND * BRENT * ADAMS *
* MacISAAC * ROSCOE *
* GIESY & SMITH *
* BECHDOLDT *
* MONTGOMERY *
* FARLEY *
* DAVIS *

THE BEST FICTION
FROM THE FRANK
A. MUNSEY LINE